Praise for *The Gun Also Rises*

"A roller-coaster of a mystery penned by a real pro. This series just gets better and better. More, please!"—*Suspense Magazine*

"Author Sherry Harris never disappoints with her strong, witty writing voice and her ability to use the surprise effect just when you think you have it all figured out!"—*Chatting About Cozies*

"This series gets better with every book, and *The Gun Also Rises* continues the trend. If you haven't started this series yet, do yourself a favor and buy the first one today."—Carstairs Considers

Praise for *I Know What You Bid Last Summer*

"*I Know What You Bid Last Summer* is cleverly plotted, with an engaging cast of characters and a clever premise that made me think twice about my shopping habits. Check it out."—*Suspense Magazine*

"Never one to give up, she (Sarah) continues her hunt for the killer in some unlikely and possibly dangerous places. Fans of Harris will appreciate both the clever mystery and the tips for buying and selling at garage sales."—*Kirkus Reviews*

"Each time a new Sarah Winston Garage Sale Mystery releases, I wonder how amazing author Sherry Harris will top the previous book she wrote for the series. I'm never disappointed, and my hat's off to Ms. Harris, who consistently raises the bar for her readers' entertainment."—*Chatting About Cozies*

Praise for *A Good Day to Buy*

"Sarah's life keeps throwing her new curves as the appearance of her estranged brother shakes up her world. This fast-moving mystery starts off with a bang and keeps the twists and turns coming. Sarah is a likable protagonist who sometimes makes bad decisions based on good intentions. This ups the action and drama as she tries to extricate herself from dangerous situations with some amusing results. Toss in a unique cast of secondary characters, an intriguing mystery, and a hot ex-husband, and you'll find there's never a dull moment in Sarah's bargain-hunting world."—*RT Book Reviews*, 4 Stars

"Harris's fourth is a slam dunk for those who love antiques and garage sales. The knotty mystery has an interesting premise and some surprising twists and turns as well."—*Kirkus Reviews*

"The mystery of the murder in *A Good Day to Buy*, the serious story behind Luke's reappearance, the funny scenes that lighten the drama, the wonderful cast of characters, and Sarah's always superb internal dialogue will keep you turning the pages and have you coming back for book #5."—*Nightstand Book Reviews*

Praise for *All Murders Final!*

"There's a lot going on in this charming mystery, and it all works. The dialogue flows effortlessly, and the plot is filled with numerous twists and turns. Sarah is a resourceful and appealing protagonist, supported by a cast of quirky friends. Well written and executed, this is a definite winner. Bargain-hunting has never been so much fun!"—*RT Book Reviews*, 4 Stars

"A must-read cozy mystery! Don't wear your socks when you read this story 'cause it's gonna knock 'em off!"—*Chatting About Cozies*

"Just because Sherry Harris's protagonist Sarah Winston lives in a small town, it doesn't mean that her problems are small. . . . Harris fits the puzzle pieces together with a sure hand."—Sheila Connolly, Agatha- and Anthony-nominated author of the Orchard Mysteries

"A thrilling mystery. . . . Brilliantly written, each chapter drew me in deeper and deeper, my anticipation mounting with every turn of the page. By the time I reached the last page, all I could say was . . . wow!"—*Lisa Ks Book Reviews*

Praise for *The Longest Yard Sale*

"I love a complex plot and *The Longest Yard Sale* fills the bill with mysterious fires, a missing painting, thefts from a thrift shop, and, of course, murder. Add an intriguing cast of victims, potential villains, and sidekicks, an interesting setting, and two eligible men for the sleuth to choose between and you have a sure winner even before you get to the last page and find yourself laughing out loud."—Kaitlyn Dunnett, author of *The Scottie Barked at Midnight*

"Readers will have a blast following Sarah Winston on her next adventure as she hunts for bargains and bad guys. Sherry Harris's latest is as delightful as the best garage sale find!"—Liz Mugavero, Agatha-nominated author of the Pawsitively Organic Mysteries

"Sherry Harris is a gifted storyteller, with plenty of twists and adventures for her smart and stubborn protagonist."—Beth Kanell, Kingdom Books

"Once again Sherry Harris entwines small-town life with that of the nearby Air Force base, yard sales with romance, art theft with murder. The story is a bargain, and a priceless one!"—Edith Maxwell, Agatha-nominated author of the Local Foods mystery series

Praise for *Tagged for Death*

"*Tagged for Death* is skillfully rendered, with expert characterization and depiction of military life. Best of all Sarah is the type of intelligent, resourceful, and appealing person we would all like to get to know better!"—*Mystery Scene Magazine*

"Full of garage-sale tips, this amusing cozy debut introduces an unusual protagonist who has overcome some recent tribulations and become stronger."—*Library Journal*

"A terrific find! Engaging and entertaining, this clever cozy is a treasure—charmingly crafted and full of surprises."—Hank Phillippi Ryan, Agatha-, Anthony-, and Mary Higgins Clark–award-winning author

"Like the treasures Sarah Winston finds at the garage sales she loves, this book is a gem."—Barbara Ross, Agatha-nominated author of the Maine Clambake Mysteries

"It was masterfully done. *Tagged for Death* is a winning debut that will have you turning pages until you reach the final one. I'm already looking forward to Sarah's next bargain with death."—Mark Baker, Carstairs Considers

The Sarah Winston Garage Sale Mysteries
by Sherry Harris

SELL LOW, SWEET HARRIET

LET'S FAKE A DEAL

THE GUN ALSO RISES

I KNOW WHAT YOU BID LAST SUMMER

A GOOD DAY TO BUY

ALL MURDERS FINAL!

THE LONGEST YARD SALE

and

Agatha-Nominated Best First Novel

TAGGED FOR DEATH

Published by Kensington Publishing Corporation

Sell Low, Sweet Harriet

Sherry Harris

KENSINGTON BOOKS
KENSINGTON PUBLISHING CORP.
www.kensingtonbooks.com

KENSINGTON BOOKS are published by

Kensington Publishing Corp.
119 West 40th Street
New York, NY 10018

All Kensington titles, imprints, and distributed lines are available at special quantity discounts for bulk purchases for sales promotion, premiums, fund-raising, educational, or institutional use.

Special book excerpts or customized printings can also be created to fit specific needs. For details, write or phone the office of the Kensington Sales Manager: Attn.: Sales Department. Kensington Publishing Corp., 119 West 40th Street, New York, NY 10018. Phone: 1-800-221-2647.

Kensington and the K logo Reg. U.S. Pat. & TM Off.

First Printing: January 2020
ISBN-13: 978-1-4967-2251-5
ISBN-10: 1-4967-2251-5

ISBN-13: 978-1-4967-2252-2 (eBook)
ISBN-10: 1-4967-2252-3 (eBook)

10 9 8 7 6 5 4 3 2 1

Printed in the United States of America

To Bob
You're the best thing that ever happened to me

ACKNOWLEDGMENTS

First, thank you to the two men who are behind the scenes with every book: John Talbot of the Talbot Fortune Agency, and Gary Goldstein, my editor at Kensington. When we started this series with a three-book contract, I never dreamed I'd be writing more and starting a new series too. Thank you both for believing in me.

To Lieutenant Colonel (Ret.) Ken Ribler for talking me through what would happen on a base after a spouse was murdered, that yes, someone like Sarah might be used, and for telling me about the "cops and robbers" meetings. I hope I got it all right.

Ashley Harris (fantastic former neighbor and military spouse), thanks for answering my questions about dining-outs and grog bowls. And always for your knowledge about online garage sales.

Jill Hoagland, another former neighbor and military spouse, who shares her stories with me.

Nancy Frost was my first friend when we were stationed in Los Angeles. We spent many a happy day going to garage sales in her Suburban and managed to be stationed in the same place twice. I miss you every day. Thank you for helping me come up with Sarah's name and the town of Ellington. Also thank you for sending a link to a real CIA agent's garage sale. It obviously inspired me.

Michelle Clark, medicolegal death investigator, once again answered my questions. Thank you for taking time out of your very busy life to help me.

Independent editor Barb Goffman once again read an early draft, talked me through many revisions, and stayed my friend when I whined. Thank you!

Mary Titone is one of the best beta readers on the planet. She spots things I missed, pats me on the back or gives a swift (virtual) kick when I need it. Your friendship means the world to me. You make the books better.

Clare Boggs, I can't write this without tears in my eyes. I miss you mostly because of the amazing friend you were, but also because of your eagle eye with my books. That can't be replaced.

Christie Nichols, dear neighbor, who dropped everything to do a final read-through for me. You made a great catch and inspired something too.

To The Wickeds—Jessie Crockett, Julie Hennrikus, Edith Maxwell, Liz Mugavero, and Barbara Ross— thank you for your support, your check-ins, and your friendship. You buoy me when I'm down and cheer me when I'm up. Life would be dull without you.

To the friends I've made through Sisters in Crime— what a ride. Thanks for your generosity.

And finally to my family. I've traveled a lot this year for a variety of reasons. You've kept the home fires burning and Lily walked and fed. I love you.

Chapter One

From the back of the base chapel I could see the large photo resting on an easel at the front of the church. Golden light from a stained glass window shone on a picture of a smiling, auburn-haired young woman, dead, murdered right here on Fitch Air Force Base.

I sat on a pew after a couple scooted over for me. The church was packed, standing room only even on a Tuesday morning. I wasn't sure if it was because they knew Alicia Arbas or were horrified at how she had died. Maybe it was a combination of both. When a tragedy hit a base, especially a smaller one like Fitch, military people pulled together.

I studied the picture of Alicia, her bright smile. She wasn't me, but she could have been. That's why her death hit so close to home. Why I was sitting back here listening to the prayers, eulogies, and singing hymns even though I hadn't known her all that well.

Thirty minutes later the service for Alicia was almost over. There had been a lot of laughter as people shared funny stories, but more tears because Alicia died at the hands of an unknown killer. Someone who lived on base or had, at the very least, been on base. People glanced at each other more often than normal. Were they trying to suss out if their neighbor could have been the one who committed a murder? I worried about what would happen to people, to a community such as this, when they couldn't trust each other.

We sang the last hymn as the casket was carried out. Alicia's husband, a young captain, followed, pale and uncomfortable looking in his black suit. The pain in his face seared my soul.

A few minutes later I stepped out of the church. The January wind slashed at my tights-covered legs and pulled at my coat. I scraped at the blond hairs that slapped my face, so I could see where I was going. Lunch was to be served in the church basement, but I was headed to DiNapoli's Roast Beef and Pizza for food and comfort. I didn't know Alicia well enough to console anyone. I had paid my respects, said my prayers, so it was time for me to go.

I crossed the parking lot to my car.

"Sarah Winston."

I turned at the voice. Squinted my eyes in the sun. Scott Pellner, a police officer for the Ellington Police Department, called to me. I almost didn't recognize him out of uniform and in a suit. He was broad and muscled, a few inches taller than me. His dimpled face grim.

"What are you doing here?" I asked. I had scanned the crowd at the funeral, curious about who'd be there. There had been a large group from the base Spouses' Club, an OSI agent—the Office of Special Investigations—who I knew, lots of military folks in their uniforms. A few of my friends, but they were too far away to join. I hadn't spotted Pellner.

"Working the case," Pellner said.

The base and the town of Ellington, Massachusetts, had memorandums of agreement. When a crime was committed on base but involved a dependent—the spouse or child of the military member—they worked together.

"Do police really go to funerals to see if the killer shows up?" I asked.

"They do in this case," Pellner said. His voice was as serious as I'd ever heard it.

"No suspects?"

"There's suspects. But no proof."

From what I'd heard, at some point in the night almost a week ago, Alicia had gotten up to take their new Labrador puppy out to do its business. We'd had a terrible ice storm that day and a thick coat of ice caked everything. The house I lived in looked like it had been wrapped in glass. And when I'd gone to bed that night I had heard tree branches across the street on the town common, snapping under the weight of the ice. Later chunks fell off the house as a warm front swept through from the south and I was grateful to be snug in my bed.

Early in the morning Alicia's husband woke to the sound of the puppy barking and crying. He found the sweet thing scratching at the back door—shivering but otherwise okay. After calling for Alicia, he found her sprawled in the backyard with a head wound. Ice shattered around her. At first everyone had thought it was a terrible accident. But later the medical examiner discovered the wound might not have been an accident. When Alicia had first been found the scene wasn't treated as a crime scene, so any evidence had melted away. No footprints, no nothing.

"Who are the suspects?" I asked. I assumed the husband. He had to be on the list as the last person to have seen her.

"Did you know her?" Pellner asked.

Of course he wasn't going to answer my question. I shouldn't have bothered asking. "We occasionally crossed paths at the base thrift shop."

"Do you know who her friends are?"

I shook my head. "No. And I don't know who doesn't like her either." That's what he really wanted to know.

Car doors slammed. We turned to see the hearse pull away. Pellner shook his head. "I need to go." His face still grim as he hurried off.

Forty minutes later I pushed my plate away from me. I'd polished off the better part of a small mushroom and sausage pizza, today's special. Angelo DiNapoli, the proprietor and my dear friend, didn't believe in pineapple on pizzas and sneered at toppings like kale. According to Angelo those weren't real pizzas. He stuck to the traditional and was excellent at what he did. Me, on the other hand? Except for anchovies I'd eat almost anything on a pizza, especially if someone else made it.

I wished I could have a glass of wine to warm me, but I was meeting a client who was interested in having a garage sale. That was a rare thing in January in Massachusetts, so I needed the business. I was still cold from talking to Pellner in the parking lot. And every time someone opened the door the wind nipped at my ankles like an overenthusiastic puppy.

I shuddered thinking again of Alicia.

"You haven't been in for a while," Angelo said. His face was warm, his nose a little on the big side, and his hair way past receding, not that he cared. By *a while* he meant five days. I'd been huddled at home.

I looked around the restaurant. It was almost empty. The right side, where I sat, was lined with tables. To the left was the counter where you ordered and behind it the open kitchen. I'd been in such a swirl of thoughts I didn't notice the lunch rush had left—back to wherever they had to go. That explained my cold ankles. Angelo DiNapoli pulled out a chair and sat down. He wore his white chef's coat, a splash of marinara on the pocket.

"Is everything okay?" he asked.

"I just left a funeral."

"For the woman who was murdered on base?" Angelo asked as he crossed himself.

I nodded. "She was like me. A younger version. Only twenty-five." Fourteen years younger than me.

"How so?"

"Active in the Spouses' Club, volunteered at the thrift shop, didn't have kids."

"You see yourself in her?"

"Yes. I know what it's like to have to move somewhere you don't want to live and far from everyone you know and love. Then do it over and over." I sighed. "I didn't know anything about the military or military life when CJ and I met. And I was always afraid I'd do something that would hurt CJ's career." I had married my ex-husband, CJ, when I was only eighteen. "During our first assignment I asked a colonel's wife out to lunch because she was so friendly. We went to the Officers Club and ate. Then there was this huge brouhaha that a lowly lieutenant's wife was out with a colonel's wife. She didn't care. I didn't care. But a lot of other people did."

"That doesn't sound easy," Angelo said.

"It wasn't at first. It's hard enough to feel judged when it's just you, but then worrying about tanking your husband's career too? It feels like you're walking a minefield of rules no one gave you."

Angelo crossed his arms over his chest. "Are you reevaluating your life?"

"Maybe I have been. I've been a bit down since I heard the news of her death. It seemed like everyone loved her." I wasn't so sure everyone had loved me when I lived on base. CJ and I had lived on Fitch for a couple of years until we divorced two years ago. We had tried to work things out, but just couldn't manage it and split up for good last spring. "If the eulogies are any indication."

"They aren't," Angelo said, "any indication. Genghis Khan would sound like a saint at his own funeral. People gloss over. They forget that people are complex."

"You're right." I knew that. It's a lesson I'd learned over and over the past few years.

"Would you change the past?" Angelo asked.

I sat for a moment thinking over my decisions, how life had led me here. I'd moved to Ellington right after my divorce and had started my own business organizing garage sales. My friends buoyed me and I was in a great relationship. I was proud of what I'd accomplished, but always feared failure. It was part of what I'd been obsessing about for the last week.

I shook my head. "I wouldn't change much. Every decision made me who I am. Even though I'm still not sure who that is."

"Then what are you going to do? Sit around and feel sorry for yourself?"

I smiled at Angelo. He didn't pull any punches. "That's exactly what I've been doing."

"What have you been doing?" Rosalie, Angelo's lovely wife, joined us. Concern creased lines around her brown eyes. Her brown hair was cut short and suited her. Rosalie held three plates with pieces of tiramisu and passed them out. "We've missed you."

I almost laughed. It would keep me from crying. Jeez, I was one big ball of emotions. "You two are the best."

"At least someone recognizes that," Angelo said.

"Oh, Angelo," Rosalie said.

He held up both hands, palms up. "It's the truth."

We ate our dessert, chatted about things that didn't have to do with Alicia. They entertained me with stories of the early years of their marriage living in a small apartment in the bad part of Cambridge.

"Did you always want to open a restaurant?" I asked them.

"Yes," Angelo said. "My *nonna* and mama taught me everything I know about food. I loved cooking from the day I set foot in their kitchen when I was three."

I turned to Rosalie. "And you?"

She smiled at Angelo. "I love him, so I supported his dream."

"She's a born hostess and a great partner," Angelo

said. He took Rosalie's hand and kissed it. "Forty-five years almost, and I don't regret a day."

"Maybe one day?" Rosalie said with a wink. "Cooking is all about love for us."

Maybe I should learn to cook a dish and surprise everyone by having them over for a meal. It's not like I never cooked while CJ and I were married. It's just that when I tried I always seemed to leave an ingredient out or overcook everything. I blanched when I remembered the episode of the undercooked chicken. That was one dinner party no one would ever forget.

Even when I'd tried using a slow cooker, I seemed to end up with mush. Now there were Instant Pots and air fryers and pressure cookers. New appliances with elaborate recipes to try to master. It was terrifying out there.

"Have you two heard any local gossip about the murder?" Lots of military and civilians who worked on base lived in Ellington. There wasn't ever enough housing on base for all military personnel to live there, and for civilians it was a dream commute— only fifteen minutes depending on traffic. Even if they didn't live in Ellington they filled DiNapoli's at mealtime.

"Nothing here," Angelo said.

I looked at Rosalie.

She shook her head. "I was at the hairdresser two days ago. There was a lot of speculation but no information."

That was strange.

"You're going to take that pizza home with you," Angelo said, pointing to what I hadn't eaten.

No one left food behind at DiNapoli's. Angelo

took it as a personal insult. Rosalie took the pizza, boxed it up, and brought it back over. After saying goodbye, I left DiNapoli's and drove over to meet my new client, pondering the lack of gossip about Alicia's death and what it meant.

Chapter Two

A tall, thick-boned woman met me at the one-story ranch on a quiet side street in Ellington. The street wasn't busy this time of day, but I knew at rush hour in the morning and evening it was used as a cut-through.

"I'm Jeannette Blevins." She had bushy brown hair held back with a sparkly headband. I knew from some of the paperwork she'd already filled out that she was thirty-three.

"Sarah Winston," I said. We shook hands. Her grip firm. We stood in a narrow hallway with a low ceiling that served as a foyer. What I presumed was a coat closet was to the right. We walked past it, took a left, and went into the living room. I was surprised to see a vaulted ceiling that made the room seem more spacious.

"Like I told you when I called, my parents died two months ago in Senegal. A tragic accident with a faulty gas line." She paused and sucked in a shaky breath. "My brother and I need to get rid of all of this stuff." She waved her hand around.

"I'm so sorry." She wasn't that old to have lost both her parents. Jeannette had contacted me through my website four days ago. Because of a past incident I now requested documentation proving the party had the right to sell the contents of the house. Since her brother was the executor and lived out of town, I'd also asked for and gotten a notarized letter from him saying Jeannette could oversee the sale. When I was satisfied that all was in order I agreed to meet with her.

"Is there anything that you want to keep?" I asked. There was so much left in here.

"My brother and I have gone through and taken what we want. I live in a two-family house and don't have room or the desire to take much. He lives in New York City in a small place."

I scanned the living room. This would be a huge job. Every bit of wall space seemed to have something hanging on it. Paintings, mosaic tiles, mirrors, samurai swords. It was an eclectic mix that gave me a bit of a headache to look at. I stepped closer to study the things hanging on the wall next to me. Everything seemed to be excellent quality, at least in this room.

"Let me show you the rest of the house."

We walked through the three bedroom, two bath house. One of the bedrooms had been converted into a study. The house was filled with Japanese furniture, a Danish modern bedroom suite in the guest room, framed maps, and shelves filled with figurines. "Your parents must have traveled a lot," I said. I snapped pictures with my phone as we went through the rooms. It would help me organize, estimate how many hours this project would take, and maybe I could even do some pricing from home.

"They did. We all did." Jeannette stopped next to a family photo. Black and white, it looked like it had been taken in Egypt, since a pyramid and camel were in the background. She hesitated for a moment. "I guess it doesn't matter now that they are gone."

I wondered what was coming next.

"They were both in the CIA."

My eyes widened. "That must have been an interesting way to grow up."

"We didn't know it. We thought Dad worked for the agricultural department and that Mom was a translator. We took all the moves for granted."

"How did you end up here?" I asked.

"My dad was originally from Boston. They met in college at Georgetown. At least that was their story." Jeannette grinned. "I think Mom was my dad's handler, although they never admitted it."

"Wow." I thought about growing up in Pacific Grove, California. My childhood had been grounded, a bit boring even. It's one of the reasons why I'd gotten married so young "Are you . . ." I stopped. It wasn't any of my business if Jeannette was in the CIA or not. She wouldn't tell me if she was.

"CIA?" She laughed. "Oh, no. I'm a teacher. I loved all the places we lived, but I wanted to settle in one place."

Having moved all the time when I was married to CJ, I understood the need for roots. It's why I stayed in Ellington when we split up.

"Did you have a favorite place where you lived?" I asked.

"Japan. I was ten and it all seemed so exotic and amazing. For some reason my mom had more free time there. We spent lots of time baking and exploring. It was great." Jeannette took the photo off the wall. "I guess I should keep this. If you find anything else like this, will you let me know?"

I nodded.

"There's so much stuff that it's hard to spot everything."

"No problem," I said. "I'll keep an eye out. Am I going to find any spy gadgets?" My voice held a little more hope in it than I'd intended. This might be a very interesting sale.

Jeannette laughed again. "I think spy gadgets are overrated. Most work was done talking to people one-on-one."

Maybe I'd find a lapel pin with a camera or a pen with a poison dart. A girl could dream. Maybe I should be extra careful sorting things, though.

We discussed payment options. With a project this big I sometimes charged an hourly fee to price items, or I could take a larger than normal commission. The first option was better for me because there was no way to tell how much all of this would sell for. On the other hand I needed the business, so I was inclined to accept the larger commission. I'd toyed with the idea of starting an online auction site for this kind of sale. Maybe it was time to implement that. But before I offered it up as a solution, I wanted to double-check what kind of website I'd need to support it. And I would have to think about all the packing and shipping costs that would involve. It didn't seem like the right time for this idea.

We settled on a larger commission and signed a contract agreeing that I do the sale in two weeks. "I'm going to start promoting this sale online right away because we want to attract as many customers as possible."

"That's a great idea. Thank you." Jeannette gave me the keys to the house.

"I'll be back tomorrow to work."

Jeannette nodded. "The will stated that my brother gets eighty percent of everything." Her voice sounded brisk.

The way the will was split seemed unusual, but it wasn't my place to ask why.

"There was a reason, in the past, why they made that decision. I want to make sure we get top dollar for him."

"That's always my plan. And I've built a reputation for doing that."

She smiled. "I know. That's why I hired you."

Chapter Three

At three thirty I parked my car in the small lot next to my apartment. My landlady, Stella, had put up a sign with a stern warning saying the lot was for residents only. Since we lived right across the street from the town common, parking could be at a premium especially during events. My apartment was on the second floor of a house with four units. It overlooked the town common with its large green space and towering white Congregational church.

I didn't feel like going home yet, so I walked the half block over to my friend Carol Carson's shop, Paint and Wine—or as I called it, Paint and Whine. The air had gotten colder and the wind stronger. My blond hair blew wildly around my face and I wished for a hat or a ponytail holder. Her shop faced the Congregational church just like DiNapoli's a couple of doors down. Carol knew most of my secrets. We often spent our time together to catch up, complain, laugh, and celebrate the little things in life. I blew into the store on a gust of wind and managed to wrestle the wood-and-glass door closed without doing any damage to it or the old panes of glass.

"That is some wind," Carol said.

"Then there's hope. You'd better let me come to the pre-sale."

"You'll be the first one to know if I schedule one." I hadn't done a pre-sale in a long time. They were usually the night before the main event. It was just for friends and family, but maybe I could use it to garner extra interest in the sale. Although with this sale, a CIA sale, I didn't think extra interest would be a problem.

"I have a class coming in an hour. Want to help me set up?"

"Sure. Who's the class for?" I started pulling stools off the tops of rectangular tables. This part of Carol's shop was a big open space with lots of long tables. Behind this space was a room where Carol painted and a small storeroom beyond it.

"A group of twelve-year-olds from the base. It's a birthday party."

"That sounds like fun." After we got the stools down we started setting up tabletop easels.

"It should be. The birthday girl is shy, so this is a way to have a party without a lot of stress."

"What are they going to paint?"

"A starry night. A simpler version of van Gogh's painting. She thought it was dreamlike and fun."

We put canvases on each easel along with paint-brushes and paints.

"Want a glass of wine?" Carol asked when we were finished.

"Sure."

Carol brought me a glass of cabernet and we settled on two stools facing each other across a table.

"I went to a funeral this morning. On base. For Alicia Arbas. Did you know her?" I asked.

"Not well. But she came to a class a few weeks ago with some family members who were in town visiting."

"A private class?"

Carol shook her head, setting her ponytail to swinging. "No. Just one of the open to the public classes. Wine Wednesdays. They've been very popular. We painted a picture of a wine bottle sitting on a picnic table with some trees behind it."

"You have a good memory."

"She told me that Brad and her husband had golfed together before. So she stood out in my mind."

Most bases have golf courses. On big bases they were right on the grounds of the base. But on a smaller base like Fitch the golf course could be off base. Fitch's was on the VA grounds in the town of Bedford. Only people who were military, veterans, DOD employees, or VA patients and employees, could golf there. Well, there were two exceptions. The high school golf team and civilians who were playing with someone who had access. Golf courses weren't funded through tax-payer dollars, but by funds raised by MWR—Morale, Welfare, and Recreation.

"Did Brad know them well?" I asked.

"I asked him after I found out she'd died. He said he and Alicia's husband had been paired up in some base golf outing last fall. Brad's old squadron and Alicia's husband's current one. They hit it off and played a couple of more times. I don't think he ever met Alicia. Did you know her?"

"Not well. I met her briefly at the thrift shop on base, but never really talked to her."

Carol cocked her head to one side. "Then why did you go to her funeral?"

I shrugged. "I just felt like that could have been me. Weird, huh?"

"Not so weird. I think most of us feel that way when someone who shouldn't have died does. Did anything interesting happen?"

"Why would you ask that?" I said.

Carol shrugged. "It just seems like interesting things always happen when you are around."

I tossed a paintbrush at her. "Scott Pellner was there. For work."

"Is that why you were really there? Your curiosity about what happened? Who did it?"

"No. NO! Absolutely not." I shook my head for emphasis. But was that why I was there?

"Methinks thou doth protest too much. Especially with all of the questions you were asking."

"Okay, Shakespeare. Think whatever you want. That's not why I was there." I shook my head again. "At least I don't think that's why I was."

Chapter Four

Stella, my landlady, threw open her door when I entered the foyer. She poked her head out, green eyes large in her olive-toned face. "Do you have time to come in? For a glass of wine?" she asked.

Her sweet little tuxedo cat, Tux, meowed at me from the door by Stella's feet. It almost sounded like he meowed "please."

"Sure. I'd love to." Seth Anderson, the man in my life, was coming over but not for a couple of hours. "Sans the wine. I just had a glass over at Paint and Wine."

I followed Stella in, hung my coat on a hook by the door, and bent down to Tux. "Who's a handsome boy?" I asked. Tux put his front paws on my knee and nudged my leg with his head. "You should be on TV," I told him as I scratched his ears. My apartment was right above Stella's, only hers was a bit bigger because it had what the locals called a "bump out," a small addition, on the back. Tux lost interest in me and curled up on a pillow on the floor. I went to the bathroom and washed my hands. Being allergic to cats wasn't fun, but as long as I was careful I didn't have many problems with Tux.

Stella was sitting on her couch when I came back. I sat in a chair across from her.

"You look tired," Stella said.

"Long day." I filled her in on the funeral. "The good news is I have a big sale to do." I quickly explained about Jeannette and her parents.

"Stuff from all over the world and they were in the CIA? That is one garage sale I'm not going to miss. I'll have to bring my mom and aunts along." She smiled briefly and fiddled with a tassel on a pillow.

"What's going on? Are you okay?" She'd looked distracted and a little blue the whole time I was talking.

"I need to find a renter for the apartment next to yours. I'm sorry," Stella said. "I need the income."

"Don't apologize. It's ridiculous not to." Stella had had some problems with her renters in the past.

"You can help me look and I'll do extra background checks. By the time I'm done with them I'll know if they have a mole on their rear end."

I grinned. "Sounds good."

"Do you know anyone on base who's looking?"

"Not off the top of my head, but I can check around." Someone from base would be good because most of them already had been checked out up to their eyeballs. And if there were problems you could go to their commander. It didn't mean you'd never have a problem with a military renter, but it helped tilt the odds in a landlord's favor.

"I thought about changing it to an Airbnb type of thing. I could make a lot of money doing that with all the tourists who come to Lexington and Concord, but it seems like a lot of work and more noise than I'm ready to handle."

"More cleaning too," I added. "And you'd have to furnish it. Although, I'd do that for you. It would be fun." I loved searching for furniture for people.

"There's all that. Anyway, if you hear of anyone, let me know."

"Will do," I said. "Is that it?" I had a feeling more than just that was bothering her.

"It's Nathan."

Oh, no. That didn't sound good. Nathan Bossum was Stella's cop boyfriend. They met last winter under unusual circumstances. I'd misunderstood his last name at the time, so he'd been called Awesome ever since.

"Is he okay?" I asked. "Are you guys all right?"

Stella looked miserable. "He's been acting so strange lately."

"What's he been doing?" If he was cheating on her, I was going to kill him myself.

"He's cranky. Nathan's always been so even tempered. Until the past couple of weeks our relationship has just been easy. Fun. Now I'm wondering about everything." Tears formed in her eyes and dripped down her face.

I moved over to sit next to her. "You're in love." I knew that Stella really enjoyed Nathan. He was over here almost every day. But now that I thought about it, I'd hadn't seen him around as much lately.

"I am. I'm such a fool. I promised myself after that mess out in California I was off men forever. Then came the whole debacle with Bubbles. What a winner he turned out to be." Stella looked down and shook

her head. "But at least I got Tux out of that situation."
Tux meowed and jumped in Stella's lap. She swiped
at her tears before stroking Tux's back. "Nathan snuck
up on me. On my heart."

Stella didn't talk about her past much. I know she'd
had some problems with drugs a long time ago. "What
happened in California? Maybe it's affecting how
you're feeling now."

Stella took a drink of her wine. "The man I loved
scammed me. Took off with my money and my heart.
It's one of the reasons I came back home."

"That's rotten." I knew at times I'd projected my
marital problems with CJ onto Seth—unfairly. They
were so different. "You could be projecting. Especially after what happened with Bubbles."

"Yeah, I have a pattern of falling for guys who don't
really care about me. It looks like I've done it again."

"Awesome is a good guy." *He'd better be, anyway.*
"Maybe it's something at work that's bothering him.
Alicia's death is weighing on everyone. I saw Pellner
at the funeral this morning. He was frustrated."

"I hope that's it," Stella said.

"Me too." I planned to have a little chat with Awesome next time I saw him.

Once home I grabbed my computer and looked
up Jeannette Blevins's family. There were extensive
articles about the death of her parents. Jeannette's
father was from a well-known, well-off Boston family.
Not a family who traced their roots back to the
Mayflower, but they arrived shortly after. There was no
mention of either of her parents being in the CIA,

only that they worked for the government. The article did say it had been determined that the explosion that killed them was caused by a gas leak. Senegalese officials were cited as saying the Blevinses had misused the system. Seeing as who her parents were, I'm guessing that story had been checked and double checked.

Chapter Five

I woke Wednesday morning to the smell of coffee and the sound of Seth humming in my kitchen. I turned over with a contented sigh and pulled my blue and white comforter tighter around me. I wasn't feeling inclined to get up.

"Hey sleepyhead," Seth said.

A kiss landed on my cheek. I opened my eyes to see a cup of steaming black coffee on the nightstand. I rolled over and looked up at Seth. The first time I'd laid eyes on him had been in a bar in Lowell, a town thirty miles north of here, almost two years ago. He had come over with dinner last night after he heard about my day. You had to love a man who brought you Chinese takeout after a rough day.

He was already dressed in a suit and crisp white shirt, looking every bit the Massachusetts's Most Eligible Bachelor he'd been named the past three years in a row. Broad shouldered, wavy dark hair, and dark eyes. And he was smart too. Seth had served as interim DA after the prior DA had gotten ill and had to resign. Seth had won his first election last fall, so could continue his work as the district attorney for Middlesex County. He was the youngest DA ever elected.

I looked a mess with bed head and no makeup. A far cry from the model types Seth had dated before me.

"You look gorgeous. I wish I could stay."

I smiled and reached out an arm. "It's warm under here."

Seth leaned down and kissed me. "Don't tempt me. I have to get to court."

"Go get some bad guys," I called to him as he left. He flashed a smile that made me want to fan myself. I propped my pillows up and grabbed my coffee. I didn't have to rush this morning, which was lovely. I blew some of the steam off the top of my cup and took a tentative sip. Black and strong. Just the way I liked my coffee.

My phone rang so I plucked it off the nightstand. I frowned at it. Special Agent Frank Bristow. Why would he be calling at seven in the morning?

"Would you come see me in my office at eight thirty?" Frank wasn't one for social niceties, which always surprised me. His voice had that nasal quality so many Midwesterners had. And my perception of Midwesterners was they were all about being nice.

"What for?" I asked. I couldn't be more surprised. As far as I knew I wasn't in any kind of trouble with the OSI. The OSI was the Air Force equivalent of what NCIS was to the Navy. They investigated major crimes. I visited the base every couple of weeks, either to see friends or volunteer at the thrift shop, but as far as I knew that hadn't created any kind of problem.

"I'd rather explain when you come in." He paused. "If you come in."

Well, that's a hard thing to turn down. My curiosity

I pushed my hair out of my face until it fell back around my shoulders where it was supposed to hang. "Blow thou bitter wind, blow," I said paraphrasing a line by Maud Hart Lovelace, one of my favorite authors growing up.

Carol looked out the window. "I heard it's supposed to snow tomorrow."

"Great."

"We've had a lot this winter," Carol said. Her light blond hair was pulled back in a ponytail. She wore a fuzzy warm sweater that wrapped around her Barbie-doll figure like it was a second skin. Jeans tucked into knee-high high-heeled boots completed her outfit. For someone who spent her life painting or teaching painting, she somehow managed to never have a speck of paint on her.

"I love the days I can sit in my grandmother's rocking chair by the window, watching it fall while I drink coffee and read. But tomorrow I have to be out in it because I have a new client."

"Tell me about your new client. That's a good thing this time of year."

"It is, and it's an interesting house. The owner was in the CIA." Being in the military meant I was used to people having top secret clearances and not being able to talk about their jobs, but the CIA always seemed a bit exotic to me. Carol's husband, Brad, had been in the military too. When he retired out of Fitch they also decided to stay here.

"Oh, have you found any shoe phones?" Carol asked. "I always wanted one."

I laughed. "No. But I haven't really dug into things yet. I just did a walk-through."

was piqued and my morning open. "I'll be there, but I'll need a pass to get on base."

"I'll have one waiting for you at the visitors' center."

He hung up without a goodbye. I sprung out of bed and pondered, as I showered, what Frank wanted. Part of me was convinced it had something to do with Alicia. But maybe I was wrong. By the time I was in my Suburban driving to base, I'd convinced myself otherwise.

At eight o'clock I had another surprise at the visitors' center, where I had to show my driver's license and proof of insurance to get the pass. Special Agent Bristow had left me a pass for thirty days, not the couple hours I expected.

"Are you sure this is right?" I asked the young enlisted woman standing across from me behind a long counter. She was part of the security police force and had worked for my ex-husband when he was active duty. I had known her for three years.

"I'll double-check," she said. She tapped away on her computer. "Yes. That's the instructions. A thirty-day pass."

The pass meant I could come on and off base as I pleased. Usually passes were more restrictive, to somewhere specific like the thrift shop or a friend's house for X number of hours.

"Is everything okay with you?" I asked. Duty at the visitors' center often meant the person working the desk was in some kind of trouble and this was part of their punishment.

"It looks bad, right?" she said. "But they are just shorthanded, so here I am."

I smiled. "I'm glad that's it."

"Me too," she said.

A couple of people walked in, so I said my goodbyes and headed over to Special Agent Bristow's office.

I kept my mouth from dropping open when I walked into Bristow's office and saw Pellner sitting in a chair across from Bristow. Someone had cleared off another chair for me. Bristow's office was cramped and dark, but it was neater than the last time I'd been there a few months ago.

In fact, Special Agent Bristow looked neater. His wife had died a couple of years ago and his grief had been plastered on his haggard face for months. Now his light brown hair, thinning but not yet thin, was neatly combed. His suit didn't look like he'd slept in it. However, his tie was askew, so not everything had changed. This case must be hard for him—another wife gone, another husband grieving.

I sat on the edge of the chair, wondering why I was there. Pellner was in his uniform and was tap, tap, tapping his fingers on his thigh.

"What's up?" I asked, looking from Pellner to Bristow.

They exchanged looks but remained silent, as though each was waiting for the other to speak.

Jeez, what was going on with these two? I decided to try another tactic to get the conversation going. "You accidentally gave me a thirty-day pass." I looked at Bristow.

He adjusted his tie. But now it was crooked to the other side. "It wasn't an accident. I need your help." He gestured to Pellner. "We need your help."

"With?" I asked.

"While we have suspects, we don't have a strong suspect in Alicia Arbas's death," Pellner said. "Or, as I mentioned after the funeral, any proof."

I sat up a little at what I anticipated was coming.

"We'd like you to find out what you can. That's why the thirty-day pass was issued. That way you can come and go as you need to," Bristow said.

"Seriously? You want me to go undercover?" First a CIA garage sale and now this. Life was getting exciting, but I tempered that thought when I thought of Alicia and her husband.

"No," Pellner said. "Not undercover." He shook his head vehemently to underscore his statement. "Like you are you."

"You know more of these people and have access to them. People like and trust you," Bristow said.

"You can mingle and look innocent in places where we can't," Pellner added.

"All we want you to do is listen. If you hear anything interesting, let us know and we'll take it from there."

"We are asking you to *only* listen," Pellner said.

Bristow nodded. "And observe."

"And report back." Pellner leaned forward, giving me the hard cop look. His deep dimples all serious.

"I get it." Yeesh, the way they were acting you'd think I didn't understand English. "Who else knows about this?"

"We just came from the cops and robbers meeting," Bristow said.

"The *what*?" I asked.

"You never heard CJ call a meeting that?" Bristow asked.

CJ had been the head of the base security-forces squadron when he was active duty. As such he attended lots of meetings. "No. That I would remember."

"It's the weekly meeting with the top brass to go over what's going on around base."

I hooked a thumb toward Pellner. "He's not top brass." I looked at Pellner. "No offense."

"None taken," Pellner said, "but we have shared jurisdiction for Alicia's death since she's a dependent and it happened in base housing. I was invited to that meeting."

"Who else was there?" I asked. I wanted to know who the players were.

"In addition to the base officials, a representative from mental health," Bristow said.

"Why?" I went over in my head what I could remember CJ saying about those kinds of meetings. Not much. But to CJ the meetings would have been part of his routine so nothing unusual.

"For two reasons. To see if any mental health issues were involved, with the victim or perpetrator, and to help coordinate efforts for extra counseling for the troops. People on base are shook up over all of this," Bristow said.

That made sense. Good sense. Sometimes I didn't give our military officials enough credit for all the parts they had to juggle. "And they all agreed to me helping. Listening? Why?"

"Most of the people knew either you or CJ," Bristow said. "You and I have worked together before."

Yeah, one of the times we "worked" together was when Bristow was trying to pin a murder on CJ.

"And we vouched for you." Pellner pointed back and forth between the two of them.

Wow. My heart felt all warm and fuzzy. "Why me? There are plenty of other spouses available. The general's wife. The husband of the new head of the security forces."

"You are a trusted source," Pellner said.

"And you won't go around bragging that we asked you for help. No one was sure the other people whose names were tossed out could do that," Bristow added.

"Okay. I'm in." In and flattered. Who knew people had such a good opinion of me? Frankly, it was nice to hear after my ego was bruised from the breakup with CJ. Last fall Bristow had told me that I'd make a good analyst. I hadn't taken him very seriously at the time. A small pump of pride went through me that two professionals were asking for my help. Even more important, I could do something for a young woman and her family. I could help find her killer.

Pellner stood up. "I need to get going. Sarah, just—"

"I've got it. Listen, observe, report." I stood up too as Pellner left.

"Wait," Bristow said. "I have one more thing to ask you."

I swear his cheeks pinked just a bit. "Okay."

"There's a dining-out on Friday night. I wondered if you'd go with me."

I kept my face as neutral as possible. This was an interesting turn of events. Dining-outs were formal military banquets held by a wing or group. Different wings had them at different times throughout the year. Women wore gowns and men wore tuxes, or if they were in the military their mess dress—the military equivalent of a tux.

"For work. For the case," Bristow added hastily.

"It will look like we are on a date," I said.

"I know it's a lot to ask since you're involved with the DA."

Involved was one way of summing up our relationship. I was surprised he knew, but maybe Pellner and Bristow had talked about this before I arrived. Pellner had taken off quickly. Maybe he didn't want to witness this particular conversation.

"If it will help you find who killed Alicia, I'm in." I was sure Seth would understand. He would want the killer caught as much as anyone, and his office might be in charge of prosecuting whoever did it. But first we had to figure out who that person was.

Chapter Six

Boy, was I wrong. Seth's fork clattered back onto the plate between us with a piece of pistachio cake still clinging to it. We were sharing the cake at the end of our lunch at DiNapoli's.

"It's unconscionable that Special Agent Bristow would involve you in this," Seth said. "And Pellner."

I sat back, surprised. But maybe I wasn't so surprised, since I'd waited until the very last minute to bring it up. Right before Seth had to leave to go back to work.

"It's not a date," I said, deliberately misunderstanding his comment.

"You know it's not that."

I glanced over and saw Rosalie tug Angelo's arm, tilting her head toward us. They liked Seth better than they'd ever liked CJ. I didn't want that to change. I relaxed my posture and smiled. I took a bite of the pistachio cake. Seth started to swivel his head. He could sense the change in my attitude instantly. I put my hand on his arm.

"Don't look. Please. Angelo and Rosalie are watching."

"And?"

"I want them to like you. To like us together." I smiled again. "They are a little overly protective of me."

Seth relaxed too. Laughed. "A little? Like grizzlies watching out for a cub."

"Bristow just asked me to observe, listen, and report back. What's the harm in that?" I took another bite of the pistachio cake. It had just the right amount of moisture and was silky smooth as it slipped down my throat.

"So, you aren't going to run around asking anyone questions?" Seth finally picked up his fork and ate the piece of cake on it.

Darn it. He knew me too well.

"I love you," Seth said. "Just promise me you'll be careful."

"Always."

As I drove over to Jeannette's parents' house to work on the garage sale, I pondered why it was so hard for me to say *I love you* back to Seth. I'd only said it once. I think I loved him. I know I loved parts of him. Whoa, that came out wrong. I loved aspects of him—his intelligence, the way he understood me and let me be myself. And he was hot, there was no doubt about that. But I'd rushed things with CJ when I was eighteen. I didn't want to do that again twenty years later. I needed to make sure I could stand on my own two feet before I made any major life decisions.

Fifteen minutes later I was inside Jeannette's parents' house. It was cool and dark since the thermostat was turned down and most of the windows had heavy drapes over them. I decided to start in the living room, and flung open the curtains. Snowflakes, the big, lovely, floaty kind, were falling. Sitting on the couch and just watching was so tempting, but one look around the place and I knew I had one huge project on my hands.

The anticipation of finding a hidden gem got me going. Every sale I'd done had been a new adventure. Even the ones that didn't include anything of great value gave me pleasure and taught me things. Sometimes it was as simple as watching human interactions. And it was always nice to have a satisfied client who made some money.

I unpacked the tote I had brought in with me. It was full of stickers with preprinted prices from twenty-five cents to fifteen dollars. There were also unmarked stickers where I could fill in the price. I had packed scissors and a measuring tape, too—the tools of my trade. My phone was fully charged so I could use it to make notes. Sometimes I needed it to check prices online or with a friend of mine who was an antique dealer. She owned a shop in Acton, which was about ten miles west of Ellington.

The last thing was a small wireless speaker so I could blast music from my phone to help pass the hours. Since no one else was here, I cranked the volume on an oldies rock and roll station. It was the music my parents had always played, made me think of family dance parties, and it was energizing.

This house was a daunting task and I might need to hire some additional help. Since I was selling everything left in the house, it was more estate sale than garage sale. Maybe I should check and see if any military spouses would be interested. It was often hard to find a job—even harder to keep a job—with all the moves. An actual career was almost impossible. And some employers wouldn't even hire a military spouse because they knew the spouse was likely a short-term employee, so why invest in training? Of course, employers would never come out and say that.

I tackled the first wall. It held a selection of masks, from Mardi Gras to African and Asian. They were beautiful. Everything from wood to porcelain to papier-mâché. Since I wasn't very familiar with masks it was slow going because I kept stopping to check prices online. And okay, I confess, I kept trying them on and checking myself out in a mirror. I might have taken a few selfies. It was spooky seeing my eyes behind some of them. But it also made me want to learn more about them.

I took some kind of sword off the wall when I heard the front door slam open.

"Jeannette?" I called. I shut off the music. When I turned I saw a man standing about five feet away from me.

"What are you doing in here?" a tall, burly man asked. He had a heavy, dark beard that covered his face and neck. It was sprinkled with snow. A knit Patriots cap was pulled low on his brow and he carried a briefcase.

"Who are you?" I asked.

He glanced warily at me. I realized I was holding the sword out, but I didn't drop it. I tightened my grip on it. I knew I had locked the door, so either he'd broken in or had a key. I was really hoping it was the latter because that meant he was supposed to be here. We stood there staring at each other.

"I'm running a sale for Jeannette." Maybe this guy was a concerned neighbor. I needed to add *notify your neighbors* to my running list of things my clients should do prior to me being at their home. I still didn't lessen my grip on the sword. My hand was starting to sweat and my arm started to shake with the weight of it. "And you are?" I asked again.

"Jeannette's brother, Troy."

"She told me you lived out of town." I gave the sword a little shake, mostly so he wouldn't see the tremor in my arm. What would I do if things went horribly wrong? Could I really run someone through with a sword? *Aim for the gut, not the ribs.* Where had that thought come from? I'd taken some self-defense classes, but none of them involved swords.

Troy stared at the sword. Took a step back. "I flew in this morning to take another look around. Before the sale. To see if there was anything I missed that I wanted."

I pointed the sword at him. "Stay right there. I'm calling Jeannette."

He nodded. I'm not sure which of us was more afraid of the other. I backed over to my phone and made the call. She answered and I hit the speaker button on my phone. We heard the chatter of kids and locker doors slamming. It was hard to hear anything she was saying. I could never work in a school. The noise alone would drive me crazy. I quickly explained about Troy's arrival.

"Troy, what the heck? You should have told me you were coming. You must have scared poor Sarah to death."

"I think it's the other way around. She's holding a sword on me."

Jeannette let out a hoot and I finally put the sword down.

"I wish I was there to see that. Way to go, Sarah. It's not easy getting one up on my brother."

After we hung up, I circled my shoulder to try to relax it after having a death grip on the sword.

"Sorry I scared you," he said.

"Yeah, back at you."

"Would you have really run me through with the sword?" he asked.

"I'm not sure. I'm glad we didn't have to find out."

He gave me an assessing look. "In that case, me too."

"You must have had an interesting childhood," I said.

He shrugged. "I guess."

"You and Jeannette don't want more of all of this?" I asked. "There are some really interesting pieces."

"It's one of the reasons I'm here. My wife decided there are some things she couldn't live without." Troy looked around. "Some carvings, masks, and other stuff."

"There are lots of carvings." I'd seen some yesterday while I was here with Jeannette. "Some are in the study. Down the hall and to the left." Yeesh, as if he didn't know. It was his parents' house.

Troy lumbered off. I went back to the living room. I picked the sword up to try to price it. Swords were way out of my realm of pricing. I checked online but didn't find anything quite like it. I snapped a couple of pictures and sent them off to my friend.

I continued to work for the next thirty minutes, listening to music, but not as loud as before. Occasionally, I heard Troy moving around. A crash sounded from the back of the house.

"Troy?" I called. I didn't hear anything. That was odd, but maybe he just knocked one of the many objects off one of the walls. It wasn't hard to do in this house. "Troy?" I said it louder this time. I heard movement and couldn't quite decide what to do. Give him his privacy or go investigate. A moan sounded from the direction of the study. I ran down the hall. Skidded into the room. Troy lay unconscious on the floor with his foot twisted at an odd angle. A cool breeze blew over me as the drapes bellowed out. The window was wide open.

I checked Troy's pulse, which beat madly. I snatched my phone out of my pocket and called 911. As I gave the dispatcher the information I studied the room. File drawers were pulled open. Files and papers spilled across the avocado shag carpet. Desk drawers were open too. Was Troy searching for something back here, dumped all this on the floor, and then slipped?

A chill shook me. One that had nothing to do with the breeze coming in through the open window. What the heck had happened in here while I was out in the other room minding my own business, pricing, and listening to music. A couple snowflakes floated in. They fell onto the folders, leaving small splotches. Why was the window open? The house was a bit stuffy, but it seemed like opening it a crack would have been enough.

I ran to the linen closet in the hall, found some blankets, and covered Troy as best I could. It was cold in the room, but I didn't want to close the window in case it had any evidence on it. Evidence of what, I wasn't sure. For all I knew Troy opened the window and went through the files. Maybe he *had* tripped and hurt himself. But for some reason I didn't think so.

I picked my way over to the window, trying not to step on anything. I nudged the curtains aside with my elbows and peered out. The storm window lay broken on the ground. Faint footprints led away from the window in the skiff of snow that had fallen. Sirens sounded close by. Tires screeched and car doors slammed. I ran back to the front of the house and yanked the door open.

Pellner shouldered by me as an ambulance pulled up. "Where is he?"

"Down the hall. To the left." I pointed, but Pellner was already in motion. The EMTs hustled in and I directed them too. I stayed in the living room out of the way. I took my phone out to call Jeannette, but hesitated. I'd rather call after I knew where they were taking Troy and what his condition was. The EMTs came back, hauling Troy out on a gurney. An IV hung from his arm and an oxygen mask was clapped over his mouth and nose.

Pellner followed and detoured over to me. I filled him in on what I knew.

"Do you think someone else was in here when you arrived?" Pellner asked.

I shook my head. "I don't think so. I would have heard them. This house isn't that big. Unless I surprised them and they were trying to quietly wait me out." There were plenty of closets to hide in.

Pellner's dimples deepened, which was never a good sign.

"Maybe Troy walked in while someone else was climbing in the window," I said. That made more sense and wasn't quite as scary. I remembered reading a Mary Higgins Clark book when I was in high school. A man had hidden in the closet of a woman's bedroom—for hours—until she came home. I'd spent a lot of time checking closets in the months after I'd read that book.

"I'd better call Troy's sister Jeannette and let her know what's going on. I'd like to meet her at the hospital if that's okay?"

Pellner nodded. "I'll lock up after we're done here. Let me know if you think of anything else."

I met Jeannette at the hospital in Burlington. A nurse directed us to a room in the ER. We rounded the corner. Troy looked gray under his oxygen mask. A doctor stood by his side.

"How's he doing?" I asked the doctor.

Jeannette looked from me to Troy to the doctor.

"You're his family?" the doctor asked.

"She is." I pointed to Jeannette, who seemed to be in shock. I couldn't imagine finding my brother in the hospital like this.

"That's not my brother," she said.

Chapter Seven

"What do you mean that's not your brother?" I asked. "That's who was in the house." My voice shook. "He talked to you on the phone."

"It was noisy when you called. Hard to hear. I never dreamed anyone would pretend to be my brother."

We both stared down at the man.

"Who is he then?" I looked at the doctor, who frowned at me. "Where are his personal things?" He must have a wallet with an ID in it.

She was already shaking her head before I finished the sentence. "Get out. If you're not his relatives you can't be in here."

Jeannette and I sat in the lobby of the ER trying to sort through the shock we'd both had. I called Pellner and filled him in.

"He had a briefcase when he came in," I told him. "He took it with him to the office. Hopefully, there will be some ID in it so we can get this mystery straightened out."

I looked at Jeannette after I hung up. She twisted a ring on her right hand, round and round. "Pellner asked me if we could wait for him here. He shouldn't be too long."

Jeannette nodded. "I'm going to call and check on my real brother. He's a venture capitalist and it can be hard to get hold of him. What if the man in that room hurt him?" Her hand shook as she held the phone to her ear. Fortunately, her brother answered the phone and they talked briefly. "He's okay. But shaken by what happened. He said he'd fly up, but I told him there was no reason to at this point."

Jeannette and I went over what Fake Troy had said to us again.

"What happened when he walked into the house?" Jeannette asked.

"After he got over being startled that I was there, he acted so confident," I said. "So casual. He said he wanted a few more things from the house." We both thought that over. "The study was a mess. Someone had been looking through the file cabinet."

"Someone?" Jeannette asked.

I told her about the open window and the footsteps leading away from the house. I didn't want to scare her, but I thought she needed to know the whole story.

"Whoever he is, he knows enough about my family to know who my brother is," Jeannette said.

After that we waited for Pellner. A half hour later he finally showed up. I'd spent most of that time pacing the lobby while Jeannette sat biting her lip.

"I'm going to see what I can find out," Pellner said. He veered over to the reception desk and then down the hall before I had a chance to ask him anything.

"Do you want some coffee? Or something else to

drink?" I asked Jeannette. I couldn't just sit here waiting any longer.

"Sure. Coffee would be great."

"I'll go to the cafeteria and be right back." I followed signs and arrows until I found the cafeteria and bought some coffee. I hadn't thought to ask Jeannette how she liked it, so I grabbed some packets of creamer, sugar, and those little plastic stirrers.

When I got back Pellner was still nowhere to be found. We sipped our coffee, which wasn't terrible. Faint praise but better than some coffee I'd consumed. As I was tossing our cups in the trash, Pellner finally returned to the lobby.

"Who is he?" I asked. He pulled a chair over to where Jeannette and I sat.

"No idea. They carted him off to be x-rayed. We didn't find his briefcase at the house. I was hoping it was here. That somehow the EMTs grabbed it. But he didn't even have a wallet on him," Pellner said. "After they x-ray his foot we'll get his prints and see if we can identify him that way."

"When will you be able to interview him?" I asked.

"Not for a while. The doctor said he'll be loopy from the pain meds they've been giving him." Pellner shook his head. "Neither of you have ever seen him before?"

We said "no" at the same time. I noticed Pellner watched Jeannette carefully while she answered. Could he suspect her? This day just kept getting weirder.

"Sarah told me that you are selling your parents' belongings," Pellner said. "What happened to them?"

I was surprised that Pellner didn't know. Or maybe he did and he just wanted to hear Jeannette's version.

She told him what she'd told me about the faulty gas line. I thought again, given her parents' past, officials would have taken extra precautions to make sure it was indeed an accident.

"Your parents must have traveled a lot, considering the interesting things they owned," Pellner said.

"Yes," Jeannette said. "They did."

I wondered if she would tell him why or if he would ask. Jeannette glanced at me. I gave her a little nod.

"They were retired CIA," she said.

Pellner's expression didn't change. He kept his cop face locked and loaded. I thought his dimples deepened just a bit, but his impassiveness was impressive. Unless he already knew and didn't want Jeannette to know for some reason.

"Do you have any reason to think what happened here had anything to do with that?" Pellner asked.

"No." She sat back and thought. "It is strange that someone with no ID came to the house pretending to be my brother. But as far as I know, that chapter of their lives was over and done with ten years ago."

"Sarah, do you have any other thoughts about what happened? Anything you forgot to mention?" Pellner asked.

"He said he came to see if there was anything else he wanted before the sale or that his wife might want," I said.

"He's not even married," Jeannette said. "Never has been."

I wished I would have known that earlier. "There must have been someone else in the house. Or he was let in. Right? I saw footprints in the snow outside the window."

Pellner nodded after hesitating.

"Any leads on who that was? How they got away?" I asked.

"One of the officers followed the footprints through the backyard, through the neighbor's yard, and out onto the next street."

"So the person either parked there or someone was waiting for them?"

"Most likely parked, because of how the footprints ended in the street."

I was surprised Pellner told us that much. Take this with what had happened in Bristow's office and maybe he was finally beginning to trust me. It made me realize I trusted him more all the time, which hadn't always been the case.

Pellner stood. "Thank you both for waiting here for me."

"Is it okay to go back to the house?" Jeannette asked.

"Yes," Pellner said. "I'd like to meet you there. To see what, if anything, is missing."

"Can Sarah come too?" Jeannette asked.

I straightened up, surprised that Jeannette wanted me to go with her.

"She's been in the house recently and did a thorough walk around," Jeannette explained. "A second pair of eyes will be helpful. She's studied everything more than I have."

Pellner had started to shake his head but stopped. "Okay. I'll meet you over there in a few minutes."

Chapter Eight

I met Jeannette back at her parents' house. We sat in my Suburban with the engine running and the seat warmers going. This past week of unusually cold weather seemed to seep into my bone marrow. We had decided to wait for Pellner out here since neither of us were eager to go back into the house.

"Thanks for agreeing to come back over here. If you don't want to go through with the sale, I understand." Jeannette looked thoughtfully at her parents' house.

On the drive over I'd had a brief thought about telling her I didn't feel comfortable doing the sale. That she should find someone else. I'd just let that man, whoever he was, waltz into the house. The whole idea of it had me unnerved.

But I had bills to pay and at least two more months of winter to get through before garage-sale season started up again. And that was only if spring came early, which wasn't all that likely considering this was New England. When CJ had tried to convince me to move to his hometown in Florida, one of the things he'd mentioned was I could run my business year round. At times I saw the sense in that, but I still didn't want to leave Ellington.

Pellner pulled up ten minutes later. It had started to snow again—tiny, mean flakes that stung my cheeks as we hurried into the house. After shedding our coats in the living room, we all headed to the study.

"Is this the only room he was in?" Pellner asked.

"I'm not sure. He was down at this end of the house alone for thirty minutes or so," I said.

Pellner frowned. I interpreted the look as he had hoped we could take a quick look around the office and then get out of here.

"Okay," Pellner said. "Let's start with the study. We know he was in there."

Jeannette and I went in the office. Pellner leaned against the door.

"I took a bunch of photos when I was here the first time," I said. "Maybe that will help us identify anything that is missing." I pulled my phone out of my pocket and sent the pertinent photos to Pellner.

"I'll go look in the master bedroom while you two search in here," he said.

"Why don't I take a quick look in the guest bedroom," I suggested. "It's the only other room back here besides the bathroom."

It only took me a couple of minutes in the guest room. A drawer on the Danish modern dresser was open slightly. I didn't remember it being that way, but it could have been. The dust ruffle on the bed was flipped up. It hadn't been that way earlier. That I was sure of. I glanced in the bathroom as I headed back to the office. The bath mat was askew, but again I might not have noticed it earlier.

When I got back to the office, Jeannette picked up

file folders while I compared the pictures I'd taken to what was in the room. Five minutes later, Pellner came back to the study.

"Any luck?" he asked.

"No," I said.

Jeannette slumped into the desk chair. "Me either, but I didn't know what papers were in what folders. Or for that matter what folders were in the files." She looked at us. "I have no idea if anything is missing or not."

Pellner and I exchanged a look.

"And then there's this," Jeannette said. She yanked open a deep drawer and gestured at the contents. It was crammed to the brim with everything from office supplies to knitting needles and yarn. "My parents weren't good at throwing things out. According to them, you could never tell when that old mint tin would come in handy."

"Are the folders that were on the floor labeled?" I asked. "Maybe the labels will give us a hint as to what someone was looking for."

"Or they could have tossed folders they didn't care about on the floor," Pellner added.

"But it won't hurt to look."

Jeannette handed Pellner the folders. I stood by his side while he sorted through them.

"Travel," he said, holding up the first one. "Complete with magazine articles about places to visit. Crafts, kids' activities, and recipes. All with articles clipped from magazines." Pellner passed them over to me.

I did a quick look through the articles, hoping there was something tucked in one of them. No such luck. We looked through more of the folders, passing them around to see if anything stuck out to any of us. Nothing did. Then we went through the files left in the cabinet to see if it would help us figure anything out. But that didn't work either.

"This seems to be a dead end," I said. "We don't have a good enough idea of what was here to say if anything is missing or what Fake Troy was doing here." I shuddered.

"Fake Troy?" Pellner asked.

"Do you have a better name for him?"

Pellner thought for a minute. "I guess Fake Troy is better than suspect number one, which is what I've been calling him." He smiled. "I'm off. If either of you think of anything, call me."

We walked with Pellner to the front door. "Sarah, could I have a quick word with you?" We stepped out onto the front porch. I shivered wondering what Pellner wanted that he didn't want Jeannette to overhear. Maybe it had something to do with Alicia.

"I have a favor to ask you. This might be bad timing."

I tried to keep my eyebrows from popping up. That's a first. It was usually the other way around. "Okay." At least with Pellner I didn't have to worry about him asking me to break some law. "What do you need?"

Pellner turned red. This ought to be interesting.

"Next month is Valentine's Day. And I'd like to do something special for my wife. I've been working so much lately that I want to make a grand gesture."

"Okay." It came out kind of long and slow. Where was this going? "Dinner at the Wayside Inn in Sudbury is always nice. You could take her for the weekend."

"Five kids, all in school activities. We'll never get away for the weekend."

"Does she collect anything?" I asked.

"She has a shelf full of some kind of blue glass she's always yelling at the kids to stay away from."

"What color? Light blue?" It could be Fostoria.

Pellner shook his head. "A little darker than the color of your eyes. She has a name for it, but I can't remember what."

"Cobalt glass." Cobalt glass was a deep, rich blue that was popular during the Depression. Everything from canisters to eyewashes was made from it. It was still made, but not as beautifully as during the Depression. Sometimes pieces of cobalt glass had been prizes in laundry detergent.

Pellner smiled. "That's it. Could you find a piece for me?"

"Sure. But I don't want to duplicate what she has. Can you snap a picture of her collection and send it to me?"

Pellner nodded.

"Oh, and I'll look for a vintage Valentine." It might be harder to find than the cobalt glass. They were popular and paper was fragile, so it didn't hold up as well as glass. "Anything else?"

"No. Thank you. I appreciate it. I'll try to send you a picture of it later today. Tomorrow at the latest."

Jeannette stood in the foyer when I went back in. She turned to me. "Was he trying to talk you out of doing the sale?"

"No, not at all."

"Like I said earlier, if you don't want to do the sale

any longer, I'll understand. I had no idea anything like this would happen."

I had continued to think about it while we were in the house with Pellner. Was it worth the risk? Was there even a risk now? I'd never backed out on a client. I thought again about how I needed the work. "No. I told you I'd do the sale for you."

"But circumstances have changed."

"Whoever was here knows someone else is going to be around. I may hire a couple of people to help out so I'm not here alone."

"I'll reimburse you for those expenses. And I think I'll get a home security system installed until the sale is over and the house is sold."

"That sounds like a great idea."

"I wonder if this has anything to do with my parents," Jeannette said.

I didn't know what to say.

"It's creepy. That man coming in here. Acting like he was my brother."

"It doesn't seem like it's some random burglar," I answered. It made me wonder what secrets this house held.

That evening at six I sat with a circle of women in a crowded townhouse on base. Gender reveal parties and baby showers were always hard for me, since CJ and I had never been able to have children. But I'd been invited, and it seemed like a perfect time to listen to gossip like Special Agent Bristow had asked me to do. Plus, it distracted me from all that had gone on today. So far though, as expected, all the talk had centered on the mother and baby. I knew the mom from the thrift shop and the crowd seemed to be made up of thrift shop people, family, and her neighbors.

We had played games, presents had been opened, we ate a light supper, and the cake was about to be cut. The inside of the cake would be either blue or pink, revealing the baby's sex for the first time. Everyone leaned forward as the mother cut into the cake. She held up a piece that had pink and blue swirls.

"It's twins," she announced proudly. "I already knew, but wanted to surprise all of you."

Everyone gasped and then leaped up to hug her. After congratulating her I took over cutting slices of cake and plating them. I took two pieces of cake over to the soon-to-be grandmothers. As I walked back I heard Alicia's name and slowed.

"I always thought Alicia and her husband were madly in love," one woman said.

"Then why did the OSI haul her husband in for questioning this afternoon?" the other said.

Whoa, that was news. Hauled him in for questioning? It made sense. Bristow and Pellner had been very vague when they mentioned suspects. Did that mean Alicia's husband had gone from a pool of suspects to prime suspect? Why hadn't Bristow told me that?

"You know what they say—you never really know anyone." The first woman shook her head.

I wanted to break into the conversation and ask if they had any specific information about Alicia's husband. I tried to transmit my thought to them, but they started talking about the base school. So much for my psychic abilities. I went back to my cake cutting duties, my thoughts more swirled than the pink and blue cake. Eventually, I cut a piece for myself and stood to one side eating it. As I ate, my friend Eleanor came over. We worked together at the base thrift shop.

"Had you heard Alicia's husband was questioned by the OSI?" I asked.

Eleanor shook her light blond hair, eyes wide. Eleanor had a round, youthful face and wouldn't ever look old. "No. Why would they do that?"

I shrugged. While I might want to hear gossip, I didn't want to spread any. "Did you know Alicia very well?"

"She was a doll. One of those go-getter types. Did you hear about the Spouses' Club cookbook? A fundraiser for scholarships and wounded warriors."

I nodded. The cookbook had been called *A is for Apple, a Tribute to the Fall Bounty of New England.*

"Alicia not only spearheaded the project, but her brother owns a printing shop, so he printed them at a discount and mailed them to us. We made a bunch of money."

"That was nice of him."

"The general's wife was really pleased. In the long run it would help Alicia's husband's career."

You would think in this day and age what a spouse did wouldn't have any effect on their husband's career, but some things never changed.

"I wish I'd known her better. She sounded amazing."

"She was. It's why it's been doubly hard around here."

***

On the way home from the gender reveal party I went to the store to buy ingredients for chicken marsala. It's the meal I decided to learn to cook because I knew it was one of Seth's favorite dishes. I'd found the recipe online. It didn't look that hard or have too many ingredients. I bought thin-cut chicken breasts so I didn't have to pound them like the recipe said to. Although pounding chicken might be good stress relief. The shallots I bought looked like baby onions. My list finished with flour, mushrooms, and garlic.

Next I went to the packie—what people in Massachusetts called a liquor store—for the marsala wine. I got there only to find out there was sweet marsala and dry marsala. My recipe didn't mention which type. Sweat started to break out on my forehead. It seemed inordinately hot all of the sudden. I unwrapped my scarf and unzipped my coat. Maybe I should just abandon this project while I still could. *Get a grip.* I took a couple of deep breaths.

"Everything okay, miss?" A curvy woman stood beside me.

"I'm a terrible cook." The woman took a step back. It came out louder than I intended it to and I sounded like a nutter. I took another breath. "I'm trying to learn how to make chicken marsala, but there are two kinds of wine. My recipe doesn't say which one."

"Ah, well I happen to be a pro at chicken marsala. I buy one of each and do half and half. It's perfection. I use unsalted butter in the pan." Her butter came out "buttah" and marsala "marsalar" with her accent. She droned on, talking about dredging, using the right amount of flour, clumping, and all kinds of other frightening things. "You can do it," she summed up, "it's easy."

Under her watchful eye I grabbed the two kinds of marsala wine and checked out. I waved goodbye and headed home, giving myself a pep talk about cooking.

My cell phone rang when I walked into my apartment just before nine. Pellner.

"Are you okay?" he asked.

I flipped on a light in the hall. "Yes. Why wouldn't I be?" I stayed put, wondering if I should run back outside. "I just got home from a gender reveal party on base."

"No one followed you?" he asked.

"What's going on? You're scaring me." I backed up to the door, looking toward my dark bedroom. I'd forgotten to leave lights on when I left. I couldn't see into my living room from here. I did forget to leave the lights on, didn't I?

"The guy from the hospital."

"Fake Troy?" I asked.

"Yes. He's disappeared."

Chapter Nine

I almost dropped my phone. "Explain exactly what you mean."

"The guy was in his hospital room and then he wasn't."

"You didn't have an officer posted at his door?" I asked.

"We're stretched thin, as always. Fake Troy, as you call him, was out of it anyway. And while this guy committed a bunch of misdemeanors, it didn't warrant the cost of posting someone."

"Or pretending to be out of it so he didn't have to talk to you." I stayed by the door, trying to decide whether to go in or go back out. "Why are you telling me this? Why are you worried?"

"He knows who you are and that you've seen him. I want you to watch your back."

My back was now pressed against the door to my apartment. I could feel the knob digging in. "How did he get out of the hospital?"

"Someone wheeled him out in a wheelchair. The security tapes caught that much. But not what kind of car he left in."

"What did that person look like?" I asked.

"Dressed in jeans and a bulky jacket with a Patriots logo. Stocking cap pulled low. Dressed like almost half the New England population in other words. He kept his head down. They're still looking for more footage, trying to identify him. Fake Troy kept his head down too."

"Could it be the person who left the footprints in the snow outside of Jeannette's house?" I asked.

"No idea," Pellner said.

That wasn't very helpful. "What if Fake Troy just slipped on all those papers and files that were on the floor? Maybe it was an accident. The other guy heard me call to Troy and left him there to fend for himself." I hesitated, feeling foolish. "Will you stay on the phone with me while I walk through my apartment? I didn't leave any lights on and I feel a little freaked out."

"Sure. Do you want me to come over?"

"No. But thank you." I walked from room to room, turning on lights, looking behind the shower curtain, under the bed, and in the closets. It didn't take long since there was only a bedroom, bathroom, living room, and kitchen. I even checked the attic space off my living room. "Okay. No one is here."

"Just keep an eye out," Pellner said.

"Trust me, I'll keep two eyes out."

I could have gone to Seth's house, but I'd be alone there too. He had flown down to a meeting for district attorneys in Washington, D.C., until tomorrow night. I'd stayed at his house for a few days last summer when he was out of town, and it had been awkward to say the least. Things wouldn't be as awkward now, but staying here seemed better. The apartment next to mine had been empty for several months and the couple who lived across from Stella were wintering in Florida as usual. However, Stella was downstairs. I could hear her singing an aria from *Madame Butterfly*.

She'd toured Europe when she was young, but now taught voice at Berklee College of Music in Boston. Last fall she'd been in a production of *The Phantom of the Opera* in Boston. The evening I attended she had filled in for the lead. She was amazing, like Tony-award-winning amazing. It made me wonder why she wasn't touring. Maybe it was because of Awesome.

And now that I thought about it, most likely Awesome would be spending the night. He usually did these days, although I worried about them ever since Stella and I had talked the other night. All in all I felt fairly safe here.

I had no way to search for Fake Troy, but desperately needed a distraction. Since it was only 9:10, I decided to call Becky Cane, who was the president of the Spouses' Club. Her husband was a colonel and second-in-command on base. She might know someone who was looking for part-time work. Even better, she was in a position to know a lot of gossip and may have heard something about Alicia or Alicia's husband. Calling her was part of what I'd promised Special Agent Bristow I would do. Sort of.

I plunged in after we said our hellos. "I'm looking for a couple of assistants to help me with a big sale. I thought you might know someone who would be interested." I was never quite sure how Becky would

take things. She'd had an issue with a woman in the
Spouses' Club last fall. I'd heard both sides of the story
and thought a bit of blame lay with each of them.
Becky, who came off as a bit snooty, had confessed how
shy she was. What a toll her role as wife to the second-
in-command had taken on her because she had so
many unofficial duties that kept her in the public—
well, base—eye.

"I'm not an employment agency," Becky said.

Not the reaction I was hoping for. "Of course you
aren't. You just know everyone. No worries. I can
ask someone else." A little flattery along with a hint
that someone else might also be in the know often
worked with Becky. Even though doing it made me
feel sneaky and not very kind.

"Let me think about it. I may be able to come up
with someone."

Whew. "How are things going?" I asked. "It must be
stressful with all that is going on with Alicia's death."

"Sarah, you have no idea. We've all taken her death
so personally." Becky's voice choked up. "She was
such a dynamo and everyone loved her."

"I heard that at the gender reveal party tonight,"
I said.

"Oh. How was it? I couldn't make the party because we had to entertain some dignitaries who were
visiting base. I hope there was a good turnout."

That was one of the parts of the military I missed.
People came to visit the base for all kinds of reasons.
Meeting them was fascinating. I'd met an ambassador
or two over the time CJ had been active duty and
people from all over the world. "The party was packed.
Lots of fun."

"I'm sorry to have missed it then."

I couldn't think of anything else to ask about Alicia that wouldn't sound overly inquisitive. Becky promised to call me soon with some names and we said our goodbyes.

Chapter Ten

I was still full of nervous energy so I decided to try making the marsala. It was better than sitting around worrying about Fake Troy showing up. I read the recipe twice, got out all the ingredients, and did all the prep work like washing the mushrooms and chopping the shallots and garlic. After I managed all that without injuring myself, I measured out the chicken broth and wine, setting them aside for later. Because I was still a bit unsure of what was next, I watched a video of an Italian *nonna* making it. She chatted and smiled and tasted the sauce as she cooked. Really, it looked easy.

But as I dredged (I'd looked the term up) the chicken in the flour, the flour kept falling off. When I put it in the pan, I dumped some more flour on each piece and packed it down. There. At last it stayed on. I set the timer and sautéed the first side for four minutes like the recipe said. When I flipped it some of the flour fell off, so I added more again to the other side. Was there some kind of flour glue that made flour stick on chicken? If there wasn't maybe I could invent it. Cooks everywhere would thank me.

After cooking the chicken on the other side I

added the mushrooms, shallots, garlic, broth, and wine. I put a lid on the whole thing and turned the heat down. As I settled in my living room my phone buzzed. A text from Pellner with a picture of his wife's cobalt glass collection. I saved the picture and then swiped it to make it larger. I counted fifteen pieces, mostly bottles like an Evening in Paris perfume bottle and what looked to be old medicine bottles of some sort. There was a vintage child's mug with a fading image of Shirley Temple's face with her mop of curly hair. They were hard to find and it could be the most valuable piece of her collection. Although it wouldn't be worth more than forty dollars or so.

I turned on the TV and ten minutes later the timer went off. It smelled delicious in here. Cooking wasn't as awful as I remembered. I lifted the lid of the skillet and stared down. The sauce was a thick, gelatinous substance with small islands of hardened flour dotting it. The chicken had curled a bit, but maybe the marsala just looked a little funny. After all, it smelled good. I got a spoon out of the drawer and dipped it in, avoiding the flour islands. I tasted, swallowed, and almost gagged. I ran to the faucet, turned it on, shoved my head under, and drank straight from it.

How could food that smelled so good, taste so awful, like some kind of flour gelatin? I looked into the pan. "You will not defeat me." Yes, I'd like to collapse into a heap and swear off cooking forever, but not this time. I shook my fist at the stove. "Not this time." Some of the ingredients would have to be replenished before I could try again. After I cleaned the kitchen and took out the trash, I read up on cooking with flour and found out too much wasn't a good thing. I'd also missed a step. I should have taken the chicken out of the pan when I made the sauce. Oh, well.

My phone rang at seven for the second morning in a row. This time I was up, dressed, showered, and drinking coffee. It was Bristow. Again.

"We've got to stop talking like this," I said cheerfully since I'd already consumed some coffee.

"I wanted to thank you for volunteering to help with the case, but we've made an arrest."

I set my coffee down, sloshing a little on the trunk I used as a coffee table. I got up and headed to the kitchen to find a towel to mop up with. "Really? Who?" That was fast.

"I can't say."

"Come on. You know as soon as we hang up I can call someone on base and find out. You might as well save me the trouble." I grabbed a blue and white dish towel off a hook and headed back to the living room. Everyone would be so relieved knowing there wasn't a murderer running around among them.

Bristow sighed, but didn't say anything right away. I mopped up the coffee while it seemed like he silently debated the truth of what I'd said. "It's why you asked me to listen anyway," I pointed out.

"Walter Arbas. Alicia's husband," he finally said. "I've got to go."

"But—" Bristow disconnected before I could say more. I pictured Alicia's husband at the funeral. He had looked so torn up. Was he really that good of an actor, or did Bristow get it wrong?

* * *

After tapping my fingers against the arm of my white, slip-covered couch for a few minutes, I decided to go to base, curious to hear what was being said about Alicia's husband. I still had the thirty-day pass and guessed that Special Agent Bristow had more on his mind than taking the time to revoke it. I'd use it while I could.

I stopped and bought a box of donuts from Dunkin's and a large coffee for me. After my talk with Pellner last night, I had jumped at every little sound. Old houses creaked a lot, so an extra dose of caffeine seemed imperative this morning. The line to get on base was almost a half mile long. We inched forward as each driver had to pause at the gate and show their ID before they could continue on. If the driver was military and outranked the guard, the guard had to salute the driver. Even that few extra seconds added up. I pulled into the parking lot behind the thrift shop forty-five minutes after I'd left my house.

When I entered the back room of the thrift shop carrying the donuts, I ran into a beautiful woman who looked like a Nigerian princess—a real one, not the internet-scamming kind. She had a graceful long neck and her posture made it look like she'd been schooled somewhere where they made you walk around with books on your head. She had a bright yellow headband wrapped around her head and a smile as wide as the Niger River.

"Hello. Can I help you?" The woman's hips swayed as she glided toward me. Watching her made me stand up straighter, wishing I moved half as gracefully.

I clutched the box of donuts, introduced myself, and told her I'd come to volunteer.

"Ah, yes. I've heard of you." She had a beautiful

British accent. Maybe she did go to some posh school where they taught posture.

Hearing of me might not be a good thing, considering some of the things I'd ended up being unwillingly involved with.

She must have noticed my concern because she laughed. "I've heard what a hard worker you are and about your garage sale business." Her eyes sparkled. "And a few other things too. I'm Nasha."

"That's a beautiful name."

"My mum is originally from Nigeria. She says it means 'arrived in the rainy season.'"

"And did you?" I asked.

"I did."

I set the box of donuts on a scarred table in the break room. We both grabbed blue bib aprons that would let shoppers know we were volunteers and put them on. The store wouldn't open for another hour, so I went to work in the sorting room. Nasha came with me. We did that whole thing talking about where we had been stationed and did you know so and so, as military spouses always do. But we didn't have very many bases or people in common. It happened. Our husbands had had different career fields. Her husband was a program manager and CJ had been with the security forces.

I sorted a box of clothing as we talked, relieved to see that someone had taken the time to wash everything in this one. A few of the pieces were name brands and would go quickly. Since Nasha and I hadn't found a connection from other bases, I started talking about people we both knew here. Hoping she'd mention Alicia. We both knew Eleanor, of course, since she volunteered here so often.

I hesitated to bring up Alicia directly, since Special Agent Bristow had warned me to only listen. But she had to be fresh on everyone's mind. Besides, as of this morning he'd told me not to bother investigating, I mean listening, so talking about Alicia one way or the other shouldn't matter to Bristow or anyone else. In my gut I was sure he was wrong about Alicia's husband. The grief I'd seen etched on his face—I just didn't believe you could fake that.

"Did you know Alicia?" I asked. I might as well be blunt.

Nasha sorted a bag of toys. Most of them were sticky and dusty, so I wetted some rags and helped clean them.

"I did. She was lovely," Nasha said. "She'd been stationed at Mildenhall too. We met several years ago."

Mildenhall was one of the bases in England. "I love England." I said it with a sigh. It would be a long time before I could afford to go back.

Nasha gave a gentle laugh. "I think you Yanks all have these romantic notions about what it's like to live there."

I laughed too. "Maybe. But I loved it."

"You've been there then?" Nasha asked.

"For two glorious years at Mildenhall. Almost ten years ago."

"Alicia's one of the few people I know who couldn't wait to get out of there," Nasha said.

"Really?" I asked.

"She said it was too cold and too gray."

I nodded. "It was both of those things, but that didn't, uh, dampen my pleasure."

Nasha smiled her beautiful smile at me. I needed to find out what else she knew about Alicia.

"Her husband seemed so broken up at the funeral." Just putting it out there seemed smartest. I didn't know if news of his arrest had spread or not.

"He was. We live near them. Our husbands are friends." She shook her head. Tears swarmed her eyes. "It's amazing how everyone is suddenly best friends with a person who passes."

"Yes." It made me think of Angelo's comment about eulogies and people being thought of as saints after they died. "I didn't know her well, but we worked the same shift here every once in a while," I said. It was impossible to think that would never happen again. Her poor family.

"She made people laugh but wasn't one to get her hands dirty, if you know what I mean," Nasha said.

We looked from the dirty toys to our hands. I laughed. "I know exactly what you mean." Most people would rather run the register or help customers. Even dusting was more fun than digging through bags of who knew what. But to me sorting through donations was almost as much fun as going to a garage sale. I liked finding the treasures that hid among the trash. Last time I was here I found a pair of designer jeans that retailed for over two hundred dollars. They were almost like new. Working back here had its advantages.

It seemed like Nasha was going to say something else, but we were interrupted by a bunch of volunteers showing up, including Eleanor. The new arrivals brought with them the news of Walter Arbas' arrest. Nasha left as soon as she heard. Chatter seemed more subdued than normal although there was still plenty of it and most of it was about Walter.

I went into the retail side of the shop since no one

else was in the back room and there was no way to overhear anything. A group of three women huddled over by the glassware, gossiping. I edged over that way to see what I could find out. I grabbed a dust rag and started dusting a set of china that had been in the store for several months. It was a good brand and when I'd first started volunteering at base thrift shops right after CJ and I were married twenty years ago, this would have flown off the shelf. Now you could barely give it away. Times change, and people like to entertain differently than they did in the past. I certainly didn't have room for it in my tiny kitchen.

But I'd been thinking about having my own garage sale next spring. I'd accumulated some stuff that I couldn't resist and stuck it all in the attic space off my living room. Maybe I should buy this for a garage sale too. I could make cake stands out of the plates, with a turned over cup from the set as the base for tiered serving trays, or even a fountain if I felt really ambitious. Lately, I noticed people were using pieces of old china in bracelets and necklaces. It was pretty, but I was no jewelry maker. I decided I would buy the china, and then realized I'd totally lost my focus.

Yeesh, I'd come over here to try and see what the women were talking about, hoping it was Alicia. I felt compelled to find out what was going on. I kept my back to them and started moving glasses around on the shelf.

"I guess he bashed her over the head and just left her there to die," one woman said.

"I never did like him. Something about his eyes."

"I agree. They seem small. Kind of feral. And that poor puppy. Can you imagine leaving that poor thing out in the cold? He'd have to be cruel to do that."

"That and murdering his wife."

"How come you're so quiet?" the woman who'd spoken first asked someone.

I wanted to look over my shoulder to see who, but didn't want to draw attention to myself.

"You know something, don't you?" the woman continued.

"What is it?" someone else asked.

"I heard it wasn't the ice that killed her. She was poisoned."

Chapter Eleven

I almost dropped the wineglass I was holding. Poisoned? I peeked over my shoulder to see who'd said it. The women surrounded a younger girl whose back was to me. Her thin hair hung below her equally thin shoulders.

"You all can't say anything. My husband would kill me."

They all flinched at that. She refused to say anything more about the kind of poison or what else she'd heard. Maybe she was wrong. Maybe she just wanted attention. Stories got jumbled. Rumors could run rampant when things happened on base. And the death of a spouse by her husband's hand wasn't just any little thing. When the group turned to walk off, I got a glimpse of a sharply sloped nose, and cheeks burning bright from the unwanted attention. If it was unwanted.

After they left, I found a box and put all the china in it, wondering if I was being stupid. But for this price it was hard to resist. It was marked down to twenty dollars for the set of eight place settings. I carried it up to the register where Eleanor was working.

"China?" Eleanor grinned at me. "Does this have anything to do with a handsome DA?"

"No." It came out a little louder than I intended it to. I was a long way from thinking about picking out china with Seth, or anything else for that matter. I enjoyed my freedom. Although I did like him very, very much. My face warmed and Eleanor laughed. I still needed to guard my heart. All that I'd gone through with CJ had left me a bit scarred and scared. Definitely scared.

"Then what are you going to do with all of this?" Eleanor asked. "I have a friend who's been left so many different sets of china that she uses it as her everyday dishes."

I told Eleanor what I planned to do with it. But maybe she was right. I could use this china and get rid of the dishes CJ and I had picked out together when we got married. Maybe the china CJ and I used could be turned into the serving pieces I'd been thinking about. And I'd have the added advantage of having one less reminder of CJ at home. "Maybe I will do that too. I don't have a dishwasher anyway, so I can't damage the gold edges." It was a pretty set. And new old things were so much fun.

"I gave up worrying about the gold around my plates. It's either, I'm never going to use them, or I can use them with the gold worn off."

"That's smart." My phone chimed. A reminder that I needed to head over to Jeannette's parents' house. "I have to run," I told Eleanor.

"Thanks for helping out," she said.

"Anytime."

Eleanor laughed. "You know I'm going to hold you to that."

* * *

I was the biggest chicken ever. I sat in front of Jeannette's house, daring myself to go in. Snow was falling softly. The snow from yesterday hadn't melted. I had sat here long enough with the engine off that the heat from the seat warmer had dissipated. I either needed to start the car or go in. Sitting here wasn't doing a thing.

I grabbed the salad I'd swung by the grocery store and picked up on the way over, got out, and slammed the car door. Resolve. It was just a house. But I trekked around it as snow clung to my coat, hair, and even my eyelashes. I wanted to make sure all the windows were closed and locked. I wished the drapes weren't drawn across so many of them. I came back around the corner and about jumped out of my pants when I almost ran Pellner down.

"What are you doing here?" I asked.

"A neighbor called in a suspicious person." Pellner frowned at me. "You're working here today? Alone?"

"Yes. I have a job to do." I wouldn't admit to him how relieved I was to see him. I could barely admit it to myself.

"Do you want me to go in with you? Do a walk-through?"

I nodded. "Please. I admit I've been a little freaked out about going in. It's why I was walking around out here. Suspiciously." I grinned at Pellner, happy to have him here. I'd been in plenty of bad situations before and hadn't been so shaken.

Pellner agreed. "Come on."

We walked through the house together. Pellner checked out the basement with me and even pulled down the attic ladder. He climbed the steps, flashed his light around, and came back down.

"The whole place is clear," he said. "You're sure you'll be all right?"

"I'll be fine. Thanks for coming in. I've turned into such a wimp."

"With good reason."

"Any news about Fake Troy or whoever he really is?" I asked.

"Nothing. Thin air so far. I'll swing back by later in my shift to check on you. Until then, keep the bolts on the door and call 911 if you get scared."

"Will do." I bolted the door behind him. I stuck a chair under the door that led to the basement and put the safety chain across the door that led to the garage. That should keep me safe enough. Then I smacked my hand to my forehead. I should have asked Pellner if Alicia had been poisoned or if that was just some wild base rumor that someone had started. Between Eleanor rattling me with her china question, me spooking myself, and then being startled by Pellner, it had slipped my mind. He said he'd swing back by; I would ask him then.

I tried calling Special Agent Bristow to see if I could find anything out. I got his voicemail and asked him to call me. I wasn't about to mention the poison in a message or he'd never call me back. I set my phone down and turned my attention to the job at hand. Jeannette's parents' house was a treasure trove. I never knew what I would discover in the next drawer or the next cupboard. It was like being at a birthday party and getting to open gifts. Fortunately, no one was around to hear me squeal with delight. It had been a long time since I'd had this much fun pricing things, even though some of the things were a challenge to figure out.

They had such an eclectic mix of items and didn't seem to have much of a system for where they put what. I opened a cedar chest in the living room. It sat under the picture window and had a cushion on it for extra seating. The cedar scent wafted out. The chest was filled with photo albums and scrapbooks. I started flipping through them to see if they were personal family albums or if they contained things that could be sold.

The first two were family albums. But the third one, oh yes, was filled with vintage postcards. I had a hard time resisting vintage postcards and these needed saving. They were in an old photo album in individual plastic sleeves that used to be so popular. The plastic would eat away at the old paper, eventually ruining the postcards. They needed to be on archival paper or in an archival box that wouldn't react with them.

I took the postcards out one by one. Some were from Boston with sites like the Boston Public Library, Boston Harbor, and a hotel I'd never heard of. There was one of South Station. On the back it said it was the gateway to the South and West. That more passengers went through it in the course of a year than any similar station in the world. It was hard to tell the age, but the cars on the postcard led me to believe it was from the late thirties.

But my favorite was one of the Old South Church. Benjamin Franklin was baptized there. I'd been to it myself when I toured Boston. The postcard called it the "Sanctuary of Freedom." I'd have to look it up and see why.

I flipped to the next page. It was full of Christmas cards. The next, New Year's Eve cards. I crossed my fingers, hoping the next would be full of Valentines. Woo-hoo. It was. I took them all out of their sleeves. Surely, one of these would be just right for Pellner to give to his wife. One was a little girl and boy with two hearts between them. It said: *Two hearts beat as one they say—But my one beats like two. In fact it beats like sixty—Whenever I see you.* Red hearts rimmed the border. I loved it. I still had to find him a piece of cobalt glass that would be unique and different than anything his wife had. I hoped I could find a vase of some sort that he could put flowers in. That would be perfect.

I took the rest of the cards out of the album— Easter, Fourth of July, Thanksgiving, along with some from New York City, and one old linen card of Fenway Park from 1933. It was likely the most valuable one of all. I did a quick price check on my phone. There was a similar one selling for twenty-nine dollars. That didn't mean it would go for that, but would give me a starting price. I would watch the card online and see what it sold for. If a lot of people swooped in at the last minute and a bidding war broke out, it could be fun to watch. I added a re-minder on my phone to let me know when the sale was almost over.

I took the Valentine with me to the kitchen, found a notepad and pen, and wrote Jeannette a note telling her I'd like to buy the Valentine card from her for a friend of mine. After looking up prices on my phone

I added what I thought the approximate value was and marked it up a bit to be fair. I also added a bit about finding the family albums and the stack of vintage postcards I'd taken out of their album.

I took a break and ate my lunch before getting back to work. An hour later my phone rang. I stood and stretched as I reached for it. I didn't recognize the number, but it was local so I answered it anyway. It might be a new client.

"Sarah, this is Zoey Whittlesbee."

Her name didn't sound familiar. "Hi," I said. "How can I help you?"

"Becky said you were looking for someone to do some part-time work for you."

"I am." *Yes!* I smiled as I explained the job and pay to her. "Are you interested?"

"Absolutely. If I can work when my kids are in school and on weekends when my husband is home."

"That's not a problem." But what I had to say next might be, but I couldn't, in good conscience, not tell her about the odd man showing up and then disappearing from the hospital. I explained the situation. "So if that changes your mind I understand completely." I waited for a couple of moments. "Zoey?"

"Oh, sorry. I got a text from my daughter. She wants me to break her out of school early." Zoey laughed. "I get at least one of these a week. The answer is always no, but she doesn't give up. I always tell myself that her persistence will pay off some day in her future."

"I'm sure it will. About the job?"

"Oh, I'm in. If we are both there how dangerous can it be?"

I hoped those weren't famous last words. She agreed to meet me at the house tomorrow morning at ten.

I sent Jeannette a quick text telling her I'd hired Zoey. Jeannette wouldn't have to worry about me being here alone for much longer. She let me know that the new security system was being installed first thing in the morning. A couple of hours later I was up to my wrists in a box of Japanese netsuke. I traced a finger over one of the small carved ornaments once used on an obi—a sash worn around a kimono—to attach and hold a small pouch for men. The one I held looked like a fish, complete with tiny scales. The craftsmanship was amazing. Some of the netsukes were jolly-looking men, others were animals that were so intricate they looked almost lifelike. They were made from everything from ivory to boxwood. I was amazed the family didn't want to keep them. This would be a great draw for the sale because collectors went nuts for them.

Pellner sent me a text saying he was on his way over and that he didn't want to scare me by just pounding on the door. I appreciated that, since I'd been jumping at every little creak and groan the house saw fit to release. I stood in the window waiting for him. It was still snowing. My Suburban had about an inch on top of it. It seemed like it took forever for Pellner to arrive.

"Alicia was poisoned?" I asked as soon as he stepped inside.

Pellner's expression didn't change, which told me

a lot. I recognized cop face from my years of living with CJ.

"I don't know what you're talking about."

"Please. I can see it in your face," I said.

"Where did you hear that?" Pellner continued to sidestep my question.

"At the thrift shop. I was there this morning."

"Ah, the base rumor mill. Even I've heard about how quickly rumors spread. It's possibly worse than the person-to-person telegraph in Ellington," Pellner said. "You can't believe everything you hear." He looked out the window. Dark was creeping over the town. Night fell early in January in Massachusetts. The snow continued unabated. "The wind is supposed to increase and temperatures drop rapidly."

"In other words, it's going to get slick out there."

Pellner nodded. "Are you staying much longer?"

"I think I'll wrap this up and head home."

"Okay. Take care."

After Pellner left I stowed the box of netsuke, made sure all the doors were locked, and headed out to my car. Wrapped in thoughts and my warm winter coat.

As I climbed the stairs to my apartment with the box of china I'd bought at the thrift shop, voices came from the empty apartment next to mine. Had Stella found a renter already? That was fast. Although rentals in this area always went fast. But what happened to checking the people out and asking me? I set the china down at the top of the steps and took off my gloves one at a time. It felt like I was getting ready for a fight. There were only two doors up here: mine to the left and the empty apartment to the right. Its door was open. I heard Stella's voice and another familiar one. It was Mike "the Big Cheese" Titone.

Chapter Twelve

I followed the voices and found Stella standing there with Mike Titone.

"Hello?" The room only had a couch in it. The front window provided the same view of the town common and Congregational church as I had. The scene made me smile. Especially with snow covering the ground. Seeing Mike, on the other hand, made me nervous.

"Sarah." Mike came over and kissed both of my cheeks. Mike was a runner, slender, tall, with icy blue eyes that sometimes scared me. "It looks like we are going to be neighbors again."

He was certainly in a good mood right now. Oftentimes he was reserved, bordering on cold.

"Oh." It wasn't much of a response to his "neighbors" comment, but when he had lived here last winter it was because he was hiding from someone in Boston. Someone who had tried to kill him. People from Boston seemed to think that Ellington was in the hinterlands, even though it was only fifteen miles as the crow flies from Boston. Maybe less. And one town blended into the next the whole way here. Mike owned a cheese shop in the North End of Boston and had connections to the Mob but had a good side too.

I was never sure which side of him would show up, but more often than not he would help me out when I needed it. Sometimes at the cost of owing him. And the cost of owing him was high. I'd like to do him a favor and get the owing part off the proverbial plate that constituted our relationship.

"You're moving back in?" I asked. Stella shot me a *don't be rude* look—maybe because of my tone. It wasn't exactly happy.

"Last night someone broke into my store, filled a metal garbage can full of cheese, dragged it out to the curb and lit it on fire." Mike's tone was light, but there must be more to the story if it was enough to make him come stay out here.

"All that cheese," I bemoaned. That's one positive thing I could always say about Mike, his cheese shop was amazing.

"Yeah, well, don't worry. Whoever did it was thoughtful enough to provide a clean trash can, so it was like an instant fondue party on the block by the time I got there."

I laughed. "You're kidding."

"Naw. You've never seen so much Italian bread in one place at one time. Everyone was happy except for my neighbor Alan. He has some weird cheese phobia."

"But you must feel like it's some kind of message if you're here," I said.

Mike shrugged.

"Do you know who did it?" I asked. Someone like Mike must have security out the wazoo.

"It was someone savvy enough to get around all of my security measures." He didn't sound happy. "I have friends checking cameras on the block, but so far it's turned up nothing solid. What with the fondue party and all."

"That and the tourists," I added. The North End was a popular place for tourists to visit with its combination of historical sites and fabulous Italian restaurants and bakeries.

"Well, we're glad to have you back," Stella said with a side glance at me.

Glad might not have been the word I used, but whatever. I wondered what Awesome would think about Mike being here. I guessed that he wouldn't be thrilled and he was already grouchy. I hoped this didn't make things worse.

"The boys will be moving a few things in this evening, Sarah. I hope it doesn't disturb you."

"No worries. I'm glad you're safe." I hoped we all would be. Someone sophisticated enough to get around Mike was a concern.

"We're taking the usual precautions. Flying and driving our cell phones to different locations. Making reservations in far-off locales. The way the weather's been, a trip to someplace warm would be nice."

"Then why are you staying?" I asked.

"To find the rat who did it."

Minutes later I was unlocking the door to my apartment and hanging up my coat. I set the box of china on the trunk I used as a coffee table. I rubbed my arms and went over to turn up the thermostat a couple of degrees. Then I looked out over the common. The snow pelted down and the skeletal branches waved frantically. I pulled the curtains across the window and shivered.

Special Agent Bristow called. "Are you still available for the dining-out?"

"I am, but I thought you didn't need me anymore," I said.

"Alicia's husband is off the hook."

"Really? How?"

"Yes, really. He has one of those smart beds that shows he was in it at the suspected window for the time of death."

"His bed gave him his alibi?" I asked. I'd heard of personal fitness devices providing alibis or placing someone at the scene of the crime, but not a bed.

"It's a whole different world. These beds can track all kinds of things."

"I'm glad it wasn't him." I didn't add that I hadn't thought it was him. "Do you have another suspect?"

Special Agent Bristow paused. I could picture him rubbing his face. "No one we can charge. We're back to the drawing board."

We decided to meet at the venue Friday night. He had offered to pick me up at my apartment, but that seemed awkward and too date-like. Bristow said a quick goodbye and hung up.

He didn't give me a chance to ask about the poison. Although a bed couldn't provide an alibi for a poisoning. Or could it, depending on the type of poison and how fast acting it was? I called him back, but he didn't answer. Again. This was all very confusing. Maybe I'd misread Pellner when I brought up the poisoning. Maybe his cop look was just that and not a comment on the validity of my statement. A gust of wind rattled the windows. I was rattled as well.

Chapter Thirteen

I got a heart text from Seth. He was working late and must be in a meeting since he hadn't called. At least he'd made it back from D.C. I fixed a quick Fluffernutter sandwich for my dinner. I'd never heard of them or eaten one until I moved to Massachusetts. Marshmallow fluff had been invented in Somerville and someone decided to pair it with peanut butter and white bread. Then it became the state sandwich of Massachusetts. It was easy and satisfying. Not as good as the food from DiNapoli's, but good enough on a cold winter night when I didn't want to venture out.

I decided I'd better figure out what to wear to the dining-out. All my fancy dresses were packed in a plastic tub in the attic. I hadn't needed them since I'd moved to Ellington. During the time CJ had been active duty, I'd attended many events that called for cocktail dresses or ball gowns. Some of them got donated because fashions changed. I shuddered thinking about the one with the enormous padded shoulders. But I'd kept others that were more classic.

I flipped the latch to the attic space, opened the door, and flipped on the light. As soon as I crawled through the door, I could stand up. Lots of boxes were tucked under the eaves. I shivered as I looked through the jumble of things I'd been collecting. This space wasn't heated and the wind howled like it was in pain. I realized once spring came I did have enough stuff to do my own garage sale. Preparing for it would help these long winter nights pass more quickly.

I moved a wicker chair someone had left out on a curb. It had been terribly dirty when I found it, but nothing else seemed to be wrong with it. I had cleaned off the dirt and cobwebs before I had brought it up here. I shoved aside a few boxes of books. Behind them I spotted the bin with my dresses in it. I had to duck-walk over to it and drag it behind me until I could stand back up.

I shoved it out of the attic space, crawled back into the living room, and re-latched the door. I set the box on the trunk by my sofa and pried the lid off. I started lifting dresses out, remembering events I'd worn them to with CJ by my side, handsome in his mess dress. I was finally getting to a place where I could remember our life together and not feel so sad. We'd both moved on with our separate lives and I was glad for him. But he'd always be with me to some extent.

After digging through the dresses, I scooped up a deep blue velvet dress, and took it to my room to try on. The wind gusted hard as I put on the velvet dress. I loved the color against my pale skin and with my blond hair. It still clung in all the right places and the slit allowed me to move easily. This was the one.

I was about to change when someone knocked on my door. I felt awkward answering in formal wear. I peeked through the peephole and saw a bunch of red roses in Seth's arms. My heart shook harder than the wind at the windows. I swung open the door, a little embarrassed by my attire.

Seth stared at me for a couple of beats before taking my hand and leading me into the living room. He twirled me a couple of times.

"I do declare, Miss Sarah, that you are the most gorgeous creature I've ever laid eyes on."

It was funny to hear his mock Southern accent with his slight Bostonian one. But that was quite the compliment since he had a history of dating models. My face warmed. Would I ever get over blushing? I did a little curtsy. "Why, thank you. You don't look bad yourself." His black suit, purple tie, and white shirt fit him perfectly.

Seth tossed the roses on the trunk, pulled me close, dipped me, and kissed me until my toes curled, which took just about two seconds.

"I'm not sure it's legal for you to be out in a dress like this," he said when he righted me. His eyes glowed. "Men will be walking into walls or falling over their own feet with one look at you."

Part of me wished that was true, but it was lovely to hear. Seth pulled me close again. "And as much as I like seeing you in this dress, I'd really like to see you out of it. Turn around."

I smiled as he slowly unzipped it and pressed kisses down my back.

Chapter Fourteen

For once I was up before Seth, and on a Friday morning no less. Troubled by what I had heard about Alicia and poison, I'd gotten up and made coffee. Now I was searching for any such news online. I sat at my small kitchen table, laptop open, drinking a cup of coffee so strong I might not need another cup all day. The wind was still looping the house, but the snow had stopped.

Seth walked in, hair mussed, buttoning his now wrinkled shirt. I clicked off the search. "Coffee?" I asked.

"You're up earlier than normal," he said.

"Alicia's death has been keeping me awake. It's just so sad," I said. "Want some scrambled eggs?" It's the one thing I usually didn't screw up. Well, that and Fluffernutters, but you could only offer a man so many Fluffernutters.

"I'd love some." Seth poured himself a cup of coffee and leaned against the counter as I took eggs, milk, feta, and chopped green onion out of the refrigerator. "Looks fancy." Seth grinned at me. "Anything else keeping you up?"

"I suppose that means you know about the mystery man from the hospital."

Seth nodded, then sipped his coffee. "This is good."

I put a pan on the burner and added a pat of butter. I started whisking the eggs, waiting for Seth to comment further. Expecting the worst—some kind of *trouble follows you, be careful* speech. I poured the eggs into the pan, added feta and the green onions, scrambling with a vengeance.

"Hey, look, whatever it is you're thinking about, you don't need to take it out on those poor eggs." Seth nudged me out of the way with his hip and took over.

Good lord, it was hard to be angry with the man. Especially when I was making up things I thought he was going to say while he just stood there drinking his coffee. "Pellner told you. Is it why you came over?"

"Pellner told me. But I would have come over anyway because I wanted to see you. Peeling that dress off you last night was the highlight of my week."

I got two plates out. "Having been peeled was the highlight of mine."

Seth divided the eggs onto the two plates and carried them to the table. I still hadn't taken off the vintage Christmas tablecloth with its bright poinsettias. My parents had come for Christmas, although they stayed over at my brother's place because he had more room. They'd met Seth, even though I wasn't ready for that, but there'd been no avoiding it. And they all seemed to like each other. My mother had only made one comment about it being too soon. I grabbed silverware and napkins and sat across from Seth.

"Mike Titone moved in next door," I said.

"Really? When?"

I tried to assess his tone. It sounded neutral. "Yesterday. He didn't tell you?" I took a bite of the scrambled eggs. The feta had melted perfectly and the green onions added just the right tang.

"No. But I saw an empty chair by the apartment door when I came over, so I wondered what was up."

I liked that he hadn't quizzed me about it. That he waited for me to tell him. I filled him in on why Mike had moved back in.

Seth reached over and laid his hand over mine. "Just take care," he said.

"I will. I hired someone to help me with the sale at Jeannette's house, so I won't be there alone."

"That's good. You're smart. It's one of the many reasons I love you."

I shoved some eggs into my mouth to cover for the myriad of emotions rushing through me at Seth saying the word "love." After I chewed and swallowed my heart rate was almost back to normal. And I figured out something to say that didn't include love. "It makes me feel safer too. But I can't imagine the guy coming back when I'm there."

"Let's hope not." We finished our eggs. Seth washed the dishes while I dried, before kissing me and leaving.

I tried one more search using "poison" and "Alicia" but nothing came up. After that I checked on my virtual garage sale. I'd set it up last winter to keep an income stream going. I sold things, got paid for ads, sold things for clients and got a commission from them. The virtual garage sale had grown more and more popular. Mostly that was great, but occasionally the large group could create problems. People wouldn't follow the rules or they'd post things I wouldn't allow them to sell, like weapons and animals.

Even worse, someone would start talking about local politics. There were plenty of other groups that did that, and I took all those kinds of posts down. But sometimes someone in the group would send a nasty message to me. Banning them was the only solution, and I knew that didn't go over well because then they emailed me through my website. It always amazed me how riled up strangers could get with each other online. Fortunately, today everything seemed to be going smoothly. I looked at a few items including an abstract oil painting, but talked myself out of buying it.

After a few minutes of mulling over the pros and cons, I put up an ISO, *in search of*, post for cobalt glass. It might save me time shopping. However, it also meant that a seller would know I wanted the item, making it harder to negotiate a better price.

By the time I was finished I had to get ready to meet Zoey at Jeannette's parents' house. I put on a pair of leggings and a warm, loose sweater. As I trotted down the stairs to leave, Stella came out of her apartment.

"Is it going okay with Mike next door?" she asked. "I've hardly seen him."

"Is Seth okay with it?" A worry line creased between her brows.

"He knows. If he's not okay with it, I'm guessing he'll talk to Mike about it and not me."

I filled her in on what had happened at Jeannette's parents' house.

"That's scary."

I described the man to her. "If you see him, call Awesome."

"If I see him, I'll faint."

I laughed. Stella was made of way tougher stuff than that.

Zoey was a petite woman, with a boisterous laugh and an unnatural tan that screamed tanning booth addict. She gripped my hand and squeezed until I almost squeaked in pain. But I didn't get the impression that she did it maliciously. She just didn't get that her grip was a bit overwhelming. If Fake Troy or his partner in whatever showed up, I thought we could take them. Zoey could shake their hands and bring them to their knees while I called the police.

"I'm so excited to be here," Zoey said.

"Great. Do you have much experience with garage sales?" I asked.

"A little. I like to go to them."

"Me too. Let me show you around the house first," I said. "They are selling everything that's left except for some of the stuff in the office that Jeannette still needs to go through."

"Holy crap," Zoey said as we walked down the hall. "Every inch of wall space is covered with stuff." She squinted her eyes. "That looks like a basket my husband brought back from Malawi. And those look like chopsticks. Who hangs chopsticks on their wall?"

"They have a lot of stuff," I agreed. I didn't want to denigrate their decorating choices out loud, even though no one would hear us. It didn't seem respectful.

After the tour I led her back to the living room, where I'd been working since I first started. The whole process had been much slower than I thought it would be. Of course I'd had some significant interruptions.

"How in the world do you decide how to price this stuff?" Zoey's voice boomed off the walls. It was loud for someone so small.

"Some of it is just from studying items at garage sales for a lot of years. Some of it is from knowing antiques. But I end up looking up a lot of things."

"Where do you look them up?" she asked.

"I'll look online. Sites like eBay. But I check other sources too. And if I'm really stumped, I set it aside and contact a friend in Acton who owns an antique store." I pointed to a box near the cold, empty fireplace. "That box is for the things I need my friend to price."

"Do you ever get it wrong?"

"Occasionally, but I've worked hard at making sure I price things properly. It puts money in my clients' pockets as well as mine."

"What do you want me to work on?" Zoey asked.

"How about clothes?" They were usually simple to price. "If anything happens to have tags, bring it out and we'll price it together. Or if anything looks unusual or is by a famous designer."

"Okay."

"If something is really worn or stained, set it aside in a separate pile." I explained how I priced regular everyday clothes.

"Sounds good. Thanks again for taking a chance

on me. It's hard to find a job that's only during school hours."

"You're welcome." I smiled at her back as she hurried down the hall. I was the lucky one. I got back to work. Having someone else in the house dispelled the boogeyman feeling that had lingered over me. I hummed my away around the room, pricing, looking up prices, and setting a few things aside for my friend in Acton. So far she'd been pricing things for free for me, but with this lot I would insist on paying her. Friendship only went so far.

"Sarah!"

We'd been working an hour when Zoey startled me by shouting. I raced down the hall, heart thumping. I skittered into the master bedroom. "What?" My eyes darted around. No bodies or blood. All of the windows were closed.

Zoey pointed to the bed. "Look at all these designer dresses."

I patted my heart. Her voice had been excited, not panicked. I had to quit thinking the worst when someone called out to me.

"There's Halston, Chanel, and an original Diane von Furstenberg wrap dress!" She held up a slinky black dress. "It's an Oscar de la Renta." Zoey's voice was almost reverent.

I smiled. "Wow. This is amazing." And they looked like my size.

"I know I don't look it today"—Zoey gestured at her leggings and baggy sweatshirt—"but I've always loved vintage clothes." She sighed. "Although none of these are my size." She looked me up and down. "They might fit you though. You have to try one on. My choice."

"I really shouldn't." There was so much work to do.

"Come on. It will be fun. All work and no play makes Sarah a dull girl."

I had been dull lately. I sometimes wondered why Seth was hanging around. "Okay. One dress."

Zoey took her time going through the dresses. "Here, this one."

It was a stunner. A sleek gold lamé number that glowed in the dim overhead light. I took it into the master bathroom and hurriedly got out of my leggings and sweater. The dress slid like liquid gold over me. The hem hit the floor, but would be just the right length with a pair of heels on. Jeannette's mother must have been about my height.

"Come out. Let me see," Zoey hollered.

I turned once in front of the full mirror. The light shimmered across the fabric. The dress was beautiful. Long sleeved with a plunging neckline, a mixture of naughty and nice. I held the dress up so it wouldn't drag on the floor and went out. "Tada," I said, throwing my arms out like I was a starlet from the forties.

"It's like it was made for you," Zoey said.

The front door banged against the safety chain. What now?

Chapter Fifteen

I held up the extra fabric of the dress and hustled down the hall.

"Sarah?"

It was Jeannette.

"Hang on," I said. "Let me take off the safety chain." I undid the chain and let Jeannette in.

She had a paper bag in her hand with food that smelled delicious. "I was knocking and got worried when you didn't answer. I saw your car so I knew you were here. Oh." Jeannette looked me over.

"I shouldn't have tried it on."

"It's my fault."

I jumped at Zoey's voice. The carpet had dulled her steps. Jeannette was so focused on the dress she didn't see Zoey come around the corner. I introduced the two of them.

"Your mom's clothes are so beautiful. I convinced Sarah to try it on," Zoey said.

"Did you think I'd be mad?" Jeannette asked. She shook her head. "I remember the night my mom wore that dress. We were in Hong Kong. I was only five or six."

"Where were they going?" I asked.

"To some fancy event at an embassy. My dad was an attaché to the American embassy." She used finger quotes around the word *attaché*.

"So CIA?" I asked.

"Everyone knows attachés are spies." Jeannette shrugged. "I'm not sure if they were CIA then or not."

"How can you remember that from so long ago?" Zoey asked.

"One reason is my mom looked so dazzling. The other is that I got in a lot of trouble that night."

Zoey and I exchanged glances.

"What kind of trouble can you get into when you're five?" I asked.

"We were staying at a hotel. We'd only been in Hong Kong for a couple of weeks and we hadn't found an apartment yet." Jeannette smiled at the memory. "My parents left my brother in charge. We got hungry while they were gone so I ordered room service."

"How did you pull that off?" I asked.

"Even as a kid my voice was deep. My brother wrote out what I should say. I ordered the pupu platter, fried rice, Szechuan chicken, which was so spicy my eyes watered, and beef lo mein noodles." Jeannette smiled again. "It was the best meal of my life, but maybe because of the subterfuge."

"What did you do when the food came?" Zoey looked skeptical.

"My brother said our mother was in the bathroom. I yelled from behind the bathroom door to let him sign the receipt. The man let him. My brother even managed to give him a good tip."

"How did you get in trouble?" I asked.

"Our parents came home and saw the remains of

our feast. We had strict instructions not to open the door while they were out."

We all laughed.

"It was just the beginning of my getting in trouble." A small frown passed over Jeannette's face. "But the last five years have been great."

I wondered if that had anything to do with the will, why her brother was executor, and the odd split. She seemed like a wonderful person now. "I'll go change and get back to work."

"Keep the dress, Sarah." Jeannette smiled at me.

"I can't do that. It's worth a lot of money."

"Please. I'm sure my mom would be happy to know someone else is enjoying it."

"I—"

"No arguing. Please. I want you to have it."

I looked down at the dress. It was stunning. "Thank you. It's a lovely gift."

"Hurry back," Jeannette said. "I brought meatball subs from DiNapoli's."

I quickly changed and went back out. By the time I returned Jeannette and Zoey were chatting away. They had set the table, passed out sandwiches and pasta salad. We all dug in. Jeannette had had the good sense to order three half sandwiches that any place else would be a full sandwich. The bun was soft, cheese gooey, and meatballs tender. "Thanks for bringing us food, Jeannette," I said.

"I had to meet the security system people this morning so took a personal day. I thought I'd check and see how you were doing. And make sure the system worked okay."

"Your instructions were perfect. I was able to turn it off without any problems." I looked over at Zoey.

"It's fun having Zoey here to help. Your parents had so many interesting things. What was your life like as a kid?" I asked.

"To me it was just normal. It wasn't until I went away to college that I realized how different it was than most kids'."

"Did you move a lot?" Zoey asked.

"Yes. Every couple of years. Not unlike what you do as military spouses."

"It just seems like it would be harder as a kid." I thought about my childhood friends. How close we had been even though we'd drifted apart since. "At least you had your brother."

"I was just enough younger to be the annoying younger sister. But he was overprotective. It's amazing I ever had a date." Jeannette smiled at the memory. "He went to college at Harvard, so I chose to go to California to college."

"As far away as you could. I hear you," Zoey said.

We finished our food and started to clean up the mess we'd made.

Jeannette picked up the vintage valentine I'd laid on the kitchen counter. "What's this doing here?"

"I left you a note," I said. "I'd like to buy it for a friend of mine."

Jeannette looked at the postcard and then me. "I don't see a note."

I pointed to a piece of paper next to where Jeannette stood. This was a bit worrisome. "It's right there."

"This?" Jeannette held up a blank piece of paper.

I walked over and took it out of her hand. There wasn't a word on it. Now she looked worried. "I swear I wrote you a note." I grabbed the pen I used originally. It was just a normal blue pen. I took the paper from her hand and rewrote my original message. "There."

We looked at each other.

"Do you think—" I started.

"Could it be—" Jeannette began.

"Disappearing ink," I said.

We stood staring down at the paper. Zoey walked over and joined us. Nothing happened so we finished putting our lunch things away.

Jeannette pointed to the piece of paper. "Look, some of the letters are starting to fade."

"Oh, whew. I thought I was losing my mind for a minute."

"So did I," Jeannette said with a grin. She took the pen. "I guess I'll keep this."

Zoey returned to the bedroom to price and I walked Jeannette to the door.

"You're sure you feel safe working here?" Jeannette asked.

"Yes. Especially with Zoey around and the new security system in place. I explained the situation to her."

"That's good." She paused with her hand on the doorknob. "Have you heard anything about the man who injured himself here? Do the police have any leads?"

I shook my head. "There's nothing new." At least if there was, no one had filled me in on it.

"How does someone just disappear like that?"

"Beats me." Maybe I should talk to my brother about it. He'd disappeared from my parents' and my lives for almost twenty years until he resurfaced last spring. He might have some insights. Jeannette left and I hooked the security chain back in place. I would talk to Luke when I got the chance.

At seven that evening, Special Agent Bristow stood beside my car in the parking lot of the All Ranks Club. There used to be an Officers Club and an Enlisted Club, but they had joined into one for economic reasons several years ago. I was doubly glad we agreed to meet here because I really didn't want him to run into Mike Titone or whoever was parked outside the door of his apartment.

Bristow opened the door of my Suburban and held a hand out for me to climb out. The Suburban was great for hauling stuff but not so good for descending out of in a long dress and high heels. I managed to get out without stumbling or ripping my dress. I wore what I'd originally planned to instead of Jeannette's mother's dress. I would save it to wear to an event with Seth.

"You are looking elegant this evening, Special Agent Bristow," I said. He was usually a bit rumpled. Tonight he wore a tux that was tailored perfectly. The shirt wasn't stained, but his bow tie was a bit crooked. I stepped in and adjusted it without thinking.

"Thank you," he said after I stepped back. "Please call me Frank. At least for this evening. It will feel uncomfortable if you don't."

"Of course." The whole thing felt uncomfortable the way it was. But if I could do some good for him, for the case, I would.

He held out his arm. "Let's get inside. It's cold out here."

I slipped my arm through his and we went in. After

we'd hung up our coats in the cloak room, I pulled Frank aside.

"I heard that Alicia was poisoned. Is that true?" I asked. I smiled and waved at a woman I recognized.

"Where did you hear that?"

The non-answer. And exactly what Pellner asked. Hadn't they talked about this? "A woman at the thrift shop mentioned it."

Frank's forehead squinched into a mass of wrinkles. Did that mean I was right and they didn't want anyone to know for some reason? Or was this the first time he was hearing this? His eyes gave away nothing. Really, I needed to give up on trying to read people who were in the law enforcement community. They were just too practiced.

"What's her name?" he asked.

"I don't know. I didn't recognize her. Is she right?"

"Special Agent Bristow, how lovely to see you." An older woman with gorgeous silver hair approached us. Talk about bad timing. We all headed into the ballroom together where the dinner was set up.

Chapter Sixteen

The toasts started right after the invocation was given by the Protestant base chaplain. We sat at round tables of ten, glasses charged with wine. Charged not filled, as the rest of the world would say. We stood as soon as the commander raised his glass.

"To the Flag of the United States of America," he said.

We all responded. "To the Colors." And took a sip of our wine. I took as small a sip as possible because you never knew how many toasts would follow and you didn't want to be stuck with an empty glass.

"To the President of the United States," the commander said.

"To the President," we answered. The national anthem played. When it was finished the commander toasted the Air Force, the Chief of the Air Staff, and on down the line, including the guest of honor, who was the lieutenant governor of the Commonwealth.

The toast that always got me was the one with water. Nondrinkers didn't use water for their toasts. They held their glass of wine and just lifted it but didn't drink. The toast with water was started by service members in North Vietnam prisoner of war camps where only water was available for toasting. The toast called "One More Roll" was from a poem to honor those killed in action, missing in action, or prisoners of war.

We responded with "hear, hear."

After the toasts the dinner began. This was my time to listen. I sat between Frank and a lieutenant colonel, making it difficult to chat with his wife or the other women at the round table. After a salad they served our entrées. I had the chicken and Frank had the beef. Although we hadn't planned it, that was what CJ and I always used to do at these dinners. That way if one meal was horrible—and trust me, I've had chicken the texture of jerky in the past—we could share.

Once the people at the table found out that Frank was OSI, the subject of the murder came up quickly. Frank deftly deflected the questions by asking questions in return. But as far as I could tell no one had any new information. And no one mentioned poison. One of the wives was very still during the discussion. When she excused herself to go to the restroom I did the same. I caught up with her as she left the ballroom.

"Tough topic for what's supposed to be a fun evening," I said.

"Yes. And here I thought I was going to get away from it all and enjoy this evening."

"I hear you. Did you know Alicia well?" I asked.

"She was my next-door neighbor."

"That must be terribly difficult." We slowed as we

walked down the corridor. The floor was a slippery tile and we were both in heels.

"We weren't best of friends. I'm very liberal and she was very conservative. Alicia was a nice person, but our life philosophies were drastically different. That said, I can't imagine anyone wanting Alicia dead. Especially not her husband. That was ridiculous."

"I didn't know her well," I said, "but would see her around. It's just so shocking. I thought I heard someone say that Alicia and her husband argued a lot." I held my hand to one side and crossed my fingers. We walked into the bathroom. There were ten stalls, huge mirrors, and flocked gold wallpaper.

She turned to me. "I can tell you for a fact that's just an ugly rumor. Our walls are so thin I can hear Alicia's husband singing in the shower if I'm in our bedroom. If they fought it was done very quietly." She went into a stall and closed the door a bit more firmly than necessary.

Since I was here, I might was well use the facilities too. I went into a stall at the end. First, I fought to get the dress up around my waist. Then I peeled off my shapewear. Being a woman wasn't easy. After I put myself back together, but before I exited, I heard voices.

"What's Sarah Winston doing here?"

"Got me. It's kind of pathetic how she keeps hanging around base even after her husband dumped her."

Ouch.

"Yeah, she thinks she's some kind of super sleuth now too."

"Or hero."

"That's not nice," a third voice said. "I don't see

either of you volunteering at the thrift shop. She works hard there and we're lucky we have her."

Thank you, whoever you are. I didn't recognize any of the voices. I waited a few more minutes until I was sure they had left. By the time I got back to the table a chocolate dessert had been served.

Frank leaned over to me. "Are you okay?"

"Yes." I took a bite of the dessert. It tasted like nothing, but maybe that was my mood more than the food itself.

"Did you find out anything?" he asked.

"Way more than I wanted to. But not about anything having to do with Alicia."

He gave me a sideways glance. Fortunately they brought out the grog bowl, so Frank didn't have time to pursue the matter, to my great relief. The grog bowl was another military tradition. All I know is that it was usually a toilet bowl (hopefully, someone had gone to a store and bought a new one) that was filled with punch and everything from cereal to spaghetti noodles. It used to be alcohol laced, but times had changed.

If service members violated a rule of the mess, they were sent to the grog bowl. There they took a mug, filled it from the bowl, toasted the crowd and said, "To the grog." Then they drank down the contents of the mug. CJ had once been sent for having his name tag on the wrong side of his mess dress. It created a lot of hilarity, but I was relieved that spouses and dates were excused from having to drink from the grog.

After the grog a DJ came out and dancing started. I'd always loved to dance and Frank was up for dancing too. Three songs in, a slow song came on. We stared at each other, then both shrugged, and Frank started twirling me around the dance floor. No shuffling back and forth in a tight grip for us. He was a very good dancer. After a couple more dances, Frank excused himself and I went back to the table to drink some water.

After I sat down, two of the other spouses joined me. We talked casually, introduced ourselves, and exchanged information about who did what—one was a nurse, the other a substitute teacher. I'd been relieved that neither of their voices sounded like those of the women in the restroom. My cheeks warmed a bit just thinking about the whole thing.

"Are you and Frank dating?" Rhonda asked. She had lots of dark braids that were woven together in an intricate pattern.

"No. We're just friends."

"It's nice to see him out," Paula said. She wore hot-pink glasses that contrasted with her sleek silver hair. "He's been so sad. Tonight he looks like he's enjoying himself."

Oh, boy. I hoped the base wives' rumor mill wasn't cranking up into high gear. News spread faster via that network than it did on Twitter.

"As I said, we're just friends." I thought about telling them I was seeing someone, but it didn't seem like the right thing to do.

"And I know he's been working long hours since Alicia died," Paula added.

"He mentioned that," I said. He hadn't, but maybe this was my intro to finding some information, or anything else, out. "It's so sad."

"Did you know Alicia?" Rhonda asked.

"Not very well. How about you?" I asked.

"We were dear friends," Rhonda said. "It's hard to even be here acting like everything is okay."

One thing I had learned was Alicia had a lot of friends. She must have been a very special person to be so well thought of. Paula reached over and gave Rhonda's hand a squeeze.

"I can't imagine how hard that must be for you," I said.

Tears formed in her eyes. "We were stationed together twice. Once a few years ago. We were so happy when we found out we'd be in the same place again."

It was how I felt about Carol. I was so grateful Carol and her husband decided to stay in Ellington too. I had a thousand questions I wanted to ask these women. But between Frank telling me just to listen and the comments I overheard in the bathroom, I kept silent. Rhonda grabbed her napkin and dabbed at her eyes.

"I don't want my husband to see me crying. He thinks I should be over it." She used air quotes when she said *over it*. "But you don't get over losing someone close to you that quickly. Alicia was so fun. She managed to make every day brighter."

"Except when you made her angry," Paula said.

Now that was interesting.

"Alicia angry was more fun than most people happy," Rhonda said.

Paula nodded. "That's true. I've never seen anyone rip Becky a new one like Alicia did."

"Well, Becky deserved it," Rhonda said.

"She did. Alicia was one of the few people who

wasn't impressed by Becky's husband's rank." Paula pushed her pink glasses up her nose.

It was like they'd forgotten I was there. I was dying to ask what had happened, but worried they'd quit talking if I spoke.

"Yeah, that whole *respect the spouse's rank* is so 1990s," Rhonda said.

Some spouses felt important because their husbands were. It was called wearing your spouse's rank.

"Not completely," Paula said. "You must have heard the rumors." She looked over at me.

What rumors? It took everything in me not to ask. I shook my head. Paula and Rhonda exchanged a look I couldn't interpret.

"Alicia bowled on a team with the general's wife in the Spouses' Club league," Paula said. "They took first place. And you know how competitive Ginger is."

"I don't think I know her. She must have come after I moved off base," I said.

"Ginger always wants to win anything she does," Rhonda added. "Alicia was in a sweet spot with the higher ups in the Spouses' Club and on base in general. She was the president of the PTA too."

Rhonda didn't sound jealous. "But Alicia doesn't have kids. Why would she be president of the PTA?" I asked.

"She volunteered as a reading tutor at the school and knew they were having a hard time finding someone," Rhonda said.

"Alicia stepped up to take on that role. Everyone was relieved." Paula smiled. "It's a thankless job."

That was interesting combined with everything else I'd heard. I remembered Eleanor mentioning the base cookbook and that Alicia's brother printed it for free. Combine that with bowling well and taking the PTA presidency and she was doing a lot. Plus she volunteered at the thrift shop and did who knew what else. Alicia must have been the golden child with the upper officer wives. And from what I could tell, all the other spouses too. I wonder if that is why Becky and Alicia argued.

"Do you know Becky?" Rhonda asked.

"I do," I said. "Doesn't everyone on base?" I didn't want to say anything mean about Becky. Besides, who knew who was listening. The ballroom was full of people.

Both of their spouses returned then and sat down at the table. It ended our conversation before I could find out anything else. Frank came back too. We danced until the DJ packed it up for the night. I felt a little guilty about having so much fun while Seth was stuck at some stuffy event in Boston.

"Learn anything?" Frank asked as he walked me to my car.

The temperature had dropped. The sky was clear, with winter stars twinkling madly. The moon reflected off the hard crust on top of the snow. I shivered in my thin wool coat. "Only that Alicia had yelled at Becky Cane at a Spouses' Club meeting."

"She's Colonel Cane's wife?" Frank asked.

I nodded. "Becky is hard to get to know. She can come off as snooty, but in reality she's shy. I'm sure it's nothing."

Frank took my keys from me and opened the door of the Suburban. "Thanks for coming tonight. It was way more fun than I expected."

"You are quite the dancer," I said as I maneuvered in.

"As are you," Frank said.

I started the car. "Sorry I haven't been more helpful."

"Every little bit helps. Good night."

I pondered what Frank meant by that as I drove home. I was volunteering at the thrift shop tomorrow so maybe I'd find out more.

Chapter Seventeen

Saturday morning Seth called before I'd even rolled out of bed. "Have you seen the paper?"

Uh-oh. What now? I was getting spoiled not having to be up at the crack of dawn every Saturday since it was the off season for garage sales. "No."

"Good. Because when you do, the picture looks worse than it was."

"What picture? What's happened?" I got out of bed. The room was cold because I always turned down the thermostat at night. "What paper?" I got my thick, velvety robe out of the closet, stuck the phone between my shoulder and cheek, and ooched the robe on.

"*The Boston Globe*."

I beelined for the thermostat and turned it up before grabbing my computer off the trunk in my living room. "There's a picture of me in *The Boston Globe*?" That couldn't be good. But I also couldn't think of anything I'd done to warrant the *Globe*'s attention. I sat on the couch and opened my computer.

"No. It's a picture of me. In the Style section."

It only took me a couple of seconds to find the picture. Seth was dancing with a dark-haired, dark-eyed international model. I'd seen her on the front cover of more than one tabloid and beauty magazine. She was stunning and they both looked very happy.

"I'm glad you had a good time," I said. Wow. I really felt that way. He might be dancing with her, but he was sleeping with me. "I was feeling sorry for you because I thought you were at some stuffy fund-raiser."

"That's it?" Seth asked.

"Yes. That could be me with Frank at the dining-out." Fitch had a newspaper but it didn't have a Style section. And even if it did, it wouldn't use a picture of me, it would use a picture of someone important on the base.

"You danced with Frank?"

I laughed. "You can't be jealous. I was with a regular guy. You were with a supermodel."

"She isn't you."

I stood and did a little happy dance. "And Frank isn't you." I went to the kitchen to make coffee. The linoleum floor was cold against my feet.

"You trust me."

"We wouldn't be talking right now if I didn't." I put the coffee and water in the pot and flipped it on. Okay, okay. I had a twinge or two when I saw the woman in the photo. Who wouldn't be a teeny bit insecure? But I'd known Seth for almost two years now. And he wasn't a cheater.

"What are you up to today?" Seth asked.

"Thrift shop this morning and working at Jeannette's house this afternoon. What about you?"

"I'll be in the office most of the day. Can I take you to dinner? Or has Frank got you booked?"

Oooh, Seth was a bit jealous. I grinned. "Let me

check my calendar." I paused as if I was checking. "I'm available."

"Then I'll swing by for you at seven."

"See you then."

I called my brother Luke. He was in Tampa, Florida, with his girlfriend, a colonel in the Air Force. It looked like she might get assigned to MacDill Air Force Base and they decided to check out the area. Last time I'd heard from him he'd sent a picture of him and Michelle at a beach bar. Jerk. I think the high was going to be thirty-two today in Ellington, and that was without the wind chill.

"It's kind of early to be calling a guy on vacation," Luke said.

"Ah, but I already saw you posted a photo of the sunrise, so you aren't going to make me feel guilty." I could hear gulls calling to each other through the phone. And it sounded like waves crashing in the background too. "I need to pick your brain."

"Pick away," Luke said, a cheerful note in his voice.

"If someone wanted to disappear, how would they do it?"

Luke paused for so long I thought he'd hung up. This was a sore subject that we were still working through in our new relationship with each other.

"It was easier when I left because there were less cameras, less laws about working a job off the books, and less dependence on credit cards."

The brisk note in his voice made me want to hug him. Disappearing hadn't been easy on him or the rest of my family.

"What's going on?" Luke asked. "Are you planning to do a runner?"

"Not me." I told him about Fake Troy and his disappearing act from the hospital.

"It sounds like what you want is to find someone who doesn't want to be found."

"You're right. You are so smart."

"Can you repeat that so I can get it on tape?" Luke asked.

"No."

"Do you have a picture of the guy? You could plug it into a reverse image lookup site."

"No picture. I can see about getting one, but I don't think it's likely." I thought about Pellner's face if I asked him for a picture and the lecture that would follow that request. "There was a murder on base and it's a small department. Fake Troy didn't hurt anyone, so it isn't a top priority."

"I read about the murder. And you can say no one was physically hurt, but you must be frightened."

"I am. I don't want to be. I thought being proactive would help push the fear back."

"You could plug everything you do know about this guy into a search engine and look for similarities with other crimes."

"That's a good idea." I also would see if I could find out about any crimes in the Blevinses' neighborhood. Ellington's crime rate was fairly low, so usually anything like this would be making headlines. However, with Alicia's death the focus had been on her unsolved case.

"See if you can make any connections between the house, the people who own it, the people who hired you, and Fake Troy. There's almost always a connection. People aren't very smart. Maybe he'll make a mistake."

"Thanks, Luke. Enjoy the rest of your vacation." I hoped Luke was right and that Fake Troy would come out of the shadows.

Chapter Eighteen

I was smiling when I arrived at the thrift shop because I was thinking about Seth.

"You are looking chipper this morning," Eleanor said. She was sorting cash into the register, which was close to the front door. No one else seemed to be around. "Is it that stinking-hot man of yours?"

"Maybe," I said.

"Did you decide he was china worthy?"

I shook my head. "You don't give up easily, do you?"

"Nope."

"Have you heard any rumors about Becky and Alicia having a fight?" I asked. I was breaking the rules Frank and Pellner had set out for me, but this was Eleanor, not some random person I barely knew who could put me in a dangerous situation.

"Didn't I tell you about the last Spouses' Club meeting?"

I shook my head again. "No. When was it?"

"About two weeks ago." Eleanor quit counting cash and rested her hands on the counter next to the register.

"What happened?"

"You know that Becky is very good friends with the general's wife."

"I didn't know that. Ginger? She's new, right?" I asked. I leaned against the glass counter where some of the more expensive items were kept. Bits of jewelry, a Waterford crystal clock, nothing too valuable, but things that someone could easily steal.

"Yes. And they've been friends for a long time. Anyway, the treasurer was giving a report and the money just didn't seem to add up."

"Oh, boy."

"Ginger started to ask a question. But Alicia, who is the parliamentarian, looked at her and said, 'The general's wife is supposed to wear beige, sit in the back of the room, and shut up.'"

"Holy crap." I would never have spoken to someone like that at a meeting, regardless of their position or who they were married to. But I had to admit that it was even less likely that I would be rude to someone whose husband was higher ranking than CJ had been. Careers had been hurt for a lot less. What had Alicia been thinking to say that? It was out of character for the Alicia I'd heard so much about. Alicia and Ginger had bowled together, so it made the situation even more peculiar.

"The room went dead silent. Becky ended the meeting a few minutes later, then asked Alicia if they could have a word. Well, she wasn't really asking. She was telling her.

"Everyone gathered up their stuff and hustled out of the room. But we all found a reason to linger outside the door. We could all hear a lot of yelling but not exactly what it was about. A few seconds later,

Becky yanked open the door, glared at all of us, and took off. Her face was redder than a stop sign."

"What about Alicia?" I asked.

"She came out and didn't look the least bit ruffled. But she didn't hang around to talk to anyone."

"Have you heard anything since then?"

Eleanor shook her head.

"Does Alicia's husband work for the general?"

"He does."

Wow. That offered up a bunch of suspects right there. Becky, Ginger, maybe even Ginger's husband if he was a hothead and was mad someone disrespected his wife. Becky's husband if he was defending his wife. All of them had some sort of reason to be upset by what had happened. Alicia's husband as well, even though his smart bed supposedly proved he was in it when she was killed. Maybe he thought Alicia was screwing up his career.

"That's almost unbelievable," I said.

"You should have been there. People are still talking about it."

Not people who talked to Special Agent Bristow. Unless he knew this already and hadn't mentioned it to me. Now that I thought about it, he hadn't mentioned anything he knew to me. Ginger and Alicia had bowled together. Alicia was supposed to be the darling of the upper echelon. What would make her talk to someone like that?

"Who is the treasurer now?" I asked.

"Cindy Mercer."

I didn't know her either. But she wouldn't have a reason to kill Alicia, because Alicia defended her.

"Are there any other interactions between Becky and Alicia that you've heard of?"

Eleanor scrunched her forehead for a moment. "Nothing specific about them."

"But about someone else?"

"You know how it can be. One person gets more attention from the so-called important spouses than others. People end up resentful or have hurt feelings." Eleanor turned to the register.

"Speaking of hurt feelings, have you heard anyone talking about me? How I shouldn't be here?"

Eleanor concentrated on counting out coins into their slots in the register. It seemed like it took a little longer than necessary.

"You did hear something. Spill it." I put my elbows on the glass counter and rested my head on my hands for a moment.

"It's all nonsense. And only a couple of women who are trying to desperately climb the Spouses' Club social ladder." Eleanor shook her head. "They don't even know you. But why are you asking me this?"

I told her what had happened in the bathroom last night at the dining-out. "It was humiliating."

"We want you here. I want you here. You're a godsend. Half the volunteers refuse to work in the storeroom and you always jump right in. Besides, other retirees' wives work here."

"But I'm not a retiree's wife. I don't have any real connection to the base any longer beyond some friends and a love of the life that led me here."

"You're overthinking things. Don't let a couple of gossips run you off. Please."

"I don't know what to do."

"While you think it over, there's box of stuff I want you to price on the desk in the office. Now go earn your pay." Eleanor shooed me toward the office.

* * *

I arrived at Jeannette's parents' house before Zoey did. I looked to see if there were signs of anyone lurking around. There weren't. The bright sunlight for some reason made me feel safer—as if nothing bad could happen on a sunny day and all bad things happened on dark and stormy nights. I wish.

Once inside, after doing a quick walk around, I called Becky under the guise of thanking her for recommending Zoey. What I wanted was her thoughts on what had happened with Alicia. I stood in front of the picture window in the living room, watching for Zoey.

"I'm glad she's working out," Becky said, after we'd exchanged greetings and I had thanked her.

"I was at the dining-out last night," I said.

"My husband's group dining-out is coming up in a couple of weeks. I'm tired of them. So tired of them."

"I didn't think I'd ever be at another one. Are you hoping your husband retires soon?" I asked.

"Yes. I want to move back to North Carolina, have an acreage, put my feet up, and read."

"That sounds good."

"Why were you there?" Becky asked. "Who'd you go with?"

"Special Agent Frank Bristow," I said.

"I thought you were seeing someone else," Becky said. "I heard you were dating some hot guy. Not that Special Agent Bristow isn't perfectly nice."

"I am. I went with Frank as a friend. Just so he wouldn't be alone." That sounded plausible. "The rumor mill works fast."

"It does." Becky sounded bitter.

Maybe this was my in. "Yeah, I heard a lot of talk about Alicia."

"Was I mentioned?" Becky asked.

I hated lying, but Becky was mentioned today, so it wasn't a total fabrication. "Yes. It sounds like you've been through a lot."

"You don't know the half of it."

I didn't, but I'd like to. I heard a doorbell chime through Becky's phone.

"Hang on. Someone's at the door."

A couple of seconds later I heard the door open.

"Can I help you?" I heard Becky ask. A male voice said something that I couldn't understand.

"Sarah. It's Special Agent Bristow and a police officer." Her voice shook. "Call my husband and tell him to meet me at the Ellington police station. I'm in trouble." The line went dead.

Chapter Nineteen

I did as Becky asked, wondering what was going on. Why in the world would Bristow and Pellner show up at her house and take her to the station? I'd mentioned Alicia and Becky arguing to Bristow last night, but that certainly wasn't enough to cause this. Getting through Colonel Cane's secretary, even on a Saturday, was almost as hard as making it through a locked bank vault. Eventually I managed, without telling her what was going on. Persistence paid off. Becky's husband sounded annoyed that he was being interrupted. After I relayed the message he hung up abruptly. I would have done the same given the situation.

Concentrating on work was almost impossible, but I forced myself to after Zoey arrived. We worked side by side in the kitchen. Zoey dug out two electric frying pans.

"Who uses these anymore?" she asked. "They can't be worth anything."

"Campers come into the thrift shop on base and buy them up."

"Really? I thought they were supposed to be roughing it and cook over campfires."

"I guess not if there is electricity available." We

grinned at each other. "Mark a couple of dollars for each one."

"Will do, boss. Doing this is certainly an education."

"I hope in a good way." I pulled out a set of Pyrex mixing bowls, yellow, green, red, and blue. "And you don't have to call me boss."

"Oh, I love those," Zoey said. "They are very collectible right now, right?"

"Yes. They are so simple yet so colorful. I'm kind of surprised Pyrex hasn't brought them back in these colors."

"They must be durable too."

The bowls had a few black marks in the inside bottom, but I could get them out with a nonabrasive cleanser and a soft cloth. I knew they'd come out with a stronger cleanser but didn't want to risk scratching the bowl. I'd leave that for whoever bought them.

"My mom had the brown and beige ones. She still might," Zoey said. "Oh, look. Here they are." The brown and beige set had three bowls instead of four. "How should I price these?"

"Why don't you go online and see what they are selling for. If you can, find them on sites where the auction is almost over. That will give you a better sense of the difference between what some people ask and what people pay. Then we have to take into consideration that this is a garage sale, so people usually expect to pay less."

"Wow. It gets very complicated." Zoey pulled out her phone.

"It does." Everything seemed complicated today. That thought led me to stew about Becky again and her saying she was in trouble. What I wanted to do was go to the police station to find out what was going on. Or to call Seth and see what he knew. But neither idea would provide me any information. It didn't seem fair to use my relationship with Seth to find things out. I wouldn't want him to, if our positions were reversed. The thought of him running garage sales made me smile.

After we settled on prices for the Pyrex, we moved on to the everyday dishes. They weren't anything special, just some mass-produced tableware. "Let's put them in boxes and sell them as a set. That will be easier than pricing them all individually, and maybe we can get rid of them all at once instead of a piece here and there."

"What do you do with all the stuff that's leftover at a garage sale?" Zoey asked as she packed the dishes into a box.

I studied Zoey's face for a minute. "It depends on what the person who hired me wants done." I pulled a bunch of mismatched glasses off a shelf. They ranged from jam jars to nondescript glassware. This kind of stuff was hard to get rid of, no matter the price. And the best time to get rid of it was in the fall when college kids were setting up apartments and in need of furnishings. "Sometimes people save it and do another sale. Lots of people donate it to a charity. I've hauled stuff to the base thrift shop for people. On the rare occasion, I'll buy some of the leftovers."

"I bet you get a good price."

"I always try to be fair."

"Has anyone ever given you stuff?" Zoey asked. "Besides Jeannette giving you the dress?"

"Sometimes." I moved more glasses from the shelf to the counter.

"What price should I put on the glasses?"

"Twenty-five cents. The jam jars can go in a free box."

"Why do you put things in a free box if you are trying to make money for your client and yourself?"

"I always check with a client first, but a free box set near the front of a sale can bring buyers in. Plus there's less to deal with afterward. If I can get someone else to haul stuff off, the less work for me and the client."

By the end of the day we had done a lot of work in the kitchen, but there was plenty to go. Jeannette's parents weren't hoarders—the house was too neat for that—they just had a lot of stuff. Fortunately, Zoey had caught on quickly how to price things. I spot checked some of the things to make sure she was on track. We cranked up some tunes and sang while we priced.

"Thanks for all of your hard work today," I said at four.

"You're welcome. I'm sorry I can't help out tomorrow."

"No worries. Enjoy your time with your family. And I'll see you on Monday." After Zoey left I locked the door behind her. I decided to work for another hour. Seth wasn't coming over until seven, so if I quit at five I'd have plenty of time to get ready. Without Zoey here the house seemed creepier. It was getting dark out and snow was falling yet again. Welcome to January in Massachusetts.

I checked my phone to see if there was any local news about Becky. Nothing. And no texts from anyone on base, so whatever was going on with her must not be out in public. Yet.

I went back into the hall that led to the bedrooms and started pricing items hanging on the walls. Pictures snapped and framed by Jeannette's parents were basically worthless. Unless a photograph was by someone famous like Ansel Adams, no one would pay much. The frames had some value but not much.

I hummed because I didn't want the radio up loud enough to cover any other noises. I guess I was more freaked out about being here alone than I realized. Surely, if Pellner had heard anything about the mystery man he would have called. I guess in this instance no news wasn't good news. I wandered down the hall to the office and looked in, as though it would have some answers for me. But all I had were unanswered questions.

Honestly, what was that guy doing in here? And the one who attacked him? What were the odds that two random men would show up here at the same time on a day that I happened to be here, after the house had been sitting empty for several months? Astronomical. The odds would be off the charts. Of course this was real life and coincidences happened all the time. You go to some random spot on vacation and there's your best friend from second grade. That sort of thing. Maybe the two of them were working together. When Fake Troy got hurt the other guy took off.

I sat down in the desk chair and looked around. My first thought was that the break-in had to do with Jeannette's parents being CIA agents. There was so much stuff to go through. Finding a stashed secret would be next to impossible. I opened one of the desk drawers. It was full of pens. I took them out one at a time and clicked each one several times. They were regular dull pens and none of them looked like the pen with the disappearing ink that I'd used two days ago.

I picked up a blue one, clicked on it, and jokingly spoke into it. "Testing, testing." I clicked the cap and it replayed my words. I was so startled I dropped the pen. It rolled off the desk and onto the floor. Thank heavens it wasn't a poison dart pen. The dart would have shot right into my leg. I rescued the pen from the floor and clicked it several times. Maybe there was a secret message that would explain the two men's presence in the house. Sadly, all it did was replay my words and then there was just a staticky sound. A recording of Fake Troy and whoever else was here would have been just too easy.

I was more careful as I went through the rest of the pens, always making sure they were pointing away from me. If any of them were gadgets they were too advanced for me to work. I heard tiny staccato taps on the window and looked out to find it was sleeting. For a second there, I'd been afraid it would be a person. Great. I didn't mind driving in snow, but ice and sleet were a whole different ball game. I grabbed my purse and headed home.

After sliding halfway home, I was grateful to be snug in my apartment. Lights were on at the Congregational church on the town common. There wasn't much traffic for Saturday night at five thirty. Carol's shop was dark, but DiNapoli's still had the lights on. Seth had said he'd take me out, but ice was already weighing branches down on the trees on the town common. Maybe I should get food from DiNapoli's and bring it back here. Besides, I had this restless energy that borderlined on being jumpy. A quick walk to DiNapoli's would do me good.

The sleet picked at my face as I headed over to the restaurant. The sidewalk was slick and even my boots with the good tread weren't keeping me from slipping every few steps. I should have stayed home, but at this point I was halfway there. I finally got on the grass and crunched along. Minutes later I was opening the door to the restaurant. The scent of spicy sauce and basil enveloped me like a warm blanket. The place was deserted.

"Still open?" I asked as I entered.

"Come in." Rosalie had been leaning a hip against the counter as she watched Angelo stir a pot on the stove. "We're still open. Angelo decided to take advantage of how slow it is and make a sauce for tomorrow."

Angelo motioned me in. "Come try this." He pointed to the sauce. "It's a new twist on my Fra Diavolo sauce. Rosalie thinks it's too spicy."

"A new twist?" I asked. I threw my coat and scarf over a coat tree next to the door. "How can you improve on perfection?"

Angelo frowned briefly at that. "Nothing's perfect and life's too short not to try something new."

Angelo often dispensed bits of wisdom through stories he told me. I wasn't always sure in the moment what his story meant, but usually I realized the lesson and how it applied to my life soon after. I went and tasted the sauce. "Water," I choked out after my taste.

"You think it's too spicy?" Angelo's brow creased as Rosalie rushed to get a glass.

"I'm just kidding. It's delicious. You've certainly put the Diavolo in Fra Diavolo."

They both laughed.

"What can I make you, Sarah?" Angelo asked.

"What do you have too much of?" I didn't want them to go to extra work. "Seth was supposed to take me out, but it seems like a better night to stay in."

"You are right," Angelo said. "How about some eggplant parmesan and a salad?"

"That sounds like heaven," I said.

"I'll fix you some garlic bread that you can just heat up when you're ready." Rosalie crossed the kitchen and pulled out a loaf of Italian bread.

"You trust Sarah to heat it up?" Angelo said. He winked at me. Even Angelo knew about my lack of skill in the kitchen.

"I'll write down the instructions. Then you set a timer, Sarah, so you don't forget." Rosalie found a notepad and set to writing down instructions.

Yeesh. I knew how to heat up bread. "Have you heard any local gossip?" I asked.

"Of course," Rosalie said. "There's a huge fight over having a dog park. Lotsa people want one but no one wants one in their neighborhood because of traffic, noise, and, uh, smells."

Not what I was hoping for, but interesting.

"People are still convinced there are nukes over on Fitch," Angelo said.

I shook my head. "No way. But I was thinking something more in line with crime."

"The way things are going over on Fitch with that poor young woman dead, it seems like there's more crime there than here in Ellington." Angelo turned the burner off under the Fra Diavolo sauce.

"What have you heard about that? Because originally they thought it was a terrible accident." I said.

"My hairdresser's cousin's youngest daughter works on base and she heard otherwise." Rosalie was making the salad I had ordered. I slipped some money onto the counter under the containers of salt, pepper, and hot red pepper flakes. They never wanted me to pay for anything. They would find it as they finished cleaning up for the night and I would be long gone by then.

Angelo pulled eggplant parmesan out of the oven, cut out a healthy portion, and wrapped it up for me. It smelled like heaven ought to. "That kid doesn't have an ounce of sense. I wouldn't trust anything she says."

"But what did she say?" I asked.

"That someone sneaked onto the base and killed that poor girl." Angelo brought the eggplant to the counter and put it in a bag. Rosalie put the salad in a container and placed it in another bag along with the garlic bread and instructions.

Rosalie shook her head. "I heard her say someone from base whacked the poor girl with a giant icicle."

Angelo crossed himself. "You can't trust anything she says."

The door opened behind me. I turned to see who else was brave enough or dumb enough to be out on a night like this. The man's head was down as he wiped his boots on the mat. He looked up. I'm not sure which of us was more surprised. It was Fake Troy.

Chapter Twenty

He bolted.

"Call the police!" I yelled. I dashed out after him. An odd scream sounded. My foot went flying up in the air on the ice. My rear end smashed down onto the sidewalk. A jolt went up my spine and made my eyes water. I scrambled to get up as a car pulled away from the curb. It fishtailed. Swerved into the other lane, righted itself, and rounded the corner out of my line of sight. Angelo came running out of the restaurant, rolling pin in hand. He slid on the ice, but didn't fall.

"What's going on?" he asked. "Rosalie has the police on the phone, but all she can tell them is that a man came in and you ran out yelling."

"I'll explain in a minute." Angelo followed me back into the restaurant. Rosalie handed me the phone. They listened intently, frowns forming as I explained to the dispatcher who the man was. A few moments later I hung up.

"The police will look for him, but my description of the car is so vague that it's not much help. Why don't bad guys drive around with stickers on their cars that stand out? *I'm a criminal* would be nice, but I'd settle for any identifier."

"Nothing stood out?" Rosalie asked.

"Just that it was a light-colored car."

"Do you need a glass of wine?" Angelo asked.

I smiled. I loved them both so much. "I'm fine. I can't believe he's still in town."

"Who is he?" Rosalie's face was creased with concern.

I briefly explained my encounter with Fake Troy at Jeannette's house and how we came to find out he wasn't her brother.

"Maybe there's more going on in Ellington than I realized," Angelo said. "Why would he still be here?"

"I don't know." And that worried me.

Seth came over at seven and was happy to have an evening in. "I can heat up the food," he said. "You open the wine."

I threw up my hands. "Really. It's not like I can't reheat food. I'm not that incapable."

Seth pulled me to him. "It's not that. I just like doing things for you. I've been gone a lot lately."

I laid my head on his chest. "I don't believe that for a minute."

He kissed the top of my head and let me go. "Believe what you want."

I hadn't told him about the man at DiNapoli's yet. Angelo had insisted on walking me home even though I was sure the man wouldn't turn back up tonight. And frankly, he seemed more scared of me than I was of him. One of us had screamed like a girl and I was certain it was him. I opened the wine while Seth turned on the oven.

"There was a little incident at DiNapoli's," I said as I poured two glasses of Chianti.

"What kind of incident?" Seth asked.

I explained what happened. I hoped a lecture about running after the guy wasn't going to follow. "It was instinct and frankly, I'm grateful to the slippery sidewalk. I'm not sure what would have happened otherwise. I'd like to envision myself leaping on to the hood of the car or yanking the guy out of it." Surprisingly, Seth laughed. "But I'm guessing I wouldn't have." I handed Seth one of the glasses of Chianti.

Seth held up his glass. "To the only woman I know who runs after the bad guy instead of from him."

"You're okay with that?" I stared over my wineglass at him.

"Of course not. If I had it my way, I'd tie you up and keep you safe at my house."

I raised my eyebrows. "We might have to try that sometime."

Seth laughed again. "You're on." We both took a drink of our wine. "I'm glad you're okay. Did you get a plate number?"

Wow. No lecture. But he wasn't that guy. Never had been. How many times did he have to prove that to me before I would finally believe it? "No plate number and barely a description of the car."

"I wonder why he's still in town. What could be his endgame?" Seth's forehead creased with lines. I hated to worry him.

Seth and I discussed it until the timer dinged saying the food was ready. We didn't come up with any solutions.

Becky called me Sunday morning at eight thirty. Seth had left an hour ago. I was sitting on an ice pack, which seemed ironic considering it was ice that caused my fall and now ice was supposed to help cure my aches.

"We're on our way to church, but could you stop by my house around ten?"

"Yes. Of course. Are you okay?"

She sighed. "No."

"But you're going to church?" I asked.

"I'm not going to hide. I'll explain the rest when I see you. Do you need me to sponsor you on?"

I still had the pass that Frank had given me. Not that I wanted to tell her how I came to have one. "No. I have a pass. I'll see you in a bit."

After I hung up, I checked the news on my phone. But there was nothing about Becky or anything new about Alicia. I guess I'd just have to wait.

I arrived at Becky's promptly at ten, curious as to what she had to say. Her house was in the newer section of base and was one of the larger ones, given her husband's position. I scurried to the door as the wind grabbed at my hood, blowing it off. It was wicked cold, as the natives would say.

After I greeted Becky and shed my outerwear, which she hung carefully in a large coat closet, we went into the living room. Becky was so thin her head always looked too big for her body. She had short black hair sprayed stiffly into place. Her cheeks were bright red. I wondered if it was stress or illness, maybe both.

I'd been here before but not often. I was always surprised by the contemporary furniture and large abstract paintings in violent primary colors. Honestly, one of them looked more like a blood splatter pattern than a painting. I sat in a chair with my back to it.

"Would you like anything to drink?" Becky asked. Her husband wasn't anywhere in sight. That was fine by me. He always kind of gave me the heebie-jeebies. He rarely cracked a smile and I never felt up to snuff around him.

"I'm fine. What happened yesterday? You said you were in trouble." I was so curious why she'd asked me to come over. I just wanted to get to it.

Becky's nose turned red. She pressed her lips together. It looked like she was trying not to cry. "I think they're going to arrest me for Alicia's murder."

"What?" Part of me was shocked, but another part had been expecting news like this. Otherwise I wouldn't have kept checking the news and searching Becky's name. "But that's crazy."

"I'm so glad you think so too," Becky said. "They took me down to the station and put me in this horrible, claustrophobic little room." She shuddered.

I'd been in one of those rooms more than once, so I understood how she felt. It was terrifying.

"Why do you think they're looking at you?"

"I was out for a walk that night. I couldn't sleep."

"Really?" The weather had been terrible. The ice storm from earlier in the day had coated everything. Wires and tree limbs had come down. And Alicia's house was at least a half mile up a steep hill from here. I didn't want to judge her though, since I was just out walking on an icy night and was still sore to prove it. "Okay." That was neutral, way better than me shouting *Are you crazy?* which seemed more appropriate. No wonder the police were suspicious. "Why were you out?"

Becky glanced down the hall and cocked her head, listening for a moment. "This is terribly private."

I nodded. "I'm not going to say anything."

"Daniel told me he wants a divorce."

Chapter Twenty-One

This time there was no holding back the tears. I grabbed my purse and handed Becky a packet of tissues. She dabbed at her face and took a couple of deep, shuddering breaths. A small percentage of colonels had a reputation for tossing out wives like old, holey socks, marrying a much younger woman, and starting a new family. Not that that was necessarily what had happened in this case. I knew how painful a divorce was, no matter the circumstances. It was almost like a death without the rituals that went along with an actual death.

"I'm so sorry," I said.

Becky nodded. "I'm hoping we can work things out. I've always been the forgiving type. It's why I'm still living here." She smiled a quick, nervous smile. "We went to church together this morning. I hope that's a good sign."

Hmmm, so maybe he had an affair, if there was something for her to forgive. "I hope it is too." I wanted to listen as long as she needed me to, but I was also curious about Becky's fear she would be arrested.

"Enough about my marital problems." Becky straightened her shoulders.

"Surely being out for a walk isn't enough to pin a murder on you," I said.

"Oh, there's more."

Becky's voice sounded bitter. But I didn't blame her for that. I would be too, under the circumstances. I waited, not wanting to seem like I was interrogating her. I'm sure she had enough of that yesterday.

"They found trace evidence of me on Alicia."

Oh, boy. That didn't sound good. "What kind?"

"My hair and my cat's hair. They can check cat DNA now." As if on cue, a yellow cat came strutting out. She reached down and stroked it. The cat arched its back happily in response. "I did one of those DNA tests so that's how they made the match and I also did one for our cat."

"How did the hair get on her?" Could someone have planted evidence to discredit Becky? She wasn't the most popular woman on base, even though she gave a ton of her time to the Spouses' Club board and other duties expected of a commander's wife. I thought again about last fall when she'd been embroiled in a controversy with another spouse.

"We had a board meeting at my house the morning before she died to follow up on business that didn't get taken care of at our regular Spouses' Club meeting. I hugged Alicia as she left. It was my way of trying to forgive her for what had happened at the last meeting. To let her know we were okay." Becky dropped her face to her hands for a moment. "If I hadn't hugged her, none of this would even be an issue."

I couldn't remember one instance of ever seeing Becky hug anyone. She was quick to thrust her hand out to shake and always seemed to keep that as short as possible. With her there was no prolonged contact. "You told the police that?" I asked.

"Yes. I think it's the only reason I'm home and not locked up." She shuddered. "I'm their prime suspect."

I knew enough about law enforcement procedures to realize that this wasn't enough to arrest someone. "That doesn't seem like enough to put you at the top of their list." I waited to see if she would mention the meeting Eleanor had told me about where Alicia had told the general's wife to be quiet. Or if she'd mention they had argued.

"Alicia and I have had words in the recent past. Plenty of people enjoyed describing them in detail to the police."

Oh, dear. Means, motive, and opportunity. Check. Check. Check. It didn't look good.

"But we'd put that all behind us. It's why I hugged her. You know I'm not a very touchy-feely person."

I did know that.

"You have to help me, Sarah."

"How?" I asked.

"Someone obviously had it in for Alicia. Someone other than me. I want your help in thinking who that could be."

Yikes. I was torn. I wanted to help Becky out, but I didn't want to point the blame at someone else. But coming up with a short list to ease Becky's mind might not hurt.

"Please, Sarah. You're good at this kind of thing. We've known each other a long time. Longer than almost everyone else I know here."

Maybe it would help Special Agent Bristow with his investigation. It's not like sitting here talking things over was like running around questioning people.

I knew I was just trying to justify this, but it seemed to be working for me.

"Okay," I said. "There's always the possibility that it's a random person. Someone who was on base but isn't part of the base community."

"Like a visitor. Or someone who snuck on base. I hope that's true. It will tear this place apart if someone on base did it," Becky said.

Becky was right. I couldn't begin to imagine the fallout.

"Aren't you going to take notes?" Becky asked.

I managed not to roll my eyes and took out my phone. I typed in *random person* into the notes app. "Everyone seemed to love Alicia. Have you heard of anyone who didn't?"

Becky frowned, concentrating. "Not really. But the argument we had involved other people."

That was interesting. "Tell me about the fight."

"Her behavior at the board meeting was so unlike her." Becky stared over my head as if she was seeing the whole thing play out in front of her.

"What did happen?" I'd play along to get her version and compare it to Eleanor's.

"It isn't important. Alicia apologized to me and Ginger. She said she was having a bad day."

"But you said other people were involved. How so?"

"Everyone heard Alicia's outburst and they were appalled. You should have seen their faces. I adjourned the meeting, but asked Alicia to stay behind. We had words. Loud words. When I left the room there was a group of women standing outside the door. Most of them looked shocked. It didn't take long for news of what Alicia had done to Ginger to make its way around base. You know how it is."

I typed a note: *spouses at meeting.* "Do you have an attendance list from that meeting? Or do you remember who waited outside?" I made a note to ask Eleanor the same thing.

"We don't take attendance, and since it wasn't a luncheon there isn't even a list of RSVPs." Becky frowned. "I was so upset when I left. I didn't even look at who was outside the door. Seeing people hanging around didn't improve my mood any. I got out of there as fast as I could."

That fit what Eleanor has said. "Are there any men in the Spouses' Club?" I asked.

"A couple. But neither of them were at the meeting. Most men don't want to join even if their wife is in the military. All the work to be inclusive and change it from the Wives' Club." Becky shook her head.

Even if most men didn't join, it was the right thing to do. "What's it been like since?"

"It divided people into two groups, team Alicia or team Becky. I knew we had to end the divisiveness as quickly as possible for the good of the organization and base."

"That was smart of you. I know how hard it can be to put aside personal feelings."

Becky nodded. "Other than that incident, Alicia was beloved. That's what makes her death so much more heartbreaking." Becky dabbed at another tear rolling down her face. "That came out awful. No one deserves to die like that. Good or bad."

I decided not to press her for any more details. At least not now. "They don't," I said.

Becky leaned forward. "I heard Alicia had a fight with her sister when her sister came to visit."

"When was that?" I asked. I made a note to read Alicia's obituary to see who had survived her.

"She had been staying here awhile and then left in a huff the day before Alicia died. But I don't know any of the details."

"She might have had a pass allowing her to get on and off base."

"Yes. She lives in New Hampshire, so not all that far away."

I typed in more notes. Things I'd pass along to Frank. "Anyone else?" I asked.

"No. It's not a very good list. Some random person and her sister. I mean, who would kill their sister?"

I shuddered at the thought. "It's not. But keep thinking. You might think of someone else." I didn't tell Becky that after I left her house I would add her husband to my list of suspects. I'd dig around to see if he had a girlfriend. Either one of them might be more than willing to set Becky up. But I couldn't rule out the general or his wife. Not that they would set up Becky on purpose.

"I heard that Alicia was the president of the PTA. Have you heard about any conflict there?" I asked.

"I'm not plugged into the community anymore, since our kids are at college. If I hear anything I'll let you know." She looked a bit happier. "It's terrible to want to pin this on someone else."

"It's not terrible to want to clear your name." I stood to go. There didn't seem to be anything else to say.

Becky stood too. At the door she gave me a big hug. Maybe she was changing. Life's low points altered a person forever.

"Thank you for coming over." She paused. "I know I'm not always the easiest person to be around. So that makes me even more grateful."

I patted her arm. "Of course." As I drove off, three words rolled over in my head—a murder, an accused, and a divorce. Which one was the thread I needed to pluck on to help Becky?

Chapter Twenty-Two

Alicia's husband, Walter, opened the door of their townhouse seconds after I pressed the doorbell. Maybe he was waiting for someone or maybe he was lonely and had seen me walking across the courtyard toward his door, not that he would recognize me. His eyes were red rimmed and had a lost look that made me want to run away. Walter's dark hair was in one of the shortest crew cuts I'd ever seen, which was saying a lot since I'd been around military members for over twenty years.

I held up a jar of dog biscuits that I had bought on the way to base this morning. "I brought these for your puppy." It seemed like a better thing to bring than food. First of all, his neighbors had probably sent so much food he'd wouldn't be able to eat it all. And second, food seemed like a reminder that he would have to eat alone. Dog biscuits were a reminder that he wasn't.

"I'm Sarah Winston."

"Walter Arbas." He stuck out his hand and we shook.

I pointed to the dog biscuits. "They're organic. From a place in Connecticut."

A chocolate Labrador puppy came scampering

toward us. Walter grabbed its collar, but the puppy strained toward me, on its back paws, its front ones pawing the air.

"Why don't you come in before Norton escapes."

I stepped into the small foyer and handed Walter the dog biscuits. A staircase was straight ahead. The painting of a wine bottle on a picnic table that Alicia had painted at Paint and Wine hung on the wall. To the left was a living room and then a space most base people used as a dining room. But here it was part eating space, part workout space, with a treadmill in the corner and free weights scattered around. Walter closed the door and let loose of Norton. He scampered over and put his paws on my knee. I rubbed his ears, murmuring the silly things people say to their dogs like *Aren't you a handsome boy.*

Walter grabbed some newspapers from one side of the sectional sofa. "Have a seat." He crumpled the newspaper and stared down at it like he wasn't sure what to do with it. Then he stuffed it between the couch and an end table. Walter sat in a chair across from me, facing the window, and ran a hand over his short military cut hair.

"Do you want something to eat?" He gestured toward the kitchen off to the left of the dining room. "I've got so much food." Norton plopped down by Walter's feet, resting his head on one of Walter's shoes. He leaned down and patted Norton. "He gives me a reason to get up in the morning. I guess that's why we got him."

"No. Thank you." I paused. "I'm so sorry."

"You knew Alicia?" His eyes lit briefly.

"We volunteered at the thrift shop together. But I didn't know her well." I wasn't sure what had even made me want to come over here. Some instinct to comfort. To acknowledge the depth of pain that came along with living one's life. He'd been through so much—losing his wife, being arrested for killing her, and even though he'd been released, a shadow would hang over him until the real killer was found. "If there's anything I can do . . ."

"Unless you can smuggle a couple of casseroles out of here without being seen, I can't think of anything." He managed a brief smile. "Thanks for stopping by. I haven't had a lot of visitors since the police hauled me in."

"I'm sure they'll get this cleared up soon." I hoped I was right. Walter was dealing with enough right now. It made me more determined to find out what happened.

Walter looked beyond me, out the window. His sad face became grim. I turned to see what he was looking at. A young woman was striding down the sidewalk toward the townhouse. She had the same auburn hair as Alicia. A long, black trench coat flapped behind her and she wore black motorcycle boots even in this cold weather, when riding a bike could only be a sweet spring dream.

"There's Alicia's sister." His voice was weary. "Fiona's been by every single day since the funeral."

"To keep you company?" I asked.

"To ease her guilt. She had a fight with Alicia the day before she died. It's a heck of a way to leave things."

That's what Becky had said. I stood. "She must feel awful."

"She does. She kept nagging Alicia, trying to get her to commit to a family reunion next summer. Yelled that Alicia didn't care about her family since she married me." Walter shook his head. "Some people don't get that we don't have a lot of control over our assignments. That we don't want to be away from our families." He grinned for a moment. "Necessarily."

"I hear you." My own family had had its share of problems in the past. We were closer now than we'd been in a long time.

Walter stood. "I shouldn't sound so mean. Fiona's helping me clean out Alicia's things. I couldn't do it on my own and I can't stand seeing her clothes in the closet. It's a constant reminder that she's not here."

We walked to the door.

"Thanks again for the dog biscuits. It was thoughtful."

Norton ran to the door. Walter grabbed his collar again before he opened it. I stepped out and said hello to Alicia's sister. She gave me the once-over and didn't seem to like what she saw.

"Who was that?" I heard her ask Walter as I headed down the sidewalk.

"A friend of Alicia's. She dropped off some dog biscuits for Norton."

"She isn't wearing a wedding ring. Is she single?"

"I don't know," Walter said.

He shut the door, cutting off anything else I could hear. But I left wondering about the free weights in the dining room. How hard would it be to put them in your smart bed and make the bed think it was a body? Walter's in particular. I didn't know enough about smart beds to know if they could tell the difference between a living, breathing human and weights. And there was Fiona. She almost sounded jealous of me being with Walter. What was going on there? Was her coming over to help a ruse for something else going on? I hated it when I had more questions than answers.

I waited for Awesome at Bedford Farms Ice Cream at eleven forty-five. I'd called him after I left Walter's house and asked him to meet me. Yes, it was the middle of winter and some people thought it was too cold for ice cream. But not me and amazingly, the store had its share of customers, nothing like summer but respectable for the middle of January. I hoped giving Awesome something sweet would help the cranky attitude Stella had mentioned the other night. A patrol car pulled up. Awesome loped toward the shop, his face set and way more grouchy looking than his usual relaxed self. Even the way he held his shoulders was different. Tense. I planned to find out why.

I'd already ordered my usual Almond Joy small size in a cup. It was a huge portion. A small here was an enormous at any other ice cream shop, but I was up for the job of finishing it. Awesome nodded at me, but went and ordered instead of coming over to me. I watched as the woman behind the counter took in his big brown eyes and long, long eyelashes. She winked at him, but didn't even get a smile in return.

"Why don't we go sit in my car?" I suggested when Awesome had his order. There wasn't much seating and there were too many ears.

Awesome shrugged, but he followed me, holding the door open for me with his long arm. After we hustled over to the Suburban, I turned it on and flipped on the seat warmer. "Your control is on the armrest." I pointed with my spoon.

"I already feel like I'm in the hot seat for something, but I have no idea what."

I chuckled. I ate some of my ice cream. Coconut, vanilla, chocolate bits. Heaven.

He took a bite. "Man this is good."

"What flavor?"

"Coffee. Now will you just tell me why we're here? And don't expect me to tell you anything about Alicia's investigation."

Now that we were here, I felt more awkward than I imagined. "What's going on with you and Stella?"

He froze, with his spoon of ice cream halfway to his mouth. His eyes widened in what looked like alarm to me. Awesome put his spoon back in his cup. "What are you talking about? We're great." He paused. "Oh, no. We must not be great if we're having this conversation. Is she dumping me?"

He sounded scared. This big, brave man. A former NYPD homicide detective. Scared. "No." I shook my head. "Men are idiots."

"What then?" he asked.

I took another bite of my ice cream to procrastinate. Probably none of this was my business. But I'd started so I had to finish. Had to help Stella. I hated seeing her sad. "She thinks you are going to break up with her."

"What? Why would she think that?"

"Because from what Stella said you've been incredibly cranky lately."

Awesome leaned his head back against the headrest. "You're right. I *am* an idiot."

I jabbed my spoon at him. "You aren't seeing anyone else, are you?"

"No. She's my one and only. I wouldn't have it any other way."

"Well, then you'd better get your act together. She's an amazing woman. You're lucky she puts up with you." I was teasing a bit. Awesome was, well, awesome. Normally, anyway.

"I am. She is."

"What's going on? Is it work?"

Awesome glanced out the window. "Yeah, that's it. Speaking of work, I have to get back at it." He opened the door and almost leaped out. Like he was running from something—perhaps me.

I looked at him. "Good talk. Whatever it is, pull it together." He nodded, slammed the door, and strode over to his car. I watched him start it and peel out of the parking lot. I hoped it was work. I really did.

Chapter Twenty-Three

On my way home I'd bought another batch of ingredients for the chicken marsala. And some wine to drink while I was cooking it. After I put away the groceries, I called Carol. "I have questions for you. And I have some news." I hadn't told her about Mike moving in next door.

"Do you feel like braving the cold? I'm at my shop."

"I have to go out anyway to work at a client's house. I'll stop by to see you first."

"Great," Carol said. "A class just left and I'm cleaning up."

I drove over since I had to go to the Blevinses' house next. This time of year I missed coastal California where the temperature was mild most of the year. It was a rare day when anyone broke out parkas, scarves, and gloves. Even if they did it was because it was fifty degrees. I hustled into the shop.

"Mind helping me wash paintbrushes while we talk?"

"Not at all." We stood by a sink, the soft oily smell of paint wafting around us.

"What's the news?" Carol asked.

"Mike Titone is living next door to me again."

"Not again." Carol paused, holding a set of paint-brushes midair. "Why?"

By the time I finished telling her about the sponta-neous fondue party, she was laughing so hard she almost choked. I was laughing because she was. Not to mention it was a wonderful relief after my very depressing talks with Becky and Walter.

"I'm not sure I like the idea of him living right next to you if someone is after him," Carol said.

"I know. That went through my mind too. But with his brothers and men around I'm safer than normal." I hoped I was anyway.

"I guess so. You said you wanted to ask me some-thing."

"Do you have any contact with the base PTA any-more?" Carol's kids had gone to school on base until they moved to Ellington two years ago. The base had a school that went from kindergarten through eighth grade. Then the students transferred to Ellington High School. Not all bases had schools and some had been closed down. The government paid the school district for each kid who attended a town's local schools. Most towns were eager to have them.

"One of my friends is still part of the PTA. I think she's their treasurer. Why?"

I couldn't ask questions without having to answer some too. "It has to do with Alicia's death. Some-one mentioned that Alicia was involved with the base PTA."

Carol gave me a long look. "You investigating

Alicia's death is worse than having Mike next door to you."

Carol might be right. "I wouldn't call it investigating."

"What would you call it? Snooping? Poking your nose in some murderer's business? An inquiry?"

"I'd call it helping a friend." I raised a hand as Carol opened her mouth. "I can't say who. But someone I know has been implicated in Alicia's death. She asked me for help."

Carol stood still for a moment then nodded. "You were there for me when I was accused. I guess I can't begrudge you helping someone else."

"Thank you." We continued washing brushes.

"I didn't ever meet Alicia, since she was so new to base. But I did hear things about her."

"Like what?" I asked.

"My friend on the board thought she was a bit of a social climber. That she only took positions that would up her profile and maybe her husband's. However, being president of the PTA is a thankless job that she took when no one else wanted it."

"It sounds like Alicia was a complex woman and a very hard worker."

Carol nodded. "Do you think it was someone who was jealous of Alicia?"

I couldn't mention Becky's possible divorce, not even to Carol, who I trusted with almost all my secrets. "It's possible, but there are all kinds of other reasons out there too." I glanced at the clock on Carol's wall. It looked like a paint palette and the hands were paintbrushes. "I have to go."

"I'll call you if I think of anything else I've heard

about Alicia. I worry about you working over at your client's house alone even though Jeannette put in a new security system."

"I hired a woman from base so I'm not alone. But it's a big project and I could use someone else. Can you think of anyone who wants some part-time work?"

Carol scrunched up her face and then relaxed it. "My neighbors' aunt is here for an extended visit. My poor neighbor broke her shoulder and hip all on the same side. It's hard for her because she can't get around easily. She appreciates that her aunt came to help, but would like a little alone time. Do you want me to check with her?"

I did some quick calculations in my head. Carol's neighbor had to be in her sixties. That meant her aunt had to be in her eighties. Beggars. Choosers. And I didn't want to be ageist. "Sure. It sounds like a win-win. More help for me and some free time for your neighbor."

Carol nodded. "Thanks for helping me clean the brushes."

"Any time," I said as I bundled back up.

"Tomorrow at ten then?" Carol laughed.

I shook my head and braced for another wintry blast.

My phone rang as I pulled into Jeannette's drive at one forty-five. Becky.

"I've been racking my brain since you left," Becky said. "To see if there was anything that might be significant."

"That's good. Did you come up with anything?" I

left my Suburban running with the seat warmer on. A nap sounded good. It had been an emotional morning talking to Becky and Walter. Talking to Awesome hadn't been easy either.

"Two things. The whole argument with Alicia started because Ginger was trying to ask Cindy, the treasurer, a question about her report."

"How much money does Cindy have control of?" Usually Spouses' Clubs were notoriously underfunded, so any money they had would be negligible.

"Our coffers are brimming over. We've already had our big fundraiser auction, and the cookbook we put out last fall was wildly successful. We've done three printings so far."

It was nice to hear the happy note in Becky's voice, the pride. "What's the money going to be used for?"

"Most of it will go to scholarships. But the good we can do with the rest of it is almost endless. We loved that you raised enough money to fly that dog over from Afghanistan last fall. It inspired us to help service members with PTSD."

That was all wonderful news, but it didn't add up to who killed Alicia. "But why would Cindy kill Alicia? They were friends."

"I said they were friendly not best buddies. What if Alicia found out the numbers were off? That maybe Cindy had been stealing from the coffers."

People had been murdered for a lot less. "Okay, I'll add her to the list." The problem was, I couldn't ask Alicia what had been going on with her and Cindy. Someone had robbed Alicia of her ability to do that. I turned off my car, got out, and paced.

"There's more. I hate to say it because no one

wants to speak ill of the dead." Becky's voice sounded hesitant.

"I get that, but this is about you. Your freedom."

Becky gasped.

"I'm sorry to be so blunt," I said.

"It's okay. I knew when I asked you to help that this wasn't some mystery kids kind of game. It's my life."

I wanted to say *So spit it out.* I'd been up and down the driveway ten times by now. I bet I looked like a lunatic. And my toes were cold. I looked at the house. It hunkered down, dark and low under heavy clouds. I didn't want to go in, and at the same time I was mad at myself for feeling that way. I shook myself either from fear or a weak attempt at warming up. I hoped Carol's neighbor's aunt would be able to help. Even if she was older and couldn't do much the companionship would be worth the money.

"Alicia and a man who was in the Spouses' Club were very close."

"Who?" I asked.

"His real name is Ed Flowers, but everyone calls him Channing because he looks like that actor who was in those male stripper movies."

Why hadn't I heard about this guy before? Usually if there was someone hot around, everyone knew. This was just another reminder that my life was becoming more and more disconnected from the base. "Are there rumors about them?"

Becky stayed quiet for a moment. "Yes." It sounded like it pained her to say it. "And his wife is rumored to have a terrible temper."

"How long have the rumors been going around?" I asked. I beeped the locks closed on my Suburban.

I had to go in and warm up. That and I had a ton of work to do.

"Walter and Ed's wife were both deployed at the same time. They both got back about a month ago. I heard Walter came back from his deployment earlier than he was supposed to."

"You think the rumors had anything to do with it?"

"Rumors wouldn't be enough to bring someone home early."

I let that settle over me as I unlocked the door to the Blevinses' house. It was cold in here too, or it was just my mood. "Okay. I'll see what I can find out." I turned off the alarm system as we hung up. Then I headed for the thermostat hoping something Becky had said would spark an idea of how to help her.

"I'm not afraid to be here alone. I'm not afraid to be here alone," I chanted as I turned up the thermostat. But I was. After seeing Fake Troy last night and knowing he was still around, I was more jittery than I'd admitted to Seth when we talked this morning.

"You're a big, strong, independent woman." Yeah, one who's talking to herself like a looney tune. For now I was going to have to set aside Becky's problems while I focused on working here.

I decided to take a few minutes and look at the office again before I went back to tackle more of the kitchen items. Maybe facing the office first thing would ease my fears. Maybe Fake Troy had fled the area after seeing me last night. That might be wishful thinking, but I'd go with it. This time I looked behind pictures and certificates that lined the walls in the office. Maybe there was a safe or hidey-hole behind one of them. Or maybe a note or key would be taped to the back—a note or key that Fake Troy was looking for. After fifteen minutes I'd found a dead spider, a lot of dust, and some cobwebs. Nothing more interesting than that.

My phone binged a text message from an unknown number. The message read: This is Harriet Ballou. My niece lives by your friend Carol. I hear you need help. Text me the address and I will swing by and see if we can work together.

Interesting. I'd wondered how old Carol's neighbor's aunt was. Not too old to text was my only answer. I sent the address and got a message back saying she'd arrive in fifteen minutes.

I returned to the kitchen. The house was so quiet I couldn't take it any longer. I turned on an old radio that sat on the counter. There was a lot of static but I finally managed to find a country station that came in fairly well. I kept the volume down so I could listen for sounds of intruders and/or Harriet's arrival. While the security system provided some comfort, it didn't cover all the windows. I sang along when I knew a song, putting on my best fake country drawl.

Jeannette's parents had been big fans of all kinds of kitchenware. But at least it was all fairly good quality and not reused margarine tubs. I found a shelf full of different sizes of cast-iron skillets. From a little bitty one that you could cook a single egg in to one that was at least fifteen inches across and weighed about a ton. Heirloom quality cast-iron cookware was always popular and hard to find at garage sale prices.

One of the pieces looked kind of dirty, so I decided to wash it. Yes, I was a full service, do-it-all business. I ran some hot water and found some old dishwashing soap under the sink. Just as I was ready to pour it in, a little thought niggled into my head. I had a feeling that there were very specific ways to clean cast iron. I set the soap down, turned off the water, and did a quick search online.

The recommended cleaning method was to make a paste out of kosher salt and water. I dug around, found some salt, made a paste, and scrubbed away, rinsing well with hot water. It didn't seem all that sanitary, but according to the directions any other kind of cleanser would damage the seasoning—whatever that was.

After I dried that pan, I priced them, and then put them back in the cupboard for now. The day of the sale I'd put most of the kitchen items on the counter and kitchen table. But I needed the space for pricing until then.

The doorbell rang and my phone binged at the same time. The message was from Harriet. "I'm here" was all it said.

I trotted to the door, opened it, and stared. "Harriet?" I asked. A tall, slender woman stood in front of me with light brown hair streaked with a bit of gray. It almost looked like she'd had it done like that. Maybe she had. Harriet was much younger than I was expecting considering the age of her aunt. She looked to be in her mid-sixties.

"Are we just going to stand here in the cold staring at each other?" Harriet asked.

"No. No. Come in. Sorry. I'm Sarah."

Harriet stepped in. Her well-worn motorcycle boots clumped on the tile as I closed the door. She whipped off a sporty-looking black quilted jacket which exposed a very fit figure encased in a black

T-shirt and jeans. I stuck out my hand to shake and was grasped in a firm but brief clasp. My mind reeled as I tried to readjust to the Harriet who stood before me and the elderly, plumb woman I'd pictured.

She tilted her head which highlighted her high cheekbones. "You *were* expecting me?" Her eye shadow gave her eyes the smoky look that I tried to achieve and usually failed at.

"Yes. It's just that I . . ." What did I say without putting my foot in my mouth? "Carol said you were her neighbor's aunt and I . . ." Harriet was going to think I was a blithering idiot.

She smiled. "My oldest sibling is twenty years older than me as are most of my nieces and nephews. We have an upside down family. So I'm younger than most of my nieces and nephews."

"Ah, that solves that then." I led Harriet to the kitchen. She flung her coat over one of the chairs at the table.

I quickly explained how much I could pay her and she didn't object. "I do need to tell you what happened here and will understand if you prefer not to work here."

"I'm aware," Harriet said. "My niece gets the paper and I read about the incident."

"The man is still in town and could be a threat."

"And you know this how?" she asked.

I explained my run-in with Fake Troy last night.

"Did he seem like a threat?"

I thought that over. "He seemed to be a little afraid of me. Or maybe just startled."

"You will have to be on your guard until he's caught in that case," Harriet said. "What do you want me to do?"

I was starting to wonder if Harriet's arrival was some elaborate scheme by Seth and Carol so I would have an assistant who would double as a bodyguard. She looked like she could kick butt and take names without a thought. And she certainly didn't seem like someone who needed a part-time job.

"Why are you here?" I asked. Might as well get it out there instead of wondering.

Harriet laughed. "Because I'm driving my niece crazy. I'm not good at sitting still and I've already alphabetized her spices, organized her linen closet, and dusted every surface in the house. Why do you think I was here?"

"Knowing my friends they think I need a bodyguard."

"Then you have good friends. You're lucky."

I was. It made me wonder about her life, but I didn't get a vibe that she wanted to be asked. "Let's get to work then. Have you ever priced things for a sale like this one?"

"Never. But I'm a quick learner. Where do you want me? It certainly seems like there's plenty to do."

I decided, like I had with Zoey, that clothes would be easiest and took her to the bedroom. After a few minutes of instruction, I left her to it and returned to the kitchen. I found a shelf with five different sets of vintage canisters. Oh, and they were beauties. At least most of them were. One of the sets was just like one my grandmother had. They were red plastic with white boxy letters that said—flour, sugar, coffee, tea. The lids were white. There was a round metal set with pictures of fruit painted on them. These provided no instructions as to what was to go inside—woe to the person who had to make that decision on their own.

There was also a turquoise set that I loved but had no space for. Then some really old, ornate glass ones and a regrettable avocado green set. However, knowing how trends circled back around, before I knew it someone would be getting nostalgic about avocado green things. I shook my head at the thought. But the rest of them—I sighed happily—what fun. Collectors would go gaga for them.

I checked each one to make sure they were empty and clean. Since not all of them were, this time I filled the sink with soapy water and washed out the traces of flour and sugar. The flour container of the avocado green set was filled to the brim with flour. Old flour with what looked like a bug or two in it. I dumped it into the trash can. A piece of floury paper was stuck inside the bottom of the canister. *What was that?*

Chapter Twenty-Four

I fished the piece of paper out picking it up by the corner. It had a series of numbers on it that meant nothing to me. Maybe they would mean something to Jeannette, so I called her. It dawned on me what the numbers were, as I explained to Jeannette what I'd found.

"I think it's a combination for a lock," I told her.

"Why would it be in the flour canister?" Jeannette asked.

I didn't answer because I thought she was musing instead of really asking. "Do you recognize the numbers?"

"It's a combination of our birthdays and my parents' anniversary."

"Not very secure," I said.

"Not in this day and age. But it might have seemed like it whenever it was written."

Frankly, I assumed CIA people were smarter than that, even back in the day. So whatever this was, it wasn't a combination to anything too important. For that matter, the flour canister wasn't that secure of a hiding place.

"I'll come over and take a look," Jeannette said. "It'll be about thirty minutes."

I clicked off and looked up to see Harriet watching me. She had a man's suit in her hand.

"I couldn't help but overhear," she said. "Can I take a look?"

I hesitated then held the piece of paper up to her. She didn't reach for it but leaned in a bit. "It could be lottery numbers."

I realized how very little I knew about Harriet. "Why does anyone need to hide lottery numbers in a flour canister?"

"People are odd." She straightened back up. "I agree that it's most likely a combination for something. I'll let you know if I find anything with a lock."

"Thanks. Did you need help?" I gestured toward the suit.

"Mint condition, handmade, silk. I couldn't figure out a price."

I did a quick search on my phone and suggested a price. She nodded and went back off to the bedroom.

I continued to work until I heard Jeannette at the front door around three thirty. I introduced her to Harriet who was getting ready to leave.

"All the clothes are sorted. All of the men's pants are together, shirts by color, women's clothing by color and category. I also placed the undergarments that can't be resold in plastic bags. Shoes are organized by style and if they are men's or women's."

My eyes grew larger with every word. "That's great. Maybe tomorrow you can price them." She did more in a few hours than Zoey did in a day.

"I already did that. I apologize, but I'm not sure I can work tomorrow," Harriet said. "I have to take my niece to a doctor's appointment in the morning and physical therapy in the afternoon."

"That's okay. I think Zoey is here tomorrow." Between the two of them things would get done in time. Harriet said her goodbyes.

"Harriet's an interesting woman," Jeannette said.

"She is."

"Cop?"

Maybe that's where I was getting the bodyguard vibe from. "I'm not sure. I was expecting a little old lady on a fixed income." I explained how Harriet had ended up here.

"Her red Porsche says otherwise," Jeannette said.

"She drives a Porsche?" I thought that over. I should have asked more questions, but time to get back to why Jeannette was here. "The numbers can't be that important," I said to Jeannette as we walked to the kitchen.

"I had the same thought, but I'm still curious. Have you found anything with a lock on it?" Jeannette asked.

"No, but I haven't spent a lot of time looking. I wonder if there is something in the office." When we got to the kitchen, I handed her the floury piece of paper.

"That's my dad's handwriting." She smiled down at it. "I haven't seen any locks either. But there's a lot of stuff in here. Do you think this has anything to do with the man who claimed to be my brother?"

"I thought that too. But this is so low tech that it doesn't seem like your parents would do this."

"You're right. Unless it's so low tech it's the last

place anyone would think to look. Where was the canister?"

I pointed to a cupboard. "There are five sets of canisters. I think this was the second to last set I pulled out. I wasn't paying that much attention."

"Right. Who would even think they'd find a note like this, hidden? There wasn't anything in any of the other canisters?"

"Just remnants of flour, sugar, tea, and coffee."

"I'll go look around the office. It's a good afternoon to do some sorting anyway," Jeannette said.

"I'll keep working in here." I pulled open a drawer and found mundane utensils. They were still in a plastic holder divided into sections, so I priced it all as one item. The next drawer was full of vintage metal cookie cutters. How fun. I found a set of four tin playing card cutters. Then the mother lode of heart-shaped ones in all sizes. Some of them looked like they were actual antiques. These would appeal to people who loved hearts, antiques, or cookie cutters. I set them aside. There were a few sets in their original boxes. The colors on the boxes were faded but the graphics screamed *I'm vintage*. Oh, good. People loved things in their original boxes. It added to the value. It took me a while to price everything, so I was startled and let out a little yip when I heard the floor creak.

I whirled around to see Jeannette standing there.

"I'm sorry if I startled you," she said.

"It's okay. I was having so much fun going through all of these cookie cutters that I forgot you were here."

Jeannette held up a Christmas tree cookie cutter from the drawer and dangled it from a finger. "It's kind of ironic that my mom has all of these because she usually just bought cookies from the bakery. Except for that year in Japan. Mom was a busy woman with a full-time job and a family."

Jeannette sounded like she admired her mom. I thought about my own mom. She'd worked part-time in an insurance office from the time I headed off to school. She loved to bake though, so our house usually smelled like cinnamon and sugar. Maybe I should take up baking along with learning to cook more.

"Any luck finding anything with a lock on it?" I asked.

"Nothing. But I did sort through a bunch of paperwork. I'm going to go back and shred it now."

"Okay." I worked for a couple more hours, but didn't find anything too exciting. No combinations. No antiques. I was almost through with the kitchen when Jeannette and I decided to call it a day.

We were in the foyer wrapping up.

"Oh, this weather," Jeannette said. "It's so bitter cold."

"It is especially brutal this year. I live by the town common and have hardly seen anyone out on the skating rink." One thing I'd learned in my time in Massachusetts was the citizens loved to talk about the weather. As if each winter the terrible weather was a surprise to them. It was so different than growing up in coastal California, where the weather was much the same all year round. A little more rain in the winter, a little more sun in the summer. But nothing drastic like here.

"My boyfriend has been wanting to go, but I keep putting him off. I'm not the best skater so it doesn't hold a lot of appeal anyway. Thanks for all of your hard work."

"Thanks for having me." I set the security system and reached to open the door. I noticed a half-inch long wire sticking out of the wall to the left of the door. "What's that?" I asked Jeannette. I didn't remember seeing it before, but usually flipped off the light before I opened the door. "Is it part of the security system?"

Jeannette shook her head slowly. "I've never seen it before in my life."

Chapter Twenty-Five

The wire had a bit of glass on the end. "I think it's a camera," I said as I studied it.

"A camera? I don't understand," Jeannette said.

"Neither do I." I pulled on the wire but it didn't budge. "It's pointed at the security system."

"Maybe I'm wrong. The security company must have installed it too. But they never mentioned it."

Now it was my turn to shake my head. "I don't know that much about security systems, but this doesn't seem right." I looked from the tiny wire to the security system panel. "It's pointed at the panel."

"Whatever for?" Jeannette asked.

"Whoever installed this can see the security code when it's typed in." That had to be it. I had a unnerving feeling Fake Troy was behind this.

"Then why didn't they get it and take the wire out? This must be legitimate."

Wishful thinking. "The angle might be off. I usually stand right in front of the panel when I punch in the code." My mind was doing fast spins, trying to figure this out. "Let's go out on the porch."

"Oh, and follow the wire to whoever did this?" Jeannette asked.

"I don't think it will go very far." I must watch way more spy shows than Jeannette did. We went out on the porch and stared at the door to the right side of the house. I tried to gauge where the wire was on the other side. It only took moments for me to spot the wire attached to a teensy box stuck on the back of the lantern-shaped porch light. I pointed to it. "Look. It's attached right there."

Jeannette came and stood next to me. She reached for it.

"Wait. Don't touch it. Maybe there's a fingerprint or two. I shouldn't have touched the one inside." I turned, facing the street. Only two of her neighbors could see the front porch from their homes.

"How will we find out?" Jeannette asked.

Jeannette was clearly traumatized and not thinking this through. I couldn't blame her. She had been through a lot with the death of her parents, the fake brother, and now this.

"Go back inside. Call the police."

"What are you going to do?"

"Knock on your neighbors' doors and see if they noticed anyone hanging out by the door." My guess was no one would have seen anything or they would have called the police like they did on me.

Fifteen minutes later, as I finished up my last conversation with one of the neighbors, Pellner pulled up. We walked up the drive together.

"What are you doing out here?" he asked.

I'm guessing he wasn't going to like my answer. "I checked with the neighbors to see if they'd spotted anyone messing around the porch light." Before he had a chance to say anything I added, "I know, I know. Leave it to the police."

"I was going to ask what you found out."

"No you weren't."

Pellner shook his head. "Just tell me what you learned. Lectures are futile with you."

That wasn't necessarily true. I'd mostly done what Bristow and Pellner asked—that I just listen for information about Alicia. I could follow instructions but decided not to point that out. "Nothing. No one saw anyone hanging out who shouldn't be here."

I showed Pellner where the camera was. Jeannette came out, carrying a stepladder, and joined us.

"I'll go back in," Jeannette said. "There's not room for all of us out here."

Pellner stood on the porch, pulled on a glove, and climbed the ladder. I held the base of the stepladder for him. The wind swirled snow around my feet. Once the camera was out, he detached the little black box from the back of the porch light and dropped the whole thing in an evidence bag. We went back inside, where Jeannette stood in the foyer waiting for us. She was wringing her hands.

"Can you take this back to the station and trace where the signal was being transmitted to?" I asked.

Pellner stared at me for a moment.

"They do that. In movies," I said, my voice trailing off as I realized how ridiculous I sounded. Now who was watching too many spy shows?

"It's not impossible. But it would be a low priority for the state techs."

"Someone drilling a hole through your wall and sticking a camera in isn't a high priority?" Jeannette's face flushed red. "Someone watching you isn't a bad enough crime?"

"It's a property crime. Not a crime against a person," Pellner said.

"Not yet." Jeannette glared at Pellner. "But who knows what they caught on the camera. Poor Sarah's been here and by herself on and off."

I hoped I hadn't scratched myself in any embarrassing places when I'd been in the foyer. How much had they seen? I hadn't spent a lot of time in the hallway, but still . . .

Pellner's dimples deepened, but not because he was smiling. "It's shut off by now. Once they saw you spot the camera, there'd be no reason to leave it on."

"Maybe they don't know yet," I said. "Maybe it isn't being monitored twenty-four seven."

"Chances are the signal has been cut off too," Pellner said.

"Don't you have hackers you can call to trace this stuff?" Jeannette asked. "Why turn it over to the state?"

"I wish. You must be confusing the police department with the CIA," Pellner said.

Jeannette got a thoughtful look on her face. Maybe she still had some contacts from when her parents were agents or employees or whatever they were.

Pellner took a deep breath. "I apologize for snapping at you. I'm worried about what's going on here."

"As are we," Jeannette said, speaking for both of us.

"Should we look around the house for other cameras?" I asked.

"Good idea," Pellner said. "I'll look around the outside while you two look in here."

Fifteen minutes later we met back in the foyer.

"We went over every inch of this place," Jeannette said. "We didn't come up with anything."

Pellner looked at me. I shrugged my shoulders. We went over as much as we could without moving furniture or taking everything off the walls.

"I didn't find anything outside," Pellner said.

"No strange vans with antennas parked on the street?" I asked.

Jeannette gasped.

"I'm joking. I tend to do that when I'm stressed." I took Jeannette's hand and gave it a quick squeeze.

"It's okay." She rubbed her temples. "I just don't get it. I'll talk to my brother and see if he has any ideas about what in the world could be going on."

"I'll try to get patrols driving by more often," Pellner said. "I need to get going."

After he took off, Jeannette and I each slumped against a wall opposite each other.

"We should change the security code just in case they recorded it," I said.

Jeannette got the instructions and updated the system. "I keep saying this, but you don't have to come back, Sarah."

"It's fine. Quit worrying about me. I've been extra careful and I'll make sure someone is here with me."

"Thank you," Jeannette said. "I'll let you know what I hear from my brother."

Chapter Twenty-Six

I trudged up the stairs to my apartment at five thirty. A man sat outside Mike's door on a folding chair that looked too small for his bulk. He leaped up when I hit the top step.

"It's just me," I said. "I live in that apartment." I pointed to the left.

"Yeah, okay. Mike gave us all a picture of you. So nothing untoward happens."

Last year when Mike had stayed in the apartment, I'd had to prove who I was more than once. It had been annoying. I'm not sure I liked the idea of these guys having my picture, but whatever. I wished I had a picture of Fake Troy to show him, to make sure he didn't show up here.

The door popped open and Mike stuck his head out. "Want to come over for some dinner?"

Wow. This was a first. While Mike and I'd had many interactions over the last couple of years, none of them had been social. I was still feeling uneasy about what had happened at Jeannette's parents' house, so company sounded good. Besides, it would give me an excuse to put off trying to make the marsala for a couple of hours.

"Sure. Do you want me to bring anything?" Maybe I could take the Fluffernutter ingredients and make some kind of appetizer. I didn't have much else in the house except the ingredients for the chicken marsala.

"No. We're good. Linguini in clam sauce in ten minutes," Mike said.

After a quick shower, which I hoped washed away my unease along with the grime from working, I dressed, swiped on some mascara, and found a decent bottle of pinot grigio to take for the dinner. Back in the hall, Mike's guy almost looked like he was drowsing in his chair. Not very good protection for Mike. But he leaped up again when I closed my door.

He knocked twice with his knuckle and Mike opened the door. I handed Mike the bottle of wine.

"Thanks, come on in." Mike stepped back.

Last time Mike had stayed here there had been a poker table in the middle of the living room and games going all the time. At least that's what it seemed like to me. This time no poker table, but his brother Francesco was there. Where Mike was thin and runner-like, Francesco was bulked up from lifting weights. They had the same thick, dark hair and blue eyes, but Francesco had a mustache that would make Tom Selleck envious.

We exchanged greetings while Mike disappeared into the kitchen. "There's cheese and grapes to get started on," he called over his shoulder.

They had moved in a bit of furniture. A big TV, comfy couch, a recliner, and a rickety coffee table of dubious pedigree. A beautiful tray of cheese, crackers, and grapes sat on the coffee table. There were small white plates, cheese spreaders, and cocktail napkins on the table too. Francesco and I sat on opposite ends of the couch and dug in. I was starving. Ice cream for lunch just didn't stick with me no matter the big serving.

"This is delicious," I said after downing several crackers with a creamy white cheese on them. Garlic scented the air and I hoped my stomach wouldn't rumble in response. Francesco and I made small talk until Mike came back out.

"We're going to serve ourselves in the kitchen and then eat out here," Mike said. "I'm sorry that we don't have a nicer setup, Sarah."

"I'd be eating a Fluffernutter if you hadn't invited me, so this is way better." I often made a Fluffernutter and ate it on my couch while I read or watched TV.

We fixed our plates. Big bowls of pasta with lots of clams and toasted to perfection garlic bread. There was also a beautiful salad with exceedingly fresh tomatoes for winter in Massachusetts. We carried our plates back to the living room. Mike put on some opera music. Even having lived near Stella for a couple of years, I didn't always know one opera from the other. But the soaring music had melancholy tones. It seemed to suit Mike's mood.

Francesco poured us all a glass of wine. We ate in an awkward silence. Occasionally murmuring things like "This is delicious" or "Pass me the pepper." When we finished, we all carried our plates to the kitchen.

"I'll wash the dishes to thank you for the dinner," I said.

"I'll dry," Mike said.

After rinsing out a couple of pots Mike had used to cook, I filled the sink with soapy water and started washing the utensils. It's how we did it at my house growing up. Utensils, plates, glasses, pots. I'm not sure why in that order, but it was still a habit all these years later.

"Where's the poker table and your playing buddies?" I asked as I handed him a fork.

"I'm keeping a lower profile than last time." Mike dried the fork with a vengeance and put it away in a drawer.

That time, I'd seen Seth over here and had been worried about their relationship. Last summer I had found out that Mike fed Seth information sometimes. It was a dangerous business for both of them.

"Do you think someone found out about your dealings with Seth?" I asked, handing him a plate.

Mike looked down at me. His blue eyes were normally unreadable. But this time I was sure I saw a trace of fear in his expression. "I hope not." His voice was quiet. "It could be many things." He shrugged, tried for and missed a grin. "Maybe it's just a rival cheese shop owner trying to run me out of town." He dried the plate. "Are you going to wash anything else or just stand there?"

I went back to washing. The unease I hoped to shake off from earlier came back, bringing with it additional worries. If Mike was somehow compromised, Seth could be in danger too.

"What about Seth?" I asked.

"He knows what happened and that I'm here."

I already knew that, since I'd been the one to tell Seth that Mike had moved in. They must have talked since though.

Mike leaned against the counter. "I don't want to worry you, but I think you deserve to know what's going on."

That was a change. I wondered why he was telling

me all this, but now understood. "What will you do if someone does find out?"

"Worst case scenario for me is the truth comes out that I'm an informant and I have to disappear."

"And Seth?"

"He'll be the hero of the law enforcement world."

I hoped that was true. "Do you think it's someone you trust?"

Mike went back to drying. "We're checking everyone out. Anything's possible."

I would hate to be the one who betrayed Mike "the Big Cheese" Titone. "Since we're laying everything out there, I should tell you about Fake Troy." I briefed him on what had been going on as we finished up the dishes.

"You have any pictures of the guy?" Mike asked.

"I wish."

"Can you get your hands on the camera you found?"

I scrubbed the last pot. "Not a chance. Why?"

"I might know someone who could have helped out with that. You find anything else, you bring it to me, not the police."

I finished washing the pot without answering.

When I got home I called Frank Bristow. "I apologize for bothering you on a Sunday night."

"It's okay. I'm always working these days. What do you need?"

"I wanted to pass along some information. And I didn't want to put it in an email."

"Best not to," Frank said.

I explained to him that Becky had called me. I

managed to leave out the part about her asking me to help out. But I mentioned Alicia's sister and that Becky's husband had asked for a divorce. If he'd known either of these things before right now, I'd never know. His responses were neutral, either "oh" or "thanks." I also filled him in on the incident at the board meeting where Alicia had spoken so rudely to the general's wife, Ginger.

"I hadn't heard that," he said. "Thanks for letting me know."

"You're welcome. It might give Ginger or her husband a motive."

"It's possible. But given their positions, they've heard worse."

I couldn't disagree with that. "Something else has been bugging me. Walter Arbas had a lot of free weights in his house. Can a smart bed tell the difference between a real person and weights? Maybe Walter put weights in the bed just long enough to go out and kill Alicia." I hoped it wasn't true. I liked Walter.

"We looked into that. But the bed didn't show him getting up at all. And changing out the weights would have indicated someone got up. Even briefly."

"He didn't say anything about going to the bathroom."

"No. He slept through the night. The bed proved that to be true."

I was glad to hear that. "You never did tell me if Alicia was poisoned or not. Our talk about that was interrupted Friday night."

"It was interrupted and I didn't tell you. Did you ever find out who the woman was who said that?"

"No. Do you want me to?"

"If you can," Frank said.

"Is it because it's true Alicia was poisoned?" I asked.

"I have another call. Let me know if you find her."

The phone went dead, which wasn't a big surprise. I wasn't sure how to go about finding her, but I'd put that aside for the moment. I grabbed my laptop and settled onto the couch to do some research. It was easy to find Alicia's obituary. Her sister, Fiona, was listed as a survivor in the obituary. I typed her name into a search engine, but I didn't find much. She was a vet tech for a veterinary clinic in Salem, New Hampshire. But none of this told me any more about her temperament than what I'd witnessed earlier today at Walter's house.

I continued searching. On page three I found a piece in a local paper saying the police had been called to her house for a domestic incident. Fiona had held her boyfriend at knifepoint. My eyebrows popped up. Wow, she must have some temper. I kept searching for more details but there wasn't anything. Maybe charges hadn't been filed. But as I continued to search Fiona, I found more and more incidents: shoplifting, resisting arrest, speeding. I called Frank back, got his voicemail, and left a message about this. He might already know it, but maybe not.

A few minutes later I got a text from Frank. He said that this didn't fall into the listen-only instructions he'd given me. That was it. Not even a thanks.

Chapter Twenty-Seven

I stood and stretched. Time for my second attempt at making chicken marsala. I knew last time I'd used too much flour, so this time I'd be more sparing. I did all the prep work followed by lightly flouring the thin pieces of chicken and sautéing them. Once they were browned on both sides I stuck them in the oven on low heat to keep them warm while I worked on the sauce. Soon I had it simmering and didn't see any lumps. I added the chicken back to the sauce to simmer. I set an alarm on my phone so I wouldn't overcook it.

I poured a glass of pinot noir, a nice red wine for a chilly winter night. I took it into the living room, sat on my couch, grabbed my computer, and looked up who was in the PTA at the base elementary school along with Alicia. Ginger was on the list. The very one who Alicia had told to be quiet. Maybe they had issues going on between them from the PTA, which had spilled over to the meeting.

I called Carol. I'd asked her when I saw her this morning if she knew anything about the PTA, but at that point I hadn't made the connection that Ginger was on the PTA with Alicia.

"What's up?" Carol said when she answered the phone.

"Me."

"Ha. Very funny."

"Do you know Ginger? Her husband is the new general and she's on the PTA board with Alicia." I told Carol what I'd heard that Alicia had said to her.

"Oh, ouch. That's an awful thing to say," Carol said. "I've met her. She seems nice enough, but I've never been around her when Alicia was around."

"Ginger must either be a lot younger than her husband or they had their kids later in life." Most generals would be of an age that they would have older kids.

"I think it's a combination of both," Carol said. I called a few friends after we talked this morning."

"And?"

"The past few weeks Alicia had been late or a no-show for a lot of events. One friend said she hadn't been her usual cheery self."

"Hmmmm. Did anyone know why?"

"No."

"Nothing?" That seemed odd.

"No. I think maybe because Alicia died so suddenly, no one wants to say anything bad."

"That's understandable." But it made me wonder what was going on. Marital problems? Or maybe she'd just bitten off more than she should have and was exhausted. I'd seen more than one wife trying to do it all and stressing out.

"Even more surprising it's respectful." Carol sighed.

"What do you know about Harriet? Your neighbor's aunt." I asked.

"Why? Didn't she work out?"

"She's fine." At least I hoped she was. "Seems very organized. I just wondered what her background is."

"I don't have any idea. I just know that she was driving my neighbor a little crazy on occasion and that she seemed nice enough."

"Not nice? But nice enough?" I asked.

Carol paused. "I just caught a hint of 'I could beat that crap out of you' behind her smile."

"Yeah. I got that too."

"If you don't want her help just tell her."

"And get the crap beaten out of me? No thanks."

Carol laughed and I did too.

"She's works hard," I said. "I just was curious."

"You of all people should be able to get something out of her."

"Maybe I will."

"So how is Massachusetts's Most Eligible Bachelor?"

"Dreamy," I said. "I feel sixteen again when he's around."

"I'm happy for you."

"Thanks. We're taking things slow."

"Are you in love with him?"

Now there was a loaded question.

"Hey, are you still there?" Carol asked after a few moments.

"I am. I was thinking."

"You don't know if you're in love or not?"

I didn't even want to talk to Carol about my difficulties telling Seth I loved him. "I love being with him. I love how he treats me. I love how smart he is."

"And how sexy."

I laughed. "That too."

"So it sounds like you are in love to me."

I smelled something. Something burning. "Ack. I've got to go."

"We're talking more about this later."

"Okay." I clicked off and ran to the kitchen. I took the lid off the chicken marsala and stared into the pan. The sauce had cooked into a hard brown residue. I grabbed a fork and poked at the chicken. It stuck like Velcro to the sauce. "I set my alarm. How could this happen?" I opened my phone and clicked on the alarm app. I'd set it all right, but for A.M., not P.M.

Aargh. I scraped what I could into the garbage. Then I filled the sink with hot soapy water and stuck the pan in. "And now for another episode of Can This Pan Be Saved." How many pans had I ruined over the years? People thought I ate out too much, but it seemed cheaper than constantly replacing cookware and groceries. I sighed as I opened the kitchen window a crack. Icy air rushed in, but at least the room would smell better. I found a cinnamon candle, lit it, and stuck it on the kitchen table.

After I cleaned up, I decided to try to do an online search for my mystery woman from the thrift shop, the one who'd heard that Alicia was poisoned. Frank wanted me to find her, and while this again was outside the realm of listening, it was just online research. No harm, no foul. Right?

I went through old online issues of the base newspaper. There weren't a lot of pictures, and most of them were of someone who'd won an award for outstanding enlisted troop or officer of the quarter. But maybe she'd done something that would make her stand out. I searched the last twelve months. If she arrived before that, I would have run into her. Even though CJ and I had been divorced for two years now, the first year I had still spent a lot of time on base. But as more and more of my friends moved away, I hadn't replaced them with new base friends, as one would if they lived on base.

Next I went on Facebook to do some research. First I searched Eleanor's friends. This seemed a little creepier than looking at the old newspapers. But Eleanor volunteered at the thrift shop and so did the woman I was looking for, so it made sense to try. By the time I'd gone through all of Eleanor's friends my eyes were beginning to water from staring at the screen. Everyone began to look alike too. Even worse, I realized that a dressed-up photo for a profile picture was going to be a far cry from how someone looked when they went to volunteer at the thrift shop.

I stood, stretched, and went to look out my front window. The moon shone on the hard crust of snow. Two people skated on the rink. They must be freezing, but they glided as one, almost like they were dancing. Ah, to be that coordinated. A white van idled on the curb across the street. It made me think back to my conversation with Jeannette. My teasing her that the camera was sending a signal to a van. A little shiver went through me, but I couldn't worry about every vehicle that was outside. I yanked the curtains shut and then roamed around my apartment looking for cameras. Fortunately, I didn't find anything.

I forced myself to go back and look through more military friends' lists of friends. I was beginning to wonder if I even accurately remembered the woman

I was searching for. If only she'd had tattoos or piercings that were memorable. Shoulder-length light brown hair and average height described a lot of people. Thirty minutes later I gave up. While an online search was a good idea, it was time consuming and yielded nothing. There had to be some other way. Had I even asked Eleanor about her? Maybe she would recognize her from my description. I sat up a little straighter. Maybe the security cameras at the thrift shop would have a photo of her. That would be the easiest way to track her down. I gave Eleanor a quick call. She couldn't think who the woman was off-hand, but agreed to meet me in the morning.

My phone rang again almost as soon as I hung up with Eleanor. "Hello?" I said.

"This is Ginger. I'm sorry to call after nine, but I was wondering if you could meet me in the morning."

I couldn't say no. I was too curious to find out what she had to say. "Sure. What time?" We agreed to meet at eight tomorrow morning at the Dunkin's in Bedford. We could have met at the one on base, but I had a feeling Ginger wanted to avoid prying eyes as much as I did. Tomorrow was going to be interesting. I was on a roll and I promised myself that I would help Becky, find Fake Troy, and identify the mystery woman from the thrift shop.

Chapter Twenty-Eight

I met Eleanor at the thrift shop parking lot on Monday morning at six thirty. Not my favorite time of day, and especially in the winter when it was still dark out. But Eleanor worked part-time as a school nurse and had to get to work.

"Here's the keys," Eleanor said. "And I sent you an email with the instructions for looking at the security cameras. Good luck with finding the woman you were talking about."

"What about the alarm system?" I asked.

Eleanor gave me the code.

"Do you remember who stuck around the day Alicia and Becky fought after the Spouses' Club meeting?"

Eleanor thought for a moment. "Ginger, Judy, Nasha, Cindy. I know there were more than that, but I can't remember everyone."

"Why do those people stand out?"

"Ginger and Judy chased after Becky when she stalked out. Cindy, Nasha, and a couple of others followed Alicia out to the parking lot. When I went out to my car Zoey and Alicia were having an intense discussion."

"Zoey Whittlesbee?" That was interesting. Becky

had recommended Zoey to me so they obviously knew each other. I wondered whose side Zoey was on.

"Yes," Eleanor said.

"Do you know what it was about?"

"I couldn't hear anything from where I was. But Zoey flounced off, slammed her car door, and took off with a squeal of tires."

So it sounded like Zoey was on Becky's side then. "Do you think there was anything funny going on with the money? The report that Ginger was trying to question?"

"No. It all got straightened out at the board meeting. Some numbers had just been reversed." Eleanor glanced down at her watch. "I've got to run."

We waved goodbye and I went into the thrift shop. I disarmed the security system and flipped on the light as I made my way to the office. I sat down in front of one of the two computers in the office and powered it up. I checked for Eleanor's email on my phone. Soon enough I had the security camera system up and running backwards. It would take a while for it to scroll back four days. I should have stopped for coffee on the way here.

The office had one of those single-cup coffee-makers, but I'd hold out for Dunkin's since I was meeting Ginger. The good thing about this system was it was motion activated so it skipped back faster than I'd hoped. Fifteen minutes later I got to the day I'd seen the woman. Then I realized this wasn't going to be much help. The cameras were pointing down at an angle that just captured the tops of everyone's heads. I'd have to tell Eleanor that the cameras needed to be repositioned. If anyone did steal things, we wouldn't have a face to help us identify them.

I spotted my head and watched as it moved toward the three women. I took a screenshot and sent it to my phone. Not that it was very helpful. One head of dark roots, one head of gray roots, and the woman I wanted to track down with her brown, neatly parted hair. If only she'd worn a headband or hat that someone might recognize. I turned off the computer and drummed my fingers on the old metal desk.

I stood up and yawned. As I headed out the door I saw a piece of computer paper with the heading "List of Volunteers." I scanned down the names. There were a bunch of names I didn't recognize so I snapped a couple of photos of the list. Maybe a process of elimination comparing names to social media accounts might work to help me find out who the woman was. It was worth a try, but I'd have to work on it later today.

I parked my Suburban in the parking lot between the Shopette, a combination convenience and liquor store, and the base gym. Becky's husband had always been athletic. And I hoped he was one of those guys who worked out every morning and then headed to the office. I wanted to bump into him someplace, and this seemed as good a place as any. At seven thirty he walked out of the front entrance. I leaped out of my car and headed up the walk toward him, acting surprised when I saw him.

"Colonel Cane, how are you?" I asked. I'd always called him colonel. He'd been above CJ when we'd met fifteen years ago. He hadn't ever once asked me to call him by his first name.

A little frown passed his face. One I interpreted to say *I'm a busy man. Don't bother me.*

"Sarah. Long time." He paused and glanced down at his shoes. "Thanks for tracking me down the other day. For keeping things quiet."

Now that he'd mentioned it, things had been quiet. Why wasn't anyone talking about Becky being questioned? How did that get squelched? But Frank was the definition of discreet, so he must have kept picking up Becky low key.

"You're welcome. Your secretary isn't easy to get by. I thought I was going to have to make up some story like I was your girlfriend." I said it in a jokey way, even though it was so inappropriate. I threw it out there, hoping to see what kind of reaction I'd get to the idea of a girlfriend.

He looked irritated. "The only girl for me is Becky." He nodded. "I have to get going."

I watched him walk off and then walked back to my Suburban on the matted-down, dirty snow. He didn't seem to react to the girlfriend comment, at least not like someone who was hiding one. But did I know him well enough to spot a lie? Probably not. I had to respect him for keeping up appearances with Becky while they tried to work out their marital problems. Church yesterday and his comment now. Even though I didn't like him much, I respected that.

I hustled into the Dunkin's a few minutes after eight, waited in line, got my coffee, and found Ginger tucked into a booth. She was a neat-looking woman in a Burberry scarf and expensive-looking wool camel-colored jacket. I recognized her from a picture I'd seen in the base paper. She looked like she was in her early forties. Ginger stood when I approached and shook my hand with her dainty, well-manicured, and very icy one.

"It's nice to meet you at last," Ginger said. She gestured for me to sit. "I've heard so much about you and am sorry you didn't live on base by the time my husband and I arrived."

She was one of those people who made you feel comfortable right away. I didn't know whether she was born with it or it was bred into her during her years as an officer's wife.

"You too." I sat across from her and waited to hear what she had to say.

She plucked at a napkin for a moment before looking back up at me. "I know about the situation with Becky."

I wondered which one—Becky being questioned, Becky asking me for help, or Becky's marital situation. I nodded, hoping I'd be able to figure it out without giving anything away.

"Fortunately, we've managed to keep Becky being questioned quiet." She smiled. "You know how difficult that can be on base."

"It is." When CJ had been escorted off base two years ago, my phone had started ringing seconds later. The thought still made me a little sick. I wondered how they managed to keep it quiet, because Special Agent Bristow showing up at someone's door, not to mention hauling them out, would usually cause talk. Lots of it.

"We spread the word around that Becky was helping Special Agent Bristow. It seemed to quell the usual gossip." Ginger took a dainty sip of her coffee. "And Becky told me she asked you for help. That you were good at getting to the truth. That's why I asked to meet with you. To see how I could help Becky."

"Tell me what happened at the Spouses' Club meeting where Alicia spoke so rudely to you." I'd heard Eleanor's version. I wanted to see if Ginger's was the same, to see if Ginger was angry enough to have whacked Alicia on the head. But minutes later when Ginger finished talking, it didn't seem like it bothered her all that much. And her story matched Eleanor's. Of course, the incident was a couple of weeks ago now, so any anger could have easily dissipated by now.

"How'd your husband feel?" I asked.

"I didn't even bother to tell him until after Alicia was killed. His plate is overflowing right now. Per usual."

If that was true, I could cross him off my list of possible suspects.

"Do you know Captain Flowers?" I asked. She's the one married to the Channing Tatum lookalike. The one who Becky said had a terrible temper and who might have been jealous of Alicia.

"Only through her reputation as a hothead. I've met her very charming husband at some of our Spouses' Club events."

"Did he seem interested or pay particular attention to Alicia?" I asked.

"Not that I noticed. He was a bit of a flirt with everyone. All in a good-fun kind of way."

Hmmm, that could stir up trouble. "Can you think of anything else that would help Becky?"

Ginger shook her head. "I've thought this through

over and over. Losing Alicia was terrible for all of us. Losing Becky would be too." She stood. "Figure this out. Please."

I decided to grab another coffee and donut to take with me to the Bevinses' house. As I headed toward the door I ran into the woman who had the gender reveal party.

"Hey, how are you?" I asked.

"Craving sugar. And steak. It's so weird."

I smiled. "I had fun at your party."

"Oh, good."

"Becky told me she was sorry she couldn't make it."

She put a hand on her hip. "That's funny because I didn't invite her."

"Oh, I must have misunderstood." I know I hadn't. Had Becky been trying to save face? It always hurt to be left out of things. "I've been hearing a lot about Ed Flowers, but I don't think I've ever met him."

"He's a doll. We live on the same courtyard as he and his wife."

"I heard she's a hothead."

"Where did you hear that? She's a doll too. She was at my party the other night. Short red hair. Talkative."

"Oh, yes. I remember her." I said my goodbyes and walked out to my car. I had a feeling someone was lying to me, but I couldn't figure out who it was.

Chapter Twenty-Nine

I sat in the driveway of Jeannette's parents' house munching a glazed donut and sipping my coffee while I waited for Zoey to arrive. I thought over all I heard at the Dunkin's. It troubled me. I also wanted to find a way to subtly ask Zoey about the fight between Alicia and Becky. And then what she and Alicia had talked about afterward.

A car door slammed. I jerked around toward the sound. A large man strode toward my Suburban. I made sure the doors were locked and restarted my car. He bent down and frowned at me through the passenger-side window.

"What are you doing parked here?" he demanded. His lips hugged together, creating deep, angry wrinkles around his mouth. He was large, with bushy hair that blew in the wind.

I realized this had to be the real Troy, Jeannette's brother because he looked like a male version of her. He must have decided to come up here after hearing about the camera hidden in the house. I rolled the passenger window down a crack. "I'm Sarah. Jeannette hired me to do the sale."

He relaxed at that. "Ah. I'm on edge with all that's been going on."

That I could relate to. Two more car doors slammed. Jeannette and Zoey got out of their respective cars. I turned off the engine and climbed out to join everyone.

"Troy, what on earth are you doing here?" Jeannette asked. She gave him a big hug. It was amazing how much alike they looked. Almost like twins.

"I was worried after we talked last night, and caught an early flight up here," Troy said. "Aren't you supposed to be at school?"

"I have a planning period this morning." Jeannette glanced at her watch. "But I have to go soon."

In the house, after quick introductions, I pulled Zoey into the kitchen.

"We need to let them have some privacy," I said. "We can work while they talk." Zoey and I worked in silence. I confess I was trying to hear what Jeannette and her brother were talking about, but could only hear the murmur of their voices. I found a stack of vintage dish towels with the days of the week hand-embroidered on them in bright primary colors.

"Look how cute these are, Zoey," I said.

"My grandmother had some that were similar. I wonder what happened to them." She paused. "I'll bet my evil cousin took them."

She smiled to soften her words, but I had a feeling she wasn't joking from the tone of her voice. "Dividing things up can be very difficult," I said.

The front door slammed. Zoey and I exchanged a glance with our eyebrows popped up. Jeannette came into the kitchen and thumped down on a chair at the table. She leaned heavily on the table.

"My brother can be impossible," Jeannette said.

"So can mine," I said.

"I always wanted one," Zoey said. "An older one with hot friends. Instead I got a younger sister with annoying friends."

We all laughed. I wasn't quite sure what to say. Jeannette was my employer, but we'd gone through so much she felt more like a friend.

"Anything I can do?" I asked.

"He's lost it over all that's happened up here. He wanted me to cancel the sale and just donate everything." She shook her head. "Just because he's loaded doesn't mean I am. He wanted me to fire you, Sarah. And find someone new. Like you were the cause of all this." Jeannette shook her head. "He's lost his everlovin' mind."

I thought of all the work I'd done, the loss of income if she fired me. Ugh, and word would get around. People might not think I'm responsible. But I also didn't want to be the cause of a rift between Jeannette and her brother. "Jeannette, I don't want to create problems for you. If it's better, you can pay me for the work I've done and we'll call it good."

"That's lovely of you, Sarah. But I'm happy with your work and all you've already accomplished. How many people would even come back after all you've been through?" Jeannette sighed. "He knows I'm right or he wouldn't have run off like a petulant child."

Jeannette left. Zoey and I worked until two with just a quick break for lunch. By then we'd finished the kitchen and moved to the dining room. It had a suite of matching mahogany furniture including a tea cart, china cabinet, sideboard, and a table with eight matching chairs. There was more china in all the side pieces. Pewter pieces, which weren't very popular right now, sat on all the side pieces. I still loved pewter and was excited to look through all of it. There was a combination of all three types of pewter in the room: polished, satin, and oxidized. The good thing about pewter is it doesn't tarnish like silver does. The satin was my favorite, unless it was a real antique oxidized piece.

"Should we polish the pewter? Some of it looks dirty," Zoey said. "I saw some silver polish under the sink in the kitchen."

"You can't use silver polish on pewter. The best way to clean the polished and satin kind is to use warm water and a gentle dishwashing liquid with a soft cloth. Some people make a paste out of vinegar, flour, and salt."

"Really? I've never heard of that."

"It works well. You rub it on with the grain, let it sit for twenty minutes, rinse it off, and dry it. You can't polish the oxidized pewter." I grabbed a pitcher as an example. It was darker than the other two and looked older, not that it was. "Polishing might take off the dark layer and that hurts its value."

"Oh, wow. I thought the darker stuff was just dirty. Should we clean it or just leave it?" Zoey asked.

"Let's go ahead and dust it. If that isn't enough we'll see if Jeannette wants us to do more." We worked for a few minutes while I tried to figure out a way to bring up the argument at the Spouses' Club. "I'm so grateful that Becky recommended you for this job." There that worked.

Zoey smiled. "Me too."

"I've known Becky a long time and she doesn't praise people lightly." Not that she had praised Zoey.

Zoey's cheeks turned pink. "She's been such a wonderful mentor to me."

"I heard about the argument between her and Alicia. I was shocked to hear how Alicia spoke to Ginger." Zoey didn't need to know I barely knew either of them.

"I gave Alicia a piece of my mind after that meeting. Who did she think she was talking to a general's wife like that. And then a colonel's wife."

"I wouldn't have at Alicia's age."

"Exactly. And I'm the kind of friend who stands up for her friends when someone attacks them."

"Becky's lucky to have you on her side." I waited for a response and was disappointed Zoey didn't add anything else, but I couldn't see any way to continue the conversation. I picked up the next piece of pewter and searched online for a price. An hour later I rolled my neck around to try to relax it.

"Do you ever do pre-sales?" Zoey asked.

I was starting to wonder why Zoey asked so many questions. I hoped it was just an innate curiosity. "You mean like a friends and family party the night before the sale?"

Zoey nodded.

"I've done them if a client wants me to. But friends and families usually expect rock-bottom prices, which isn't good for the client."

"Or you," Zoey said.

"That's true. But the client is always right. I give them my opinion and let them decide how they want to handle things. It's better to have an after sale. Let your friends and family come at the end and haul off what they want. That makes less work for the client and me."

By four we'd finished the dining room. "Thanks for all of your hard work, Zoey."

"Sales are a lot of work," Zoey said as she stretched her arms above her head.

"They are. I always need a nap when I'm done with one." After Zoey took off, I did a quick trip around the house to make sure everything was locked. Then I set the alarm and headed out too.

Chapter Thirty

On my way home I swung by Ellington High School where Eleanor was the school nurse. I signed in at the front office even though school was out for the day. Eleanor's office was just down the hall and to the left. There were still lots of students around. Some were basketball players, some cheerleaders, and a group of kids were painting a mural on a wall. I could hear an orchestra playing somewhere.

Eleanor sat at a desk, frowning at some paperwork.

"Knock, knock," I said.

She smiled when she saw it was me. "Come on in."

"I'm dropping off the thrift shop keys. I wasn't sure you'd still be here."

"Some days I stay until the late bus leaves. Did you find who you were looking for?" Eleanor asked.

"No. And you need to adjust the cameras. They are only taking shots of the tops of heads. No faces to be seen."

Eleanor frowned at that. "That's not good. I know they weren't that way a few weeks ago because we had a shoplifter and caught them on camera. Face and all."

"Let me show you what I found." I went to the

photos on my phone, found the photo I'd taken of
the security camera, and held it out for Eleanor to
see. She studied the tops of the heads.

"Not helpful at all, is it?" she said.

"Not really, but it was worth a try. I was hoping that
neat part might look familiar, but I knew it was a long
shot." Plenty of people had neat parts.

"No worries. I'm glad you realized the cameras
were out of whack." Eleanor thunked her hand to her
forehead. "One of the volunteers at the thrift shop
mentioned the layer of dust on the security cameras.
She must have moved them when she was cleaning
them."

A teenage boy burst in. "Josh passed out in the
gym."

Eleanor jumped up. "Gotta run."

I drove through Dunkin's on the way home and
got a coffee. I decided to stop at a new thrift shop in
Ellington that wasn't far from base. It had opened up
a few months ago and raised money to fund historical
sites in the area. After all that had been going on, I
needed a diversion. It only took fifteen minutes to get
there, which wasn't bad considering Great Road could
turn into a parking lot between four and seven. It was
a cut-through from the 95 to the 495.

The store wasn't anything to write home about, but
those were usually my favorite kind. I didn't recognize the woman behind the counter. No one else was
in the store, which wasn't too surprising since they
closed in thirty minutes. I bypassed the clothes, because I didn't need any right now. I headed to their
furniture section, one of my favorites. There wasn't

anything in particular I needed other than a respite from all the recent craziness.

This section of the store was a jumble. It looked like people had just stacked things on top of each other. I did a quick scan to see if there was anything worth wading in for. It didn't take long for me to spot a set of outdoor furniture back behind a stack of end tables. I hoped they looked as good close up as they did from here. I moved a couple of the end tables and squeezed through a small space.

The furniture was fake wicker, some kind of plastic-coated wire, but looked darn good. No pieces were broken, which would have been impossible to repair. There were two chairs, a love seat, and a table. I shook each piece and it all seemed sturdy. This would be perfect for Stella's porch. She was a great friend and my rent was lower than normal for the area. It would make an excellent thank-you gift for all she'd done for me and maybe it would cheer her up. I found a price tag that said the set was sixty dollars. Amazing.

Voices drifted toward me from the front.

"I'll give you ninety-five," a woman said. Her back was to me. I saw hair swept up in an elegant chignon, a wool, winter white suit, and a peek of red shoe soul that meant the woman was wearing Christian Louboutin shoes. They started around seven hundred dollars and went up from there.

"It's a Tiffany bracelet," the saleswoman said.

"A several years old, used Tiffany bracelet," the woman in white said.

Her voice was familiar, but . . .

"Two fifty is the best I can do." The saleswoman sounded nervous. "It was originally five hundred."

"Look right there. It's missing a tiny little piece

that looks like a lock and has Tiffany engraved on it. Ninety-five is generous. Maybe eighty would be better."

"It's platinum," the saleswoman said. She looked toward the back of the store like she was hoping help would show up. I took a step forward.

"It's not. It's sterling silver. See right there? That's the mark for sterling. Really seventy would be more what it's worth in this condition. You don't even have the original box."

"Okay. Seventy it is."

I was astounded. Who was the bargaining wonder woman in white with the familiar voice? I headed to the front of the store as the saleswoman rang up the bracelet.

The customer turned toward me. Bright red lips stood out on an impeccably made up, classic-looking face.

"*Harriet?*" I asked, astounded. Or did Harriet have a twin who was a motorcycle mama?

"Sarah. Nice to see you." She took the bag from the lady. "Thank you." She winked at me and left.

Who the heck was Harriet?

The saleswoman looked at me. "I can't believe she wrangled me down like that. I figured I should quit while I was ahead or I'd be paying her for the bracelet." She shook her head. "I've done this for a lot of years. That was impressive."

I chuckled. "It was." Maybe Harriet would work Jeannette's sale with me.

"Can I help you with something? I'd better warn you I'm usually made of tougher stuff than that." She stood up straighter as if to prove her point.

Great. Harriet ruined my chances of getting a great deal. I led the employee to the back and showed her the outdoor furniture set I had been looking at.

"If you're interested in that set there are cushions for the chairs and settee, right behind you."

I turned. The cushions were covered with a vintage barkcloth, dark burgundy with white tropical flowers and bright green leaves. I tried to hide my delight, but I think I failed miserably. I didn't want to give up my ace bargainer card, so I had to ask for less. I quickly calculated ten percent off. "Would you take fifty-four for the set?"

"I would, but furniture is half off today so it's only thirty. If you want to pay more than that you're welcome to." She grinned at me. "It will make up for the money I just lost on that bracelet."

"Half off? I need to do some more looking."

"As you can see, the room is full to its gills with furniture. We need to move some of this out of here before the fire department decides to swing by and declare us a fire hazard."

"I have a virtual yard sale site. You are welcome to post your sales there." I took a business card out of my purse and wrote my phone number on the back of the card. "You can call me if you have any questions."

The woman took the card. "Thanks, we obviously aren't marketing geniuses." She gestured again to the furniture.

I could see why most of the furniture was here. A lot of it was made out of poor quality particleboard. But in the right hands, with some paint, it could be refurbished and made serviceable again. I carried the pieces I wanted out of the fray, which cleared a little space. Fifteen minutes later I was up at the register. I had found a beautiful mirror with a white frame. It was a three-foot rectangle with some simple carving on it that was meant to be hung horizontally. I also found a sweet mission-style end table. Its simple lines and sturdy oak were impossible for me to resist. I wasn't sure if I'd keep it all for me or stick it in my attic space for when I threw my own garage sale.

"You don't happen to have any cobalt glass, do you?" I asked. "I'm looking for a vase."

The woman's face reddened. "I'm not even sure what that is."

I explained to her what it was and showed her the picture that Pellner had sent me of his wife's collection.

"I think I might have some," she said. "Follow me."

We weaved through the store to plastic shelves cluttered with all kinds of dishes. I found a few pieces of the pattern called Royal Lace by the Hazel Atlas Company. They were from the thirties and forties. In the very back of a shelf I found a beautiful foot-tall vase. Its clean lines looked Art Deco and Pellner's wife didn't have anything like it. Plus he could fill it with his wife's favorite flowers before he gave it to her. Perfect.

"I'll take this one," I said. It was a steal at ten dollars. "You should put the rest of this somewhere that it's easier to see. It's harder to find than it was twenty years ago." Maybe that's why it didn't seem as popular right now. It was scarce because it was already privately owned. While she rang up my purchases, I went to my virtual garage sale site and took down my ISO post that I was looking for cobalt glass. A few people had responded, but either the price was too high or I didn't like the piece they had.

A few minutes later I had paid, filled the back of my Suburban with furniture, put the cobalt glass on the passenger seat, and felt ready to track down my mystery female. But since I was over by the base, I was going to do one other thing first.

I parked by a dirty snowbank on the far side of the headquarters building where Colonel Cane worked. A place where I could see the door but my giant Suburban didn't stand out too much from all the other SUVs and minivans. I couldn't go in, not that I wanted to, because there were guards at the door and passes that had to be swiped. This wasn't a building for the likes of me. But I knew he was still there because his blue car was in a special reserved spot with the license plate CANE 2. I told myself I wouldn't wait more than a half hour. This was probably a fool's errand anyway. However, he came out fifteen minutes later.

I followed him at a discreet distance as he left base. He took a left on Great Road toward Ellington. We meandered along in the stop-and-go traffic. People bustled in and out of restaurants and dry cleaners doing end of the day tasks. Colonel Cane drove by the town common and took a right into a shopping area across from the CVS Pharmacy. He parked and went into an Asian restaurant. The smell of spicy and fried foods wafted through the air. I backed into a parking spot as far from him as possible, but where I could still see the door.

Lots of people went in. I wondered who was meeting Colonel Cane. Sitting here wasn't going to give me any information, so I called in a takeout order. I knew from having eaten here before that I'd have a good view of the restaurant when I picked up my food. Ten minutes later I strolled in, keeping my head down as much as possible.

After giving the hostess my name, I glanced out from under my eyelashes and scanned the room. Colonel Cane was at a table with four men. Fortunately, he was seated with his back to me, so I could straighten up a bit. Two of the men also wore military uniforms. The fourth man was one of the town selectmen. In other words, nothing to see here.

I took my food back to the car, two appetizers—spring rolls and beef on a stick. Foods that were easy to eat while I waited. I called Pellner after I ate.

"Did you have any luck with the camera we found at Jeannette's house?" I asked.

"Nothing yet. Like I said the other day, we probably won't find anything out."

I sighed. "I found a gorgeous cobalt vase for you and a vintage Valentine."

"Thanks, Sarah. I have to run."

Thirty minutes later the men came out, shook hands, and went their separate ways. Colonel Cane looked at his phone and seemed to be texting someone. When the other men had gotten in their cars and driven off, Colonel Cane went into the florist shop that was two doors down from the restaurant and uncomfortably close to me.

Five minutes later he came out of the store with a bouquet of red roses. Maybe following him hadn't been a waste of time after all. I watched him walk to his car and toss the bouquet onto the passenger seat. Who were those flowers for, Colonel Cane? He took off and I managed to get out on Great Road a few cars behind him. I was on pins and needles wondering where he was going. But it didn't take long to figure it out. Base.

It didn't seem like he'd have an affair with someone on base. There were too many eyes watching. Kids always complained if they got caught doing anything wrong, their parents would know about it before the kid got home. I continued to follow though, just in case. But soon enough he pulled into his driveway, opened the garage, drove in, and disappeared from sight as his garage door closed. As I drove home, thoughts plucked at me. Something's off. Something's wrong. But maybe he was just trying to make things work with Becky. Or was he trying just a bit too hard to make it seem that way?

Chapter Thirty-One

When I got home, I arranged the furniture on the covered porch. It would have some protection from the elements and since it wasn't actual wicker it should be just fine outside. I hoped Stella liked it. As I finished arranging it, a white van pulled up across the street again. I moved closer to the door. A sprightly white-haired woman came around the side and opened the back. She hauled out a cake, closed the door with her foot, and carried it into the church.

Yeesh, I was becoming way too paranoid. Listening to my gut was one thing. Being suspicious of everyone was just plain stupid. I hauled the cushions for the porch furniture upstairs and tucked them in the attic. They would go out when it was nice enough to sit on the porch. No sense exposing them to the harsh Massachusetts winter. After that I hauled the other furniture up to my apartment. I was sweating by the time I was done, despite how cold it was outside. Mike must be out somewhere because no one was sitting outside of his apartment. He hadn't gone too far though, because the chair was still set up by his door.

I moved everything off the end table I was using, including a lamp with a cobalt-glass base, a vintage cut-glass coaster, and a small postcard-sized painting that looked like a Monet. I slid the end table from its position on the left side of the couch over near my grandmother's rocking chair by the window. Then I carried the mission-style one and put it by the couch. I stepped back to see if I liked it there or not. It was wider than mine, which might not be best in the small apartment. But I liked how it looked so I found a dust cloth and some polish to clean the piece up. My phone rang as I finished.

"This is Judy Bruce."

"Hi?" I couldn't imagine why Judy would be calling me. She'd always been one of those spouses who lived up to the reputation of the power hungry, snooty wife. Maybe she wanted to do a garage sale though, and I could certainly use the business.

"Quit spreading rumors about Becky's marriage."

That's not what I'd been expecting. "I haven't been," I said. Other than the one conversation with Frank. I couldn't imagine that Frank would run around telling anyone what I'd shared with him. Although if he'd looked into it, talked it over with someone, and someone overheard that conversation, I guess it was possible.

"They returned from their dream cruise about a month before Alicia died. Becky's husband told me that he fell more in love with her each and every day. So just knock it off with your nastiness."

How was that possible? Was he trying to cover up whatever was going on? Maybe something had happened after the cruise. I thought about the bouquet of roses. "But—"

"My husband and I just went out to dinner with

them a couple of nights ago. They are so freaking sappy with each other it's almost embarrassing."

"Who told you I was spreading rumors?" I needed to know who to defend myself against.

"I don't gossip."

Yeah, right, Judy.

"For some reason Becky thinks highly of you and I don't want this to get back to her. But if I hear one more word about this you will regret it. Why are you even hanging around base anyway?"

She didn't wait for my answer, she just hung up. I slumped onto my couch, still staring at my phone. What was that? Would Becky share a confidence with me that she wouldn't with one of her best friends? She said they were trying to work things out. He'd taken her flowers. Becky was a private woman. She must have told me in a moment of extreme stress.

I sprang up, went to the window, and opened the curtains to stare out. The church steeple's sharp shadow loomed across the town common and looked like a dagger slashing through the snow. Maybe Becky was trying to save face while she and her husband hopefully worked things out. But why would he make those comments and then turn around and tell Becky he wanted a divorce?

My conflicting thoughts on what Becky had told me versus what everyone else but Ginger had said, were interrupted when Stella stopped by a few minutes later. She headed straight for my grandmother's rocking chair and sat down. There was just something comforting about sitting in that chair. "There's new furniture on the front porch. Do you know anything about it?"

I sat on the couch. I should find another chair for in here. If it wasn't too big, one could fit on the other side of the window. "Do you like it?" I thought I'd make sure before I admitted to buying it.

"It's great."

"I found it at a thrift shop I went to. All their furniture was half price. Hang on a second, there's more." I crawled into the attic space and dragged out the cushions. "What do you think?"

"They're perfect. Thanks. You didn't need to do that."

"You've been an amazing landlady and friend. You haven't raised my rent since I moved in two years ago. I wanted to do something nice for you."

Stella waved away the compliment. "You found the old sheet music I framed for my apartment. Besides you always take care of Tux for me if I'm gone."

"That's what friends are for." I'd lucked out when I'd moved here.

"I heard you had dinner with Mike and Francesco the other night."

Something in her voice alerted me that I might not want to hear what was going to follow. "I did. It was nice of him, but kind of awkward too."

"How so?"

"I guess we haven't ever just socialized before. There was always some purpose for any interaction." Usually me wanting his help for one reason or another.

"Hmmm," Stella said with a little smirk on her face.

"What? What's that 'hmmm' mean?"

"I think he's interested in you."

"I bug him often enough." I chose to avoid what she was hinting at. Because that seemed crazy to me.

"Romantically," she added. "Remember how happy he was when he saw you the day he moved in?"

I slumped against the couch. Maybe I had realized that the other night on some level, but hadn't wanted to admit it to myself. I'd tried to chalk up the awkwardness to not knowing each other all that well. "But he knows I'm with Seth. He must have seen him here." Mike and Seth's real relationship was a closely guarded secret. I couldn't fill her in or say anything like *Mike knows a lot about Seth and me.*

"Doesn't mean he isn't interested."

Now I was going to feel awkward around Mike. "If he ever brings it up to you, please tell him there's no way." Seth or no Seth. "How's Awesome been?"

"Better, but I can tell there's something on his mind that he doesn't want to talk about."

"Are you okay with that?"

"For now." Stella stood up. "Thanks again for the furniture."

"You're welcome." Awesome better get his act together and quick.

After eating a bowl of canned soup, I poured a glass of wine and went into the living room. I grabbed my computer. Maybe action would make me quit thinking about Mike possibly being romantically interested in me. My search for the mystery woman started by using the list of volunteers I'd found in the thrift shop office. Maybe she was the key to all I had heard, all I was questioning. I took the name of each of the volunteers that I didn't know and typed their names into a search engine. I quickly crossed off the names of several women who were active on social media. Their pictures didn't match my memory. One woman I couldn't find much on. But my guess was the mystery woman was young enough that she would use lots of social media platforms, so I kept going down the list.

I typed in the name Delaney Cooley, and there she was at last. She lived on base, didn't have kids, and loved cats. Her Facebook feed was full of cat videos. Delaney had two of her own and volunteered at an animal shelter here in Ellington. I checked the list from the thrift shop again. It looked like she volunteered on Tuesday and Thursday mornings. I'd swing by the shop tomorrow. Hopefully, at long last, I'd get some answers.

My phone rang right as I climbed into bed. Becky.

"I can't believe you tracked down my husband at the gym."

Becky didn't sound happy, and being on the receiving end of an unhappy Becky wasn't ever fun. "I bumped into him."

"What were you doing there? I know you can't work out on base."

That was true. Since CJ and I divorced, the number of things I could do on base was limited to volunteering at the thrift shop or visiting a friend. I couldn't use any of the facilities like the pool, bowling alley, base exchange, or the commissary. This was awkward.

"I was meeting a friend who had some things she'd bought from me on my virtual garage sale." I didn't like to lie.

"I don't believe you. Stay away from him. Our lives are difficult enough right now without you butting in."

She disconnected. Wow, think how mad she'd be if she knew I'd spent my evening following him around. But she's the one who asked me for help and if she didn't like what I found out, that was her problem. And right now I was positive she wasn't going to like me much at all.

Chapter Thirty-Two

I called Frank at eight o'clock Tuesday morning. He'd just gotten into the office. I'd spent part of the night thinking about the nasty comments of the women at the dining-out and Judy Bruce's when she had called about Becky. I remembered Angelo's remark about nothing was perfect when he was trying a new recipe for his Fra Diavolo sauce. Nothing was. Frank had asked for my help, as had Becky. Eleanor liked having me work at the thrift shop. I wasn't going to let a few nasty women stop me.

"I found the mystery woman last night. I was on Facebook and saw her picture on another friend's page." It wasn't too big of a lie. It could have happened that way.

"Who is she?"

"Her name is Delaney Cooley. I'm volunteering at the thrift shop this morning. If she's there I'll listen and see what she has to say." I emphasized the word listen.

Frank didn't say anything for a moment. "Okay. Just be careful. And thanks."

At least this time I got a thanks.

* * *

By nine I sat in my car across the street from Walter's townhouse. I was hoping to catch his sister-in-law, Fiona, coming or going. I'd bought Norton a chew toy as an excuse to stop by. Weak, but hopefully it would work. After I sat for about fifteen minutes, I decided to just take the toy to Walter. I knocked on his door. Fiona opened it. She gestured me in, closed the door, and gave me the once-over like she had the last time.

I looked right back at her. Fiona's caked-on eyeliner was cracking. Her eyes were red from crying and she smelled like cigarettes. She wore a *Sons of Anarchy* T-shirt and a black rose necklace.

"I bought Norton a toy." One of us had to break the stare down.

"What's your story?" she asked. "Are you after Walter?"

"No." Jeez. What was *her* story? "I'm in a relationship." That sounded awkward to me. Like I was making it up. Defining Seth and me in four short words felt wrong. We were so much more than "in a relationship."

"Then why are you back here?"

"Like I said, I bought Norton a toy. Just a friendly gesture." Norton scampered in when he heard his name. I patted his head.

"In my experience there's always obligations behind friendly gestures." She did the air-quote thing.

What to say here? I'm sorry that's been your experience? That's not how it is on a base? However, since Walter had said people had quit stopping by after he'd been questioned, that might not hold true.

And I felt a little guilty because there was something behind the gift. I wanted to talk to Fiona. I held up the chew toy. "I'll just leave this then." And get the heck out of here. I tossed the toy and Norton chased after it.

"Listen, blondie—"

"It's Sarah." I might want out of here, but I didn't have to be spoken to so rudely.

"I can tell plain as day, you're dying to ask me a question. Spill. What's the worst that could happen?"

Darn, my expressive face. Knowing her background, I didn't want to tell her what I thought the "worst" could be. But why not just throw the real reason I was here out there. "I heard you and Alicia had a fight right before she died."

Fiona's face changed from tough to tragic just for the flick of a moment. "So. Sisters fight sometimes. Is your family perfect?"

"Hardly." Really, this didn't seem like any of my business, but I'd started so I might as well press on. "I heard that your fight was so bad you left in a huff."

Fiona patted her pockets like she was looking for a cigarette. "I've been around enough to know how you should act on a base. I told Alicia she needed to pull it together."

That didn't make sense. "Pull it together about what? From what I heard, Alicia was well liked."

"I'm sure she was. Everyone always loved Alicia." Fiona didn't make it sound like that was a good thing. "She didn't think she needed to apologize."

"To who?" I asked.

"That snooty woman she fought with. Our fight was nothing compared to that one."

Every nerve in my body simultaneously leaped to attention. "What woman?" Maybe a neighbor.

Fiona shrugged. "She didn't know I was here. But she ranted on about paying your dues and being respectful. And about a bunch of other nonsense I didn't even understand."

"Do you know her name?"

"No. I was in the kitchen. I didn't want to get involved in whatever was going on between them. Alicia used to be cool. Before she met Walter."

"What did the woman look like?" I asked.

"I didn't see her. I was in the *kitchen*." She drew each word out for emphasis. Her voice indicated that she thought I was stupid.

"Would you recognize her voice?"

"Maybe. Snooty. So darn snooty."

That didn't narrow my pool of suspects much. Most of Becky's friends were snooty and sometimes people from Massachusetts came off as condescending even when they weren't. "Alicia didn't tell you anything about the woman or the fight?"

"She had enough on her mind and didn't want to talk about it."

I wondered what that meant. "Did you tell the police?" Did Pellner and Bristow know this?

"Why would I bring it up?"

"Because your sister was *murdered*." I was beyond astonished.

Fiona thought for a moment. "You can't trust cops. They twist everything. Believe whoever they want."

I thought about the long list of arrests I'd read when I was digging up information on Fiona.

"The cops who are looking for Alicia's killer are good men."

"Yeah, just like the ones that believed my ex-boyfriend when he told them I attacked him with a knife. I was sleeping when he called."

"You have to tell them. It might be important." I'd certainly be telling them, but it would be better from her.

Fiona stared at me and then shrugged. "Okay. Now excuse me, I have things to do."

She yanked the door open and more or less pushed me out. Our conversation only added to my growing sense of unease.

I showed up at the thrift shop at ten sharp. Last night I'd messaged Zoey to tell her I wouldn't be at Jeannette's house until noon. I put on a blue bib apron and tied it around my back. The shop was already open and filled with volunteers and shoppers. I grabbed a feather duster and went in search of Delaney, but didn't find her. I asked Eleanor if she'd seen her.

"Last I saw her she was carrying things in from the shed outside," Eleanor said. "You might have walked right by her."

"Thanks," I said as I headed toward the back. When the shop was closed people could leave items they wanted to donate in the shed. By the time I returned to the sorting room, Delaney was coming in the back door juggling several bags and a box.

"Let me help you with that," I said. I tossed the feather duster aside and took the box out of her arms and set it on a shelf. Delaney set the bags down with a plop. Her nose was red from being out in the cold. "I'm Sarah Winston. I can help you with this." I gestured to the messy sorting room.

Delaney introduced herself. "I could use the help. Lots of people clean out after Christmas. We're overflowing with decorations right now."

"Maybe we should have a two-for-one sale to see if we can reduce the inventory," I said as I opened one of the bags. I pulled out a plush teddy bear dressed as Santa.

"That's a great idea," Delaney said.

We worked together quietly for a while before I asked her where she grew up and how she met her husband. I didn't want to grill her about what I'd overheard right off the bat.

"How come you volunteer at the thrift shop?" Delaney asked.

I thought again about what Judy Bruce had said to me about hanging around base. "I've volunteered here for four years. It's a way to see friends and help out at the same time. My ex-husband used to be the commander of security forces. We lived up on Offutt Road." It was funny to think that after leaving base only two years ago there were people around who didn't know CJ. It was like we'd been erased. "Right across the street from where Alicia lived." It hadn't been right across the street, but close enough. "I still can't believe she's . . . gone."

"Did you know her?" Delaney asked.

"Just a bit from volunteering here," I said.

"She's the one that talked me into volunteering. And now she'll never be here again. I wish I would have done it sooner."

"People must be so scared because they haven't caught who killed her." I almost shuddered at the thought.

"Things have been a little tense. People aren't talking as much. But every day that goes by makes life return to normal a little bit more."

"We can't live in fear all the time," I said. "I heard she was poisoned."

Delaney looked around to see if anyone else was in earshot. "Me too."

"Who told you that?" I asked. "It's all been very hush-hush."

Delaney looked around again. "Becky Cane. Do you know her?"

Chapter Thirty-Three

If stomachs could drop, mine just did. "She told me too, but asked me not to tell anyone." I hated lying to this young woman. "When did she tell you?"

"She was sobbing in the bathroom after the funeral. I don't know her that well, but couldn't leave her in there alone. That's when she told me. Becky was hysterical and kind of just babbling. She swore me to secrecy, saying that no one was supposed to know because it could hamper the investigation." Delaney glanced down. "I feel bad because I mentioned it in front of a couple of volunteers the other day. It just slipped out."

"I wouldn't worry about it." As far as I could tell it hadn't gotten around or I would have heard.

"You're the only other person who knows about it."

I nodded. Thoughts swirled, eddied, and slipped away. I took this in and combined it with Judy's phone call from last night saying that Becky's marriage was just fine. I thought about Colonel Cane's comments about loving his wife, and the flowers. That negated Becky's excuse for being out walking in the terrible ice storm that night. I had this dreadful feeling that the only way Becky would know about the poison was if she was the murderer. Everything she'd been telling me had been a lie. I'd been running around looking for other people to point the finger at. *What an idiot.*

"Are you okay?" Delaney asked. "You look kind of pale."

"I don't think my breakfast agreed with me. I'm going to have to go."

"Do you need a ride?" Delaney's forehead was creased with concern.

"I'll be fine." I grabbed my coat and went out to my Suburban. Only then did I realize I was still wearing my volunteer apron. I would have to return it later.

As I drove over to Frank's office I had another dreadful thought. Delaney knowing about the poison could put her in danger. Maybe I should go back and warn her. A horn honked behind me. I had stopped in the middle of the road without realizing it as I'd debated whether to go to Frank or turn back to Delaney. I chose Frank—let him deal with all of this.

I was convinced that Becky had murdered Alicia. It was like I'd been peeling layers off an onion only to find it was rotten inside. CJ's voice came into my mind because he'd said it more than once. *You have theories, but no proof.* I needed to go to Frank with proof. I felt stupid for believing Becky. For believing that I could solve this when Frank, Pellner, and their team couldn't. I thought about Ginger. She believed Becky too. That thought didn't give me any comfort though.

After I arrived at Frank's office, I waited impatiently

for thirty minutes because Frank was in a meeting. I'm sure I was driving his administrative assistant nuts with all my standing, pacing, sitting, and sighing. I flipped with no enthusiasm through an old base newspaper. Everything I thought I knew was through the filter of what Becky had told me. I had believed her. Finally, finally he came out along with a man I didn't recognize. He wasn't in uniform, so there was no name tag for me to read.

Frank gestured for me to come in. "I don't have a lot of time. The cops and robbers meeting is in a half hour."

"Thanks for seeing me." Then I spilled everything that I'd learned from Delaney this morning. I told him about all the little lies Becky had told me from not being invited to a gender reveal party to saying Ed Flowers's wife had a terrible temper. And then I added the big ones about her marriage, why she said she'd been out the night Alicia died. I poured out everything I had pieced together.

"You've been poking around?" he asked.

"What part of *Becky is lying* didn't you get from what I just told you?" I stared at him for a moment. "Becky killed Alicia." The thought chilled me. I'd trusted Becky. I'd been alone with her. I'd been suspicious of everyone from Colonel Cane to Zoey. "Although, you've never, ever admitted to me if Alicia was poisoned or not."

Frank loosened his tie, then immediately tightened it back up. I'm sure a body language expert would have a field day interpreting that. "We're waiting for lab results still. At first it was presumed that someone used a chunk of ice to kill her. You were the first one to bring up poison. It shook us all up."

"That must be very difficult for Alicia's husband, Walter."

Frank nodded. "But he wants to find out who did this. There's still suspicions and rumors going around about him."

"I can't imagine. You lose your wife and then people point the finger at you."

"I'll look into what you've told me."

"Becky's DNA was on Alicia," I said. Frank frowned at me. "She told me. Gave me a plausible explanation." I ran through what she'd said, that it happened at a meeting where she'd hugged Alicia.

"Yes. She told us the same thing." Frank stood. "I have to get going."

"What about Delaney? She could be in danger because of what Becky told her," I said.

"Or Delaney could be the one who did it and is casting doubt on Becky. These things are complicated. You could be the one in danger from one of them. It's why I asked you to just listen."

I didn't believe that. "I did just listen. Delaney told me something, which is why I'm here."

"Thank you for that. For your own safety, I'm releasing you. No more listening. I never meant to put you in a bad situation."

"You'll talk to Delaney?" I asked.

Frank nodded. "Don't worry about this. Please."

I nodded. Now I could head over to Jeannette's house and get some work done.

* * *

I stopped at the grocery store and bought a couple of lobster rolls to eat for lunch on the drive over to Jeannette's house. This had all become way more complicated than I was prepared for. But I couldn't let it go yet. I had one more call to make, one that might help Frank. Once I got to Jeannette's house I called Eleanor.

When she answered, I asked, "Do you remember that last Spouses' Club board meeting the day before Alicia died?"

"I remember going," Eleanor said. "Why?"

I wasn't even sure why I was calling. Oh, that was a bunch of hooey. I knew exactly why I was calling. Despite what I told Frank, what I told myself, I had to follow through. I was in it one way or another. *Forgive me, Frank.* "I'm not sure. Did anything unusual happen?"

Eleanor paused. I could hear school announcements in the background. "Becky seemed to be having a bad day. Although to tell the truth, that's not a stretch for being around Becky lately."

"What makes you think that?"

"She always makes us some kind of smoothie when she has us over. They are delicious and spiked with alcohol. Becky brought some of them out on a tray, passed them around, in order of the spouse's husband's rank, if you can believe it."

"I can believe it," I said.

"She had given everyone theirs except for Alicia."

"Why didn't she give one to Alicia?"

"Because she dumped it over by accident. She went and made another one. In a few minutes she came out looking flustered and apologized."

in her hands. "This is worth way more than you'll ever get for it."

"It is." I guess I wasn't going to pry anything else out of Harriet.

She put a price on the mask and hung it back up. I would double check her pricing later. I didn't want to question her too much now.

"I worked for the FBI," Harriet said.

"Wow. That must have been interesting." Well maybe not. Lots of people in the FBI spent their lives in offices doing research. Not everyone could be a field agent. Although she said she moved and traveled a lot. "What did you do?"

Harriet studied me for a moment and shrugged her shoulders. "I was a hostage negotiator."

My eyebrows shot up and I burst out laughing. Harriet frowned at me.

"That poor woman." I laughed again.

"What woman?" Harriet asked, still frowning.

"At the thrift shop," I said. "She didn't have a chance with you and that bracelet." I finally managed to quit laughing, but I swiped at my eyes to get the laugh tears out of them.

A strange look passed over Harriet's face and then she laughed too. "Force of habit. My dear husband always said he never had a chance with me when it came to disagreements."

"Does he still feel that way?" I asked.

"He died a couple of years ago."

"I'm sorry."

"Me too. Retirement isn't anything like I expected it to be."

"I guess that explains all the drastically different

outfits." Harriet frowned again. Oh, boy. I might have overstepped this time.

Then she grinned at me. "You're right. I feel like I'm trying on different personas to figure out who I am now that I'm single and retired."

"Which one feels most like you?" I asked.

"The first one. The black, with a little of the thrift shop outfit on occasion. But this outfit?" She gestured to her clothes. "It is definitely not me."

"So shed some of it."

Harried grinned again. She had a beautiful smile. And those cheekbones. Harriet unwrapped the three scarves and stretched her neck.

"Oh, that is so much better." She took off all the bracelets. "I'm free. Let's get back to work."

When we finished the hall Harriet announced she had to go.

"Would you be able to help out the day of the sale?" I asked.

"Sure," Harriet said. "As you know I love to bargain."

"But you'll have to do the reverse of your thrift shop performance. Drive the price up."

"No worries. I can handle it."

As I walked Harriet to the door I had no doubts that she could.

After Harriet left, I went to the cedar chest in the front room and pulled out the family albums that I had seen the day I found the vintage valentines. Luke had said to look for connections between Fake Troy and the family. I set the albums down on the couch and started flipping through them, viewing snippets of the Blevinses' family life. Jeannette's parents looked so ordinary. I watched the kids grow up. Jeannette became a sullen teenager who always stood a bit away from everyone else. Then I found an album of pictures of Troy at college. He was on the crew team and they were posed in front of their boat, oars in hand. I was about to flip the page, but took a second look. I stared at the guy on the end. It was Fake Troy.

Chapter Thirty-Four

Troy and Fake Troy in a photo together. I continued to stare down at it, trying to make some sense of what that meant. My conclusion was it wasn't anything good. I took the photo out of the album before I called Pellner. "You've got to come over to Jeannette's house right now."

"What's going on? Are you safe?" he asked.

"I'm fine. I found a picture of Fake Troy. In Jeannette's brother's things. They were on a crew team together at college."

"You're sure?"

"I am. You have to come see this."

"Is there a name on the photo?" Pellner asked.

I flipped it over. "There's nothing but maybe there's a yearbook around here. At the very least someone at the college should be able to identify him."

"Troy should be able to identify him."

"Don't contact him yet."

"Why not?"

"What if Troy put him up to coming into the house? Or what if it was Jeannette's brother who got Fake Troy out of the hospital?" I studied the photo a bit away from everyone else. Then I found an album of pictures of Troy at college. He was on the crew team and they were posed in front of their boat, oars in hand. I was about to flip the page, but took a second look. I stared at the guy on the end. It was Fake Troy.

Chapter Thirty-Four

Troy and Fake Troy in a photo together. I continued to stare down at it, trying to make some sense of what that meant. My conclusion was it wasn't anything good. I took the photo out of the album before I called Pellner. "You've got to come over to Jeannette's house right now."

"What's going on? Are you safe?" he asked.

"I'm fine. I found a picture of Fake Troy. In Jeannette's brother's things. They were on a crew team together at college."

"You're sure?"

"I am. You have to come see this."

"Is there a name on the photo?" Pellner asked.

I flipped it over. "There's nothing but maybe there's a yearbook around here. At the very least someone at the college should be able to identify him."

"Troy should be able to identify him."

"Don't contact him yet."

"Why not?"

"What if Troy put him up to coming into the house? Or what if it was Jeannette's brother who got Fake Troy out of the hospital?" I studied the photo again. "Troy was just here in Ellington yesterday. Maybe he's been in town longer."

"Why would he send someone to his parents' house?"

"I don't know. I hope I'm wrong. Just come over. Please." I really hoped I was wrong. Jeannette had already suffered the unexpected loss of her parents. Losing a brother would be devastating.

"Okay, I'll swing by and get the photo."

I snapped a picture of the photo with my phone, then I flipped through the rest of the album to see if there was anything else in it that would give me Fake Troy's name. There wasn't. I debated calling Jeannette, but decided to wait until Pellner showed up and we could talk all of this through.

I went through more albums while I was waiting for Pellner, looking for other photos of Fake Troy. A noise at the door made me grab the photo and run to the front door. Jeannette's brother stood there.

"Troy," I said. I put the picture behind my back like a kid hiding contraband from a parent. "I thought you left town."

"What's behind your back?" he asked, stepping forward as I took steps back.

He didn't ask in a friendly way. It was more threat than question. The foyer wasn't large, but I wasn't far from where I could run to one of the other rooms. Pellner should be here any minute.

"Nothing. Just a picture." It felt like all of my suspicions and worries flitted over my face even as I tried for a neutral "nothing to see here" look.

"Are you stealing from my folks? From Jeannette and me?" he asked.

"No. It's just a photo." I pulled my hand out from behind my back and waved the picture around, not so he could see what the picture was of, but so he could see I was telling the truth. "I was sorting through things when I heard you at the front door."

He put his hand out. "Let me see it."

I didn't have a choice. *Pellner, where are you?* I handed Troy the photo. "I didn't realize you did crew in college."

"Why would you?" he asked. He looked down at the picture. A brief smile flickered over his face. He glanced from me to the picture and back again. "You seem to think this is important. Why?"

"You know Fake Troy."

"What are you talking about?"

I pointed at Fake Troy in the picture. "That's him." I didn't add *as if you didn't know.*

Troy stared at the photo. His face went from white to deep red in an instant. "We need to talk," he said.

His voice was grim. The way he said *we need to talk* didn't make me think he wanted to talk at all. I bolted. For the kitchen. The kitchen led to the garage. But I knew the safety chain and extra dead bolt were fully engaged. I hoped I could free them before Troy caught up with me. He pounded after me.

I grabbed a box off the kitchen table and tossed it at him. It was full of plastic containers. He batted it away as I tried to release the safety chain. Troy grabbed my arm. He was huge.

"Let her go." Pellner stood there. His hand rested on his gun. His dimples said *I mean business,* as did his voice. I knew from personal experience just how scary Pellner could be. We hadn't liked each other much, or at all, when we first met two years ago.

Troy let go of my arm. Put his hands up and stepped away.

"What's going on here?" Pellner asked.

I slipped past Troy and over to Pellner, well behind Pellner.

"I don't know," Troy said. "I asked her what she had in her hand and she was acting all fishy. Then she ran in here so I followed."

"Sarah?" Pellner asked.

I nodded. That more or less summed up what had happened except for the fishy part. "He's the one who was acting fishy."

"She ran. I chased her."

"Do you have the picture, Sarah?"

"Troy has it. He said *we need to talk* in a threatening voice. It scared me, so I ran. Then he grabbed me." I didn't add the *thank heavens you showed up when you did*. I think both of them got that.

Pellner pointed to the kitchen table. "Sit."

I did, but Troy continued to stand.

"Both of you," Pellner said.

Troy sat at the opposite end of the table. We stared at each other over a sea of glasses that Zoey and I had priced. Pellner took the chair between us.

"I want to see the photo." Pellner leveled his steely cop look on Troy.

"I don't have to give you anything," Troy said.

"I took a picture of it with my phone." I swiped my phone open and brought the picture up. Pellner took the phone from me and I pointed to the guy I thought was Fake Troy. "That's him."

Pellner studied the photo and nodded. He enlarged the picture and showed it to Troy. "Who is this?"

Troy handed Pellner the real photo. I noticed his hand wobbled a little. What was with him?

"It was a long time ago. I was a stupid kid."

Pellner leaned forward. "Do we need to go down to the station to talk about this?"

Troy's face twisted. "No."

"Then why don't you tell me what's going on."

I sat quietly, trying to stay out of Pellner's way, trying to make sure Troy would keep talking.

"Why don't you ask her what's going on here?" Troy flicked his head toward the photo. "I think she's up to her ears with him."

Chapter Thirty-Five

"*Me?*" I sat straighter. "I just met him. If you could call our interaction meeting. He lied about who he was. Said he was you."

"So you say," Troy said. He looked at Pellner. "How'd he even know about the sale? Jeannette told me that was his story when he showed up here pretending to be me."

Pellner and Troy both looked at me.

"I started advertising it right away. That's how he must have known."

"Who is he?" Pellner asked. "Let's start there."

"His name is Sam. Sam Cousins."

"How do you know him?"

"We were on the crew team together."

As if we didn't already know that from the picture.

"And?" Pellner asked.

I didn't know how Pellner remained so calm. I wanted to shout at Troy. I tucked my hands under my legs to keep me from blurting out questions.

Troy glanced down at his lap. "Sam was a year ahead of me. The quintessential big man on campus. Girls loved him. Guys loved him. I wanted to be him."

I nodded. Who didn't want to be someone else when they were young?

"I bragged to get his attention. About the money my parents had. About some other things they had. I wanted to impress him."

I felt kind of bad for that young Troy. Insecurity was a terrible thing and even at this age, I'd almost let some nasty comments do me in.

"What things?" Pellner asked.

"My parents had a box of coins, some loose jewels, rings my mom would wear. I talked about them around Sam. A lot." Troy looked at Pellner. "Sam dropped out of college during the winter of my freshman year. I haven't seen or heard anything about him since."

Pellner gave a slight nod. "And why do you think he has a connection to Sarah?"

"Sam could have read about my parents' death, remembered my stories, and got hold of her to help him find them." He glanced at me, frowning. "They might·have already stolen the coins and jewelry."

"Then why would I still be here?" I asked.

"To look for more valuables? To keep up appearances so you can do the same thing at the next person's house." Troy turned to Pellner. "She's been arrested before."

I paled at that and wondered how long that incident would haunt me. "Arrested, not charged, and cleared of any wrongdoing. Besides, I've never seen that man before. And I certainly wasn't working with him to steal from you." My temper flared in a way it usually didn't. "I wouldn't last a month in this town if I was stealing. It's too small. Everyone would put it together."

Pellner nodded. "You may be right about Sam. But you're dead wrong about Sarah."

Troy looked at me and shrugged. Pellner's statement might have helped, but I'm not sure Troy was completely on board with my innocence yet.

"How come you didn't recognize him from the photo from the security footage at the hospital?" I asked. Maybe Troy was the one who was in on it and was afraid he got caught.

"You've seen the picture," he said. "All blurry, with his head down and in a baseball cap. I wouldn't recognize Jeannette like that."

"You're right. I'm sorry. I'm sorry about all of this."

"Apology accepted."

"Could your parents have put the coins and such in a safety deposit box?" I asked.

"Jeannette and I checked. We didn't find anything."

"Did they keep them in anything in particular?" I had a friend whose parents kept old coins in a vintage tobacco tin.

"Nothing I remember." He thought for a moment. "For a while they used an old lacquered box. Have you seen anything like that?"

I stared straight into his eyes. "I haven't. But I'll watch for it. Why do you think Sam went through the office?"

Troy shrugged.

Pellner leaned in. "He could have been looking for car titles, deeds, stock certificates. If they couldn't find the coins and gems, they might have wanted to find other valuables."

"Could your parents have sold them?" I asked Troy.

"It's possible. But if they did, they sure never mentioned it. And some of that was family jewelry. Hard to believe they'd part with it."

Pellner scooted his chair back and stood. "I need to get going. Let me know if either of you thinks of anything that could help us find Sam."

Troy stood too. "I have to go check in with my office."

"Are you okay with me being here alone?" I didn't want to cause any strife between Jeannette and Troy.

"If the police think you're okay, I guess I do too."

Not a ringing endorsement, but good enough for now.

After they left I got back to work. I was glad Zoey wasn't around to hear any of this. I shook my head. I'd found out a lot of interesting, sometimes terrible, things about people's lives doing garage sales. What a day. I went to the guest room to tackle things in there.

As I went through things I continued to think about the coins and gems. Why hadn't the Blevinses put them somewhere obvious or left a note? That was what you were supposed to do, but they'd died unexpectedly. I wondered again if they had a home safe. I should have asked Troy. Jeannette didn't seem to know anything about one. That made me think of the combination I'd found in the flour. Maybe they had a safe somewhere in the house even though Jeannette and Troy didn't know about it.

Or maybe her parents didn't trust Troy for some reason. They would have realized that Jeannette would be the one to clean out the house. Putting the combination in the flour was their way of making sure she'd find it. Maybe they had left clues somewhere else too—in places they didn't think Troy would look. Jeannette and I had talked about her favorite place to live. It had been Japan because her mom had more time there for baking. That would tie in with putting a note in the flour. Jeannette had also said she loved Japan because it was exotic.

They had several pieces of Japanese furniture in the house. I went to the living room where there was a Japanese chest-on-chest. My friend the antique dealer had priced it for me. I'd looked inside when I first saw it, but it had been empty. I went and took a closer second look. Nothing. There was a smaller piece that they used as a nightstand in the master bedroom. It had two drawers that pulled open. I searched it, even upending it to make sure there wasn't anything underneath.

Then I remembered the step chest in the basement. Its real name was *kaidan-dansu*. They were modular storage units that could easily be reconfigured and used as a staircase. In Japan people positioned them for attic access or for caring for silkworms under thatched roofs. I ran down to the basement.

This step chest had eight drawers and four sections with doors. I searched all the drawers, even taking them out and turning them over. After that I went through the other sections. I found Japanese dolls, some silk fabric, and children's clothing including small embroidered shoes that Jeannette must have worn at some point. But no clues. I thought I'd been on to something.

I moved back to study the step chest to see if there was anything I'd missed. The steps led to the two-foot square drop ceiling tiles. The space between the ceiling and floor above would make an excellent hiding place. I tested the first step. My foot was longer than it was, but it would hold my weight. The steps were taller than a standard American staircase. I climbed the steps and pushed on the tile right at the top. It slid out of the way easily. I went up two more steps so my head was above the drop ceiling.

It was too dark to see anything so I pulled my phone out of my back pocket and turned on the flashlight. Oh, boy. Cobwebs draped from the criss-cross of wooden beams that supported the floor above. I hoped those furry things on the ceiling panels were dust bunnies and not mice. I shined the light, swiveling it back and forth. There it was—a lacquered wooden box with handles and a lock, just out of reach wedged in between a beam and the floor above. I went up to the top step and rested my hand against one of the wooden beams so I didn't topple forward. Crashing through the drop ceiling onto the concrete floor wouldn't be fun.

I reached, brushed the box with my fingertips and reached again. This time I managed to grab one of the handles. I hefted it toward me, being careful to keep it on the metal pieces that the ceiling tiles were resting on. The box was surprisingly heavy. I didn't want to damage the ceiling. When I got it close enough I took a step down, and another, so only my head and shoulders were above the ceiling tiles.

"Whatcha got there?" a man said.

I recognized the voice even before I looked down. My hands shook. I didn't want to drop the box. Fake Troy, or Sam as I now knew him to be, smiled up at me, but it wasn't a nice smile. I thought about trying to shove the box back into the rafters. But to do that I'd have to go up a step and Fake Troy would know something was up. "Probably whatever it is you're looking for." Most likely the coins and gems. I sorted through options. There weren't many. I was in a precarious position on the small steps.

"Hand down whatever it is you found," Sam said.

How had he gotten in here? I thought I'd locked the door after Pellner and Troy left but maybe not. Or maybe he could pick locks.

"Okay," I said. I lifted the box, managed to get it and myself out of the drop ceiling. Sam reached up for it. I shifted slightly and threw the heavy box on his head. Sam yelped as he crumpled to the floor. The box crashed beside him but didn't break apart. I scrambled down the steps to retrieve it and get the heck away from Sam.

"Sam, I got the new camera set up in case they change the security code again," a man called from upstairs. "They'll never spot this one."

Oh, no. Sam wasn't alone. I held my breath. *What now?*

Footsteps tromped across the floor upstairs. "Sam? What's going on down there?"

I snatched up the box and stashed it in one of the sections of the step chest with the doors. It's the best I could do on short notice. Then I ran back up the step chest. I grabbed one of the beams, pulled myself up, and wedged between the beam and the floor above me. As I clung to the beam I reached down, stretching, stretching toward the drop ceiling panel. Footsteps pounded down the stairs. If I didn't move the ceiling panel back in place he'd find me before I could get help. My arm burned as I clung to the beam and reached down. Finally, my fingertips swiped the panel and I eased it back in place.

I carefully slid my phone from my pocket. A heavy tread sounded on the basement floor.

"Sam? Sam?" The man's voice came closer.

One-handed I texted 911, grateful Ellington had upgraded their system to accommodate texting. Typed *help* and the address. I slid the phone back into my pocket as I wrapped both arms around the beam. It smelled of old wood. Splinters dug into my arms and the wood was hard against my chest and abdomen. Sweat beaded on my brow. It rolled slowly across my forehead and dripped down onto the ceiling tiles. Each drop sounded like an explosion to me but was lighter than a mouse's whisker.

"Sam," the man exclaimed. "You are such a klutz. First you slipped upstairs the day we first came and now here. What happened?"

It sounded like he was right below me. I clung to the beam. Literally hanging on for dear life. The man didn't seem to know I was in the house. That was good. Very good. Sam didn't respond, so he must still be unconscious. Oh, no. I hoped he was only unconscious. Not dead. That thought made me shake. I couldn't afford to shake, clinging like I was. One wrong move and I would crash right through the ceiling.

I heard a groan. It had to be Sam. At least I hadn't killed him, but he would know to look up here. I felt steps vibrating from above before I heard voices. Then there was lots of shouting. People yelling, "Hands where I can see them" and "On the floor, now." I heard Awesome's voice then Pellner's. It quieted down, but still I clung.

"Sarah? Where the hell are you?" It was Pellner.

"Up here. Above the drop ceiling. I'm coming out." I let loose with aching arms, moved the panel, and shakily made it down the steps before collapsing to sit on the last one. "Thank you."

Chapter Thirty-Six

The two men were being prodded up the basement steps when I had come down from my hiding place above the drop ceiling. I'd followed Pellner upstairs once he told me they'd been stuffed in patrol cars and driven away. I stood in the living room waiting for the questions to come. And they did. Fortunately, it didn't take long to explain what had happened.

Seth showed up. Roared up, screeched up, slammed the car door so hard that it rattled the living room window. I still shook even with his arms wrapped around me. I tried to tell myself it was muscle fatigue from clinging to the wooden beam. My fingers had a few splinters in them, but I'd deal with them later. For now I just wanted to reorient myself. Catch my breath. Feel safe. Pellner retrieved the box from the basement, set it on the coffee table.

"It's locked. A combination kind. We'll need to contact Jeannette."

"I know the combination." For some reason I'd memorized it the day I found it in the flour. I explained to them why I knew.

"I still have to call Jeannette first." He quickly

made the call and got Jeannette's approval to open the box.

I recited the combination as Pellner put it in. It clicked with the last number. Pellner slowly lifted the lid. He took out a folder, glanced in, and looked over at me.

"It's a will," he said.

I hoped it was a more recent, more equitable one. A thin piece of wood covered whatever else was in the box. "What else is in there?"

Pellner pried out the piece of wood. We all stared down and then at each other. Diamonds, rubies, sapphires, and other jewels twinkled at us from one side of the box. Some of the stones were set in rings from Art Deco to Edwardian to modern. The other side was filled with gold and silver coins. It looked like the treasure chest I'd always dreamed of finding as a kid. Jeannette and Troy were going to be rich.

I plucked one of the rings out. It was a pink stone, possibly a sapphire or ruby, set in gold. Stunning.

"I wonder why they hid them in the basement," Seth said.

"I've had friends who hid things in odd places when they travel. No one ever expects to die. I guess we won't ever know for sure why this was hidden." I squatted down to take a closer look. "Amazing."

Eventually, I convinced Seth to go back to work. That I was safe here now and that I needed to work too. At three thirty, I decided to leave. Jeannette hadn't been by so I left her a note. This time I made sure it was a pen with normal ink in it. I told her I'd be back in the morning around eight and to call if she needed anything. Pellner had taken the jewels with him when he left. None of us thought it was a good idea to leave them here.

On my drive home, I decided to swing by the cemetery where Alicia was buried. I'm not sure why. I got there, trudged along a snow-packed path, and found her grave. I stopped under a pine tree five feet away. I said a little prayer.

"I hope they find justice for you, Alicia," I said softly. A gust of wind blew. Branches shook the snow clinging to them down on me. I shivered and went back to my car. After starting it and turning the heater on full blast, I sent a couple of texts including one to Becky saying I had news. Asking her to meet me at the Dunkin' Donuts on Great Road in Bedford. It should be quiet there this time of day. Becky sent a text back that she'd be there in thirty minutes. Maybe I needed to help justice along a little.

Chapter Thirty-Seven

Traffic on Great Road was slow. I inched along, passing Bedford Farms Ice Cream, the turn to the high school, and Wilson Park, where they had the pole capping ceremony every spring near Patriots' Day. I saw Becky pull into the Dunkin's just ahead of me. I waited until she was inside before I headed in so I didn't have to talk to her outside. I wanted witnesses around if need be.

Becky sat in a far corner with a cup of coffee in front of her. I ordered a large coffee regular, which meant it would come with four creams and four sugars. I'd learned that from the locals, because there was no little station in a Dunkin's where you could add your own. Although I usually just drank my coffee black, right now I needed the extra boost from the fat and sugar. I slid into the bench seat across from Becky. Dark shadows rimmed beneath her eyes. Her hair was slicked back and greasy, so un-Becky-like. But other things had been unlike her too. Delaney saying that Becky was sobbing in the bathroom and the hug she gave Alicia. All so out of character.

"What have you found out?" Becky asked.

Her tone was flat. You'd think if she thought I had

news, she'd be a little more excited. "I have a theory about what happened."

"It was Delaney, wasn't it?" Becky leaned forward. "I take no pleasure in saying that."

Of course she'd say that. "How did you figure it out?" I asked. Might as well play along and see what she had to say.

"After Alicia's funeral I found Delaney crying in the bathroom. She was just this side of hysterical."

That was the exact opposite of what Delaney had said. I shifted on the hard bench seat.

"She told me that Alicia had been poisoned. She hastily added that she'd been told that." Becky glanced down at her coffee and back up at me. "But she wouldn't tell me who had told her. The only way she could know about the poison is if she did it herself."

I put my hand to my mouth. The way Becky told it, her voice, it chilled me. *Take a sip of coffee.* I picked up my cup, hoping Becky would think my shaking hand was from what she'd just said. The sip I took scalded my tongue. I set the cup back down.

"That doesn't explain the wound on Alicia's head." *Or why you were out walking in the middle of the night, because it wasn't that your marriage was breaking up.*

Becky shrugged. "Maybe the poison wasn't working fast enough. I told you I was out walking that night. I saw Delaney drive past me. Fast. Going away from Alicia's house."

Could that be true? "If it was dark, how did you know it was her?" I asked.

"She's given me rides before. She has an old blue Thunderbird. It's hard to miss."

I hoped that Delaney had some way to prove where she was the night Alicia died, because Becky was convincing. Even though I knew deep in my soul every word was a lie. "Why would she kill Alicia?" That's what I couldn't understand—why Becky would kill Alicia. Because even though she was trying to pin it on Delaney, it didn't fit. What had Alicia done that was so horrible that Becky's solution was to kill her?

"She was jealous of Alicia. Ginger fawned over her because she was a good bowler. Can you imagine that?"

I shook my head. "That doesn't sound like a good enough reason to kill someone." But what did I know about why people killed someone?

"Of course not. But think about it. Alicia's new here, young. She gets all this praise and recognition because her brother prints the cookbook for free. All she did was make one freaking phone call." Becky's voice rose. "No matter that she wasn't the one who did all the hard work of collecting the recipes, testing them, typing them all up. That she put in years of hard work to promote her husband's career." Becky made a laugh-sob noise. "She sacrificed. Lost who she was. Then he doesn't even get the promotion they both worked for. No star for him. And no one gives a damn. No one."

I didn't know that Colonel Cane hadn't gotten promoted to general. Anytime someone didn't get promoted it stung. It felt like a personal affront to their family. I'd seen it many times.

"Then when you try to talk to her about it, she tells you to move on, that there's a new generation of mil spouse. Mil spouse. She doesn't even have the decency to say military spouse."

Becky's fists clenched.

So that's what her fight with Alicia was about. Not being respected. It must have infuriated Becky, who was used to being in charge, to people doing what she said.

"Delaney is young," I said. "As is her husband. He's not close to getting a star. Not even a major yet. They are just starting their military lives."

Becky grabbed her purse and started to stand.

"Sit," I snapped at her, surprised when she did. "You killed her, Becky. You were talking about yourself. I'm calling Scott Pellner. You call your husband and a lawyer."

"No. You're wrong. I was using my own life as an example," she pleaded.

I shook my head. "Give up. It will be better for you."

"You have no proof. It's just she said, she said. I'll say you're lying."

"They'll get the lab results back soon. They know about the smoothies and how you 'spilled' Alicia's drink and then went back into the kitchen to get her another one." I thought about the phone call from Judy. "Your husband loves you, so the excuse you used for being out that night doesn't work."

"Like I said. It's your word against mine."

"No, it's not." A woman spoke from behind me. It was Harriet. I'd texted her on my way over here, but didn't know if she'd make it with the traffic and short notice.

"I heard every word." She looked at Becky. "Call the lawyer. It sounds like you are going to need a good one."

In the end, it was quiet. No one else at the Dunkin's even knew that Becky was turning herself in for committing a murder. It took over an hour before Becky's husband showed up with a lawyer. It seemed like much longer as we sat across from each other with nothing to say, the grim truth our only other companion. Pellner along with Frank Bristow waited outside. Harriet left once they arrived. Becky turned herself in to them—lawyer on one side and her husband on the other. Although, I didn't think it would help Becky that much. Her husband had tears streaming down his face. He really did love her.

I stewed at Becky's attempt to use me to accuse someone else of the murder. It had almost worked. Almost. I had let my pride at being good at solving things get in the way of my common sense. At least I'd used what bit of smarts I had to put together the case against Becky and to trick her into tripping up.

Chapter Thirty-Eight

Stella stopped by my apartment Wednesday morning after Seth and I had breakfast and he left for work.

"You look happy," Stella said.

"I am." Seth and I had talked late into the night about Becky.

"Then I hope I don't wipe that big old smile off your face."

"Why would you?"

"Have you read the paper?" she asked, holding up the local paper.

"Not yet. I've been busy." I smiled at her.

"Look at the ad on page five."

Stella handed me the paper. I opened to page five. There was a quarter-page ad for Zoey's Tag Sales. I looked up at Stella. "Unbelievable."

"Do you know her?" Stella asked.

"I trained her. She's been helping me over at my latest project." I shook my head. "She asked me tons of questions."

"Aren't you mad?" Stella asked. "You sound so calm."

"Part of me is. But I had a sneaking suspicion that her questions had a purpose to them." I took a deep breath and let it out slowly. "I'm not going to let her get to me. People know me in town. I have a good reputation."

"You might want to read the rest of the ad."

It read: *Don't trust your business to someone who wants to buy what wasn't sold or offers to haul it off for nothing. It's a scam to steal from you. I won't put my friends above your profits. Call me for pricing. Trust me, it will beat the competition.*

"She twisted things I told her." Ack. First Becky and now Zoey.

Stella tilted her head toward the apartment next door. "Mike's still there. You could talk to him about this."

I was shaking my head before she even finished. "I'm not afraid of a competitor. I've got this." In the grand scheme of things, in light of what had happened to Alicia and Jeannette, this wasn't so bad.

"You are a better woman than I am," Stella said.

"Always have been," I said with a laugh. Stella grabbed one of the throw pillows off the couch and threw it at me. I caught it and tossed it back. "Thanks for letting me know."

"Anytime," Stella said as she left.

I spoke to both Pellner and Frank during the day while Harriet and I worked at Jeannette's parents' house. Jeannette had called to thank me for finding the hidden box.

"Any word on what's going on with Sam and Sam's partner?" I asked Pellner.

"Sam and his partner have both been charged on a

number of counts ranging from assault, to trespassing, to burglary."

"And they haven't made bail?" I asked.

"Not yet. They are both so busy pointing fingers at each other I don't think they've made arrangements yet."

"But they could make bail."

"It's possible, but let's hope they don't. I've heard that the DA is going at them hard."

That made me smile. Although, from what I knew of Seth, he dealt with every case like it affected him personally.

I called Frank. "Are the lab results on Alicia back yet?"

"Nothing yet. But Becky told us she used acetaminophen."

I remembered a class CJ had taken about household poisons. Acetaminophen was such a common painkiller. But even doubling the dose in one day could cause liver failure and death. It was even worse if combined with alcohol. Eleanor had told me the smoothies they drank had alcohol in them.

"Why would she tell you that?"

"She knew what we would find when the lab results came in. Combine that with the other evidence and the case against her was about as airtight as a case can get."

"Then why did Becky hit Alicia on the head?" I asked.

"She thought the poisoning would happen quicker. When it didn't she went over and watched her house. Waited for an opportunity."

"That means it's premeditated. If she'd just hit her on the head it might have been a moment of insanity."

"Yes. It's so horribly sad," Frank said. "The worst part is Alicia was dying anyway. Cancer. Only she and her husband knew at that point."

"So Becky robbed her of her last precious days."

"Of her being able to say her final goodbyes." No wonder this case had hit Frank so hard. And maybe it's why Alicia had spoken her mind at that Spouses' Club meeting. That incident seemed to have set Becky in motion.

I remembered Walter, Alicia's husband, saying that the puppy would give him a reason to get up in the morning. They'd found Norton together. It must have comforted Alicia to know that Walter wouldn't be completely alone.

"It's one of the reasons we asked for your help. We couldn't let this one go."

"How long have you known?" I asked.

"Since the beginning. Alicia's husband came to us right away. We asked that he not share that information with anyone else. And he agreed. At first we thought maybe he didn't want to see her suffer. It's one of the reasons we arrested him."

There was nothing more to say. We said our soft goodbyes. I was grateful to have work to keep me busy.

After spending the day working at Jeannette's house, I came home and took another stab at making chicken marsala. After chopping, dredging, sautéing, and simmering, I took the lid off on my latest batch. It smelled good. The sauce was smooth as silk instead of clumpy like it had been on my previous attempts.

I dipped a spoon in, almost afraid to taste it. I blew on the spoon to cool the sauce and waited a couple more moments. *Now or never.* I sipped. It tasted good. Delicious even. I did a little happy dance after I turned off the burner. Next, I cut into the chicken. It was tender, not like the jerky I'd inadvertently made the time before. Last time I'd been so determined to make sure it wasn't raw in the center that I overcooked it. Cooking wasn't easy. So many things could go wrong and they usually did for me.

I transferred half of the contents to a Pyrex container for later. This batch was good enough that I could pour it over the pasta I had boiling and share it with Mike. I drained the pasta and put half the pasta into the gently simmering pan on the stove. I topped the other pasta with oil and butter for later. Once it cooled I'd stick it in the fridge. I gave the marsala on the stove a quick stir. I took the pan and carried it carefully to the door to take over to Mike.

I balanced the heavy pan against my hip as I went to open the door. Ouch. It was hot. A thump from the hall was followed by a groan. My heart started hammering as I heard a banging sound and yelling. I opened my door and peeked out. Francesco was out cold on the floor. A man stood in Mike's doorway with his back to me. His arm was out and he had a gun pointed at Mike's face. A face that was paler than the snow on the town common.

Chapter Thirty-Nine

"Hey," I yelled. I ran a few steps. The man turned, swinging the gun toward me. I flung the contents of the pan at him. He screamed as the hot liquid splashed onto his face. I bolted at him and whacked him upside the head with the heavy pan. To my astonishment he fell to the floor next to Francesco.

Mike and I stared at each other for a second. Then Mike had the good sense to grab the gun up off the floor where it had fallen. Mike took the gun into the apartment and came back out.

"Who is that?" I asked, pointing a shaking finger at the man. Marsala dripped from his thick curly hair. He wore a disheveled black pinstripe suit.

"A nobody," Mike said.

"A mobster?" I leaned against the wall. My apron suddenly too tight around my waist. Had I just thrown chicken marsala in a mobster's face? Was I going to be the one that would have to leave and go into hiding? "He's got to be somebody and he's not going to be happy with me when he wakes up."

Mike came over and grabbed me by the shoulders. "It's okay, Sarah."

"He had a gun pointed at your face." I stabbed a

finger dramatically at Francesco, who groaned. "He tried to kill Francesco. None of this is okay."

"Let's go back to your apartment. Get you out of the hall," Mike said.

Francesco sat up. Mike looked at him. "Keep an eye on him."

"Is that—"

"Yes," Mike said. "I'm taking Sarah to her apartment. She's a little upset."

"What's on his face?" Francesco asked.

"Chicken marsala," I said. "I made it. And it was good."

Mike put his arm around my shoulders and walked me back to my living room. I peeled the apron off and just dropped it on the trunk by my couch. I sat down in my grandmother's rocking chair and stroked the wood of its curved arms. It was good, solid, comforting. What had I just done?

"You have to tell me what's going on," I insisted.

Mike sat on the edge of the couch, turned toward me. He put his forearms on his knees and clasped his hands together. "I went out with that guy's younger sister," he said. His face was composed and sincere looking.

I wasn't sure I trusted that sincerity. He'd lied to me before. "How much younger?" I asked.

"Just a couple of years younger than me. Jeez, what do you think, I'm a cradle robber?"

"No. Sorry. I'm just a little upset right now."

"She broke up with me. But her brother out there"— Mike jerked his thumb toward the door—"decided it was because I'd hurt her in some way. But I treated that woman like a princess. To tell the truth, it hurt when she broke things off."

"He was going to kill you because you aren't dating his sister?" What was he going to do to me then?

"No, Sarah. It wasn't even a real gun."

I'm not sure I believed that. That gun looked real to me. I'd been around guns since I'd met CJ because of his jobs with the Air Force. Why was Mike so pale if it wasn't real?

"He's just a little strange," Mike said. "Great with computers, but strange. I'm going to call his sister and take him to her."

"What about me?" I'd be furious if someone threw hot chicken marsala in my face.

"Don't you worry. He's not going to come around here again."

"He's the one that broke into your store and made the fondue?" I asked.

"Yeah. I finally got a look at him on a neighbor's security camera this morning. We've been searching for him all day. I'm a little embarrassed to admit that I let a guy like that run me out of town."

I wondered again if Mike was lying. He had looked rattled and had hustled me out of the hall quickly. Was it because he didn't want Francesco to say anything else to me? Something that would contradict what Mike was telling me right now? Was I going to have to move? Go into witness protection? Or trust Mike was telling me the truth. I guess for now that's what I'd have to do.

"How did he find you here?"

"Like I said, he's a genius with electronics. We must have slipped up someplace and he found me."

"Should we call the police?"

Mike shook his head. "There's no reason to."

"He could charge me with assault."

"He's not going to admit to anyone that a woman got the best of him."

"I have to tell Seth."

Mike opened his mouth, but I cut him off. "I'm not keeping secrets from him." I stared right into those icy blue eyes. I'd kept a secret for Mike once before and I wasn't doing it again with Seth.

"He's not going to be happy. It might put him in a compromising position, him being the district attorney."

"I know. But I don't care. I'm not lying to him."

"Not telling him about this isn't lying."

I shook my head. "No secrets."

"Everyone has secrets." Mike headed toward the door and then turned back. "You're something. You were going to save my life even when you thought the gun was real." He gave me a long look. "I owe you." With that he walked out.

Seth and I sat on opposite sides of the couch while I recounted what had happened in the hall earlier this evening. By the time Seth arrived there weren't any signs of chicken marsala on the floor or walls in the hall. The place was scrubbed clean. Even the pan was gone. No one sat outside Mike's door, so they must be out somewhere. I watched Seth's face as I told the story. Concern, relief, and interest skimmed across it as I explained what had happened.

"You cooked chicken marsala?" he asked.

"That's what you got out of all of that? That I cooked?"

He laughed. "No. I'm glad you're okay. I'll talk to Mike."

"I hope this doesn't put you in an awkward position."

"It's okay. So you cooked. For Mike."

Seth sounded a bit jealous. I blushed. "I cooked for you. I know it's your favorite. But there was so much I took some to Mike."

"There's some left?"

"Yes. Stay right there. I'll heat it up." I went into the kitchen, grabbed a pan, and started the process of heating the marsala. While it heated, I put a clean vintage tablecloth on my small kitchen table. It looked French provincial with its red roosters and fleur-de-lis. After a quick search I found a candle and stuck it in a wine bottle I had in my recycling. I checked on the marsala and gave it a stir.

I bustled out to the living room. Seth looked up from his phone and smiled at me.

"Just a few more minutes," I said. I opened the small door to the attic and crawled through. I found the box of china I'd bought at the thrift shop and took out a few pieces. I smiled. Maybe Seth was china worthy. Back in the kitchen I washed and dried the dishes, then set the table. It all looked lovely. Now to taste the marsala. I grabbed a spoon, dipped it in the sauce and blew on it before I tasted it. I did another silent happy dance.

After doling out pasta and marsala onto our plates, I lit the candle and called to Seth. "It's ready." Fingers crossed the chicken hadn't dried out.

Seth's eyes lit up when he saw the table. He swooped me into a kiss. "Want me to open some wine?"

"Yes, please. The bottle of chardonnay you brought

last time is in the fridge. The one you said had a buttery finish. It should go with the creaminess of the sauce."

"Sit," he said. He pulled out my chair and gave me a swift kiss on the cheek when I sat. "Thanks for this." He gestured toward the table.

"You might not want to thank me until after you eat."

"It smells great."

I didn't want to tell him, based on past experience, that just because it smelled good didn't mean it was. He opened the wine, poured two glasses, and set them on the table. He moved his place setting and chair next to mine.

Seth held up his glass. "To you."

We took a sip of the wine and it did indeed have a buttery finish. I sat nervously as Seth cut into his chicken. It looked juicy still, but perhaps reheating, even on low heat, wasn't its friend.

He took a bite and set his fork down.

Uh-oh.

"It's delicious."

I took a tentative bite. Seth was right. I sighed with relief.

"Thank you," Seth said.

"You're welcome." I thought back to my lunch with the DiNapolis. Maybe this is what they had been talking about—that cooking was love, because I felt warm with happiness.

Chapter Forty

Thursday afternoon Jeannette and I sat in her living room. "How are you doing?" I asked her.

"Okay. I can't believe this mess with that Sam and his friend." She shook her head. "My brother feels so guilty."

"It's crazy. And you are sure you want to sell some of the jewelry?"

"Yes. I kept a few pieces that I remember my mom wearing. But most of it I'd never seen."

"Okay. The friend I told you about, Charlie Davenport, is going to come price it for us. She agreed to be here the day of the sale too." I'd met Charlie through another friend last spring. She was a Vietnam veteran, who was a bit hard of hearing, but loved karaoke. After she'd come home from Vietnam she'd worked in the family jewelry store until she'd retired. The store had a great reputation here in Ellington, so we were lucky to have her onboard.

Jeannette handed me a black velvet box. "Here's the jewelry that can be sold."

"Charlie said she could keep it at the jewelry store until Saturday."

"That would be great. I have to run."

"Okay, I'll make sure everything is locked up tight before I go."

After Jeannette left I took the rings with me and worked in one of the bathrooms until I heard the doorbell ring.

Charlie hugged me, when I answered the door bashing me with her big purse and a tote bag. With her Afro and unlined face she looked too young to have served in Vietnam. She wore an African print caftan in bright greens over a pair of jeans.

"Come in," I said, pointing to the living room.

"Dum sim?" Charlie looked puzzled. "You want to eat Chinese food? I came here ready to work."

I tried not to chuckle because I knew the dish was called dim sum. "I said, come in." This time I said it louder. We went to the living room and sat down on the couch.

Charlie laughed. "Darn hearing aids. Battery must have gone out again. Hang on." Charlie pulled a little case out of her purse and did some quick switching around of things. "There. That ought to be better."

"I'm not sure how you handle those tiny batteries without dropping them." I still spoke louder than normal.

"Don't need to shout. I've got this now. As for the batteries, I've been working with watches and jewelry all my life. Gives one a certain dexterity. Now let's see what you've got."

I grabbed the box I'd stuffed in a bathroom drawer when I answered the door. I was still a little freaked out about all that had gone on here. "Here you go," I said, handing Charlie the black velvet box. Jeannette was still pondering what to do with the coins and unset jewels.

Charlie set the box on the coffee table, opening it carefully. About twenty rings winked and sparkled at us, lined up in slots in the velvet. "Umm, umm. This is going to be fun." She nodded her head. "I've been missing this more than I realized."

I plucked the pink ring I'd admired the other day out of the box and put it on my ring finger. Perfect fit. "What kind of stone is this?" I asked. I held out my hand like girls always did when showing off an engagement ring, watching the stone catch the light. The ring was set in swirls of gold filigree with tiny diamonds in the swirls.

"Let me get my loupe."

I continued to hold out my hand while Charlie studied it with her loupe. She nodded and then looked up at me. "Pink ruby. One minor flaw. It's a beauty."

I took it off and placed it in Charlie's upturned palm.

"Do you need my help?" I asked. Jewelry was so much more fun than bathrooms. There were some towels and washcloths that could be sold. I'd been dumping out tubes of old toothpaste, cold cream, and makeup.

"You know how to appraise rings?" Charlie asked.

"No."

"Well, then you just go do whatever you need to." Charlie extracted a small scale and some other equipment from the tote bag she'd brought with her.

Friday evening I came home from putting the finishing touches on Jeannette's garage sale. Harriet had been a huge help and I'm not sure I could have finished pricing without her. I sat on my couch with a glass of cabernet and turned on the local Boston news. Ellington was too small to have its own television station. There was a breaking news story that Jimmy "the Chip" Russo had been fished out of Boston Harbor in what looked like a mob hit. They showed a picture of him.

I choked on my wine and set my glass down. It was the guy from the hall—the one Mike knew. The reporter said it looked like he'd been tortured first because he had burns on his face and a lump on the back of his head.

Tortured? What I'd done was now being called torture? I'd saved Mike and maybe Francesco. I should have insisted that Mike call the police. I threw on my coat, grabbed my purse, and ran down to my car. Thirty minutes later I stood in Il Formagio, Mike's cheese shop. I recognized the girl behind the counter and she recognized me from previous visits.

"Get Mike over here now. Or he's going to have a bigger fondue party than the last one."

The girl got on the phone. After she hung up, she told me that Mike was on his way. I paced around the shop, declining offers of cheese, crackers, or a drink—the nonalcoholic kind. A real drink I might have considered. Fifteen minutes later Mike strolled in.

"Let's go for a walk," he said.

I assumed this was because he was worried someone was bugging the place—either other mobsters or the FBI. Who knows, maybe both.

Out on the sidewalk streetlights shone on the now dirty snow. Mike moved like he didn't have a care in the world. Snow was melting, people milled about, standing in lines waiting to get in restaurants. It was the first decent day we'd had in over a month.

"I had nothing to do with what happened to Jimmy," Mike said. He nodded and smiled at a little Italian grandmother dressed all in black. "I promise you."

"It said he'd been tortured. They think what I did was *torture*."

"What you did was save me from hurting a man I would never want to hurt."

That made me pause. It relieved a little of the pressure that had been gripping me since I'd seen the story. But this was Mike. He wasn't necessarily a reliable narrator. "Never want to, but would if you had to?" I asked.

"No. Don't twist my words. I liked Jimmy. I told you he was good with computers. It's how he got the name 'the Chip.' He managed to hack my security system. Scared me enough to get out of town."

"I got all that. Now he's dead in the harbor."

"If I'd done it he wouldn't have been found."

That wasn't comforting.

"But I didn't do it. He must have messed with the wrong person's computer. Found something that put him in danger." Mike stopped and turned toward me. "Go home. This isn't your fight. I'll look into it for the sake of his sister. And I'll let you know what I find out. If I find out anything."

I opened my mouth to protest.

"I swear." Mike held up his hand like he was giving an oath. "And look where we are."

We stood in front of a Catholic church.

"I wouldn't lie to anyone here."

My phone buzzed. A text from Seth asking if we

were still meeting for dinner at DiNapoli's. I was going to be late. I sent him a text saying so.

"If I find out different I'm going to the police," I said.

"You won't. I promise." Mike nodded to a couple who walked by. "It won't be easy for me to find an answer to this. But I will. Just don't expect a call tomorrow or even next week."

I gave him my best intimidating stare, which on a scale of one to threatening was probably a minus five. Then I walked off.

Chapter Forty-One

On Saturday, the day of the sale, I woke up earlier than normal. The weather had been warming. It looked like we'd hit the January thaw. That was good news for the sale. I'd been worried about a blizzard hitting. What did my mom always say? Worrying never solved anything. I needed to practice that more often.

I snuggled up against Seth. My world was happy again. He turned and threw an arm around me and kissed my neck.

"I have to get up," I said. It would be much more fun to stay here with Seth.

Seth groaned. "I don't want to get up, but I know it's the day of the big sale. I'll drop by if I can."

"You can stay. Go back to sleep." I turned to face him. His dark eyes were sleepy and beautiful at the same time. "I love you." There. I did it. I said it first and it felt fantastic instead of scary.

He traced a finger across my cheek and a slow smile lighted his face. "I love you back."

I jumped out of bed to avoid the rush of emotions sweeping through me. I guess I wasn't completely over being scared. "I'll make coffee."

Seth nodded and closed his eyes. "Scaredy cat."
I couldn't argue with that.

I unlocked the front door at eight to let customers in. Charlie sat in the living room behind a locked case with the jewelry and some other valuables in it. I'd hired high school students to man the exits. Until the other day I'd been counting on Zoey to help out, but ended up asking Eleanor and Nasha to come work along with Harriet. Eleanor was in the basement. Nasha and Harriet would roam and keep an eye on things.

People streamed in. I'd put an ad in the local paper to counter Zoey's ad. I had mentioned in the ad that Charlie would be here answering questions about the jewelry. The prices were high for many of the pieces and I wasn't sure they would sell. We'd decided that we weren't going to go below ten percent of the value that Charlie had appraised them at. There would be other opportunities to sell them. In fact, I think Charlie might be interested in some of them for the family store.

Harriet, who showed up wearing all black, was working it. I didn't have much time to watch her because I was busy too. But Harriet had a way of making people happy they were paying more. If this kept up Jeannette would be thrilled with the results.

Pellner had come by and I'd given him the valentine and cobalt vase. At ten Awesome showed up.

"What are you doing here?" I asked.

"I saw the ad about the jewelry," Awesome said. He sounded nervous.

"I don't think there are any men's rings here." I

looked at his paler than normal face. I grabbed his arm and pulled him close. "Are you looking for a woman's ring?"

Awesome glanced around before he nodded.

I dropped my voice to almost a whisper. "An engagement ring?"

"Yes. Will you help me pick a ring out? I didn't want just a run-of-the-mill mall ring. Stella's too special. She deserves something unique."

I squealed and hugged him. "This is why you've been so cranky?"

"Yes. What if she says no?"

"She won't, you big idiot. Come over here." I dragged him over to where Charlie sat and quickly filled her in.

Awesome studied the rings. I waited impatiently beside him. Trying not to jiggle around and distract him. Charlie took different ones out and told him about them. She handed him a blue sapphire with diamonds on each side. Then a simple triangle-cut diamond in gold. He handed each back and pointed to another ring.

"What about that one?" he asked.

"Good eye," Charlie said. She handed him the ring, which looked small in his big hands. "This emerald is in a platinum setting with a halo of diamond accents. Milgrain lines every edge."

"What are milgrain lines?" Awesome asked. His brows were pulled together in concentration.

"Milgrain is derived from the French *mille grain*, which translates to 'a thousand grains.' It's a close-set row of metal beads used as a border. I'm sure you've seen it before and just didn't notice."

Awesome shook his head and smiled. "I haven't

paid a lot of attention to rings until recently. What do you think, Sarah? Is this one special enough for Stella?"

"I love it." Tears pushed at my eyes. "I think Stella will too. When are you going to ask her?"

"We're going to Maine next weekend. I rented a house on the coast. I'll do the whole candlelight dinner thing." He stared down at the ring for a moment. "How's that sound?"

"Perfect."

I heard the front door open and more people moved into the living room. I turned, my eyes popped, and I turned back to Awesome. "Awesome," I whispered, "Stella just walked in. With her mom. And aunts." I'd forgotten she told me this was one garage sale she wouldn't miss.

Awesome gritted his jaw. He hadn't had an easy relationship with the family. "I'll take it," he said to Charlie.

I was trying to think how I could run interference. Get them to head in another direction, but it was too late. They had spotted him.

"Nathan, what are you doing here?" Stella asked as she came up behind him.

Awesome turned and dropped to one knee. Stella stared down at him in shock. Her mom and aunts clustered behind her. Everyone who was milling around stopped what they were doing to watch.

"Stella, I know I'm not perfect. There's that whole thing about me being a Yankees fan living in Red Sox country." He grinned at Stella and then her mom and aunts. He refocused on Stella, his expression serious. "And I'm a cop. Being a cop's wife isn't easy."

Stella put her hands to her mouth.

"I'm a lot of other things too. But I'm also the kind of man who looks for a reason to stay instead of looking for a reason to go."

Stella nodded, but kept her hands over her mouth. Her olive skin looked pale.

"And I certainly didn't intend to do this at one of Sarah's garage sales. But I love you. Will you marry me?" He held up the ring.

It seemed like everyone in the room was holding their breath. We waited for one moment, then two. Stella finally pulled her hands from her mouth.

"Yes. Of course, I will marry you. Yes."

Awesome jumped up, grabbed Stella, and swung her around while kissing her. Then he put her down and put the ring on her shaking finger. He looked over at her mom and aunts a little warily.

They rushed forward.

"We'll have to convert him to the Red Sox," one aunt murmured.

"And burn his Yankees hat," the other aunt said.

"Welcome to the family," Stella's mom said.

The room broke out into cheers and congratulations. Jeannette found a bottle of champagne in the refrigerator and popped it open. I grabbed champagne glasses off the kitchen table, price tags and all. We stretched the bottle as far as it would go.

"To the happy couple," I said, holding up my glass, tears in my eyes.

"Here, here," everyone answered.

Winter Garage Sale Tips

Want to have a garage sale in the middle of a Northern winter? It can be done, but there are factors to consider.

Where to have it? Think about your options:

1. You could hold it in your garage with a space heater or two (use extreme care if you use space heaters) to keep the space warm. If you can't move everything out of your garage, divide it with sheets, or throw sheets over things that aren't for sale.

2. Get together with neighbors and friends. Find a public space to use, whether it's a neighborhood community center or a church that is willing to let you use a room.

3. Don't have it in your house! I've seen this done and the risk of having strangers traipsing around outweighs the reward. (It's one thing to have an estate sale when the occupants are moved out and have taken their personal items with them.) My only exception to having it inside your home is if you have a room with a separate entrance and people to guard the access to the rest of your house.

How to deal with winter weather:

1. While forecasts are unpredictable, watch for a window of good weather and get the word out quickly. This is harder to do if you use a public space.

2. Make sure all sidewalks and the driveway are clear of snow and ice.

3. Be prepared to cancel if necessary.

What are the advantages of a winter garage sale?

1. Little to no competition.

2. Garage sale fanatics (guilty, raising hand) are itching to get out there.

3. You are ahead on your spring cleaning so you can get out there and enjoy spring!

If all of the above is too daunting, consider doing an online garage sale.

Keep reading for a special excerpt of
LET'S FAKE A DEAL,
a Sarah Winston Garage Sale Mystery
by **Sherry Harris!**

SHE'S GOT THE GOODS . . .
As a former military spouse, Sarah Winston's
learned a little about organizing, packing, and
moving. Her latest project sounds promising:
a couple of tech-industry hipsters, newly arrived
in her Massachusetts town, who need to downsize.
Unfortunately, when Sarah tries to sell their stuff, she
discovers it's all stolen—and she's the unwitting fence.

**BUT SARAH'S PROBLEMS
ARE JUST BEGINNING**
Michelle, an old friend of Sarah's from the
Air Force base, is in line for a promotion—but not
everyone is happy about it, and she's been hit with
an anonymous discrimination complaint. When
one of the men she suspects is behind the
accusations turns up dead in Michelle's car,
Sarah needs to clear Michelle's name—as well as
her own for selling hot merchandise. And she'll
have to do it while also organizing a cat lady's
gigantic collection of feline memorabilia, or they'll
be making room for Sarah in a jail cell . . .

Look for **LET'S FAKE A DEAL,** *on sale now.*

Chapter One

Two police cars squealed to a halt at the end of the driveway, lights flashing, front bumpers almost touching. I stared at them and then at the half dozen people milling around the garage sale that had started fifteen minutes ago at 7:30 a.m. Everyone stopped browsing and turned to stare, too. Doors popped open. Three officers jumped out. Unusual in these days of budget cuts and officers riding alone that two were together. I didn't recognize any of them because I was in Billerica, Massachusetts, just north of where I lived in Ellington.

"Who's in charge here?" one of the officers called. His thick shoulders and apparent lack of neck looked menacing against the cloudy late September sky.

"Me. I'm Sarah Winston." I gave a little wave of my hand and stepped forward. It seemed like the carpenter's apron I was wearing with SARAH WINSTON GARAGE SALES embroidered across the front was enough to identify me.

The officer put out a hand the size of a baseball glove to stop me. "Stay. The rest of you, put everything down and see the two officers over there."

What the heck? I stayed put, having had enough

experience with policing through my ex-husband's military and civilian careers in law enforcement to know to listen to this man no matter what I thought. Several people glanced at me but did as they were told. I stood in the center of the driveway all by myself. One by one the people spoke to the police officers and scurried off. Five minutes later it was me and the three cops. Thankfully, it wasn't hot out here like it would be in August.

"What's going on?" I asked.

"Do you have any weapons?"

"No." I looked down at the carpenter's apron tied around my waist. It had four pockets for holding things. "There's a measuring tape, some cash, and a roll of quarters in the pockets." Ugh, would he think that was a weapon? I'd heard that if you held a roll in your fist and punched someone, it was as good as brass knuckles. "Oh, and my phone. Do you want to see?"

"Put your hands on the back of your head and then kneel," he ordered.

I started to protest but shut my mouth and complied. Something was terribly wrong. Thank heavens I'd worn jeans today instead of a dress.

"Now lay face-first on the ground."

I looked at the distance between my face and the ground. I couldn't just flop forward. It would smash my nose. I hunched down as much as I could, rolled to one side, and then onto my stomach. The roll of quarters made their presence known, digging into my already roiling stomach. The driveway was warm and rough against my cheek. A pair of highly polished black boots came into sight. I felt the apron being untied, and I was quickly patted down. Then I was yanked up by the big officer. My carpenter's apron looked forlorn laying on the driveway.

"Please tell me, what's this about?" I asked again.

The big guy glared down at me, hands on his hips. His left hand was a little closer to his gun than made me comfortable. If this was an effort to intimidate me, it was working on every level.

"We had a tip that everything being sold here was stolen."

Chapter Two

Cold. Cold like someone had just dumped one of those big icy containers of liquid over my head. The kind they dumped on the winning coach at a football game. Only I wasn't the winner here. The cold reached through my skin and gripped my heart. "Stolen? That's not possible."

"Is anyone else here?" the officer asked. His nameplate said JONES.

"Yes. The two people who hired me are in the house." I pointed, thumb over shoulder, to the large two-story colonial house behind me.

"Do they have any weapons?"

"No. No one has weapons. It's a garage sale. I won't let anyone sell weapons at the garage sales I run." I stared at the officer, hoping I'd see some sign in his face that he believed me. I didn't. "I was hired to run this garage sale. It's my job."

"By who?" The other two officers headed to the house. One stood by the front door and the other went around the side of the house toward the back.

Why did this guy sound so freaking skeptical? "A young couple. Kate and Alex Green." I remembered the day we met at a Dunkin' Donuts in Ellington. I'd instantly labeled them as hipsters with their skinny jeans, flannel shirts, fresh faces, and black-rimmed glasses. Kate and Alex had been shy but eager at the same time. Alex had just gotten a job at Tufts University in tech services. "They just moved here from Indiana and didn't realize how expensive everything is. They owned a huge house in Indiana but once they got here realized they were going to have to downsize."

I almost chuckled thinking about their wide-eyed explanation of how the money they got for their home in Indiana would only buy a small cape-style house far from Boston in this area. Sticker shock was a real thing for anyone who moved here.

"Once they realized they had to get rid of two thirds of their stuff, they decided to reduce their carbon footprint," I said, "and to buy one of those tiny houses. Me? I couldn't live in one. Not that my one-bedroom apartment is that big, but those loft bedrooms? You have to climb up some little ladder. The bed's just a mattress on the floor. How do you make the beds without hitting your head?" I shuddered. "Claustrophobic, don't you think?"

Officer Jones stared at me. I was rambling. Just answer the question he asked, I reminded myself.

"So where did all of this stuff come from?" he asked, sweeping his arm toward the carefully set out tables full of items.

"From the Greens. They put it all in storage when they got here from Indiana." I remembered their excited faces as they told me that they'd moved into a one-bedroom apartment in a complex on the north side of Ellington to prepare for their new lifestyle.

"I priced everything at the storage unit, and then they moved it over here. This is their friends' house." I waved a hand at the house. "And their friends decided to sell some stuff, too. Stuff I didn't know about." I pointed to a group of tables that held computers, TVs, and cell phones. Then over to a bunch of furniture. "They priced all of the electronics. Personally, I thought their prices were a little bit high, but I don't usually deal with electronics."

"What do you usually *deal* with?" Jones asked. He stepped in closer. His coffee breath swept over me.

He sounded like he expected my answer to be "drugs." I glanced toward the house, hoping the Greens would be out here in a second to explain all this to Officer Jones. How they owned all of this stuff and it was some kind of terrible mistake. But the only person by the house was the officer knocking on the door.

"My favorite things to sell are antiques, furniture, linens, old glassware, but I sell pretty much whatever my customers want me to. And you wouldn't believe the stuff some of them want to sell." Officer Jones didn't crack a smile. "The rest of it they said to price as people expressed interest. Personally, I think everything should be priced in advance, but the customer is always right." I shut up. I was volunteering too much again.

"I'll need you to let us into the house so we can talk to the Greens," Officer Jones said. He glanced over at the officer standing at the front door.

"I'd be happy to," I said as we walked to the front door. "They went in to make some coffee for everyone since it's chilly out here. Then they were coming back out to help run the sale." If they worked the sale, then I didn't have to hire anyone to help me, which meant we all pocketed more money.

The officer by the door stepped aside as I opened the door but followed Officer Jones and me into the foyer.

"Kate?" I called. "Alex?" No answer. "The kitchen is just down the hall." They should have heard me. Why didn't they answer?

The two officers exchanged a look. One that gave me prickles of discomfort.

"Miss Winston, would you mind stepping back outside while we take a look around?" Officer Jones asked.

The prickles turned into waves. I called to the Greens again. Nothing. "I'd be happy to wait outside."

Officer Jones looked at his fellow officer. "Go with her."

The other officer didn't look happy, but Jones's message seemed clear. *Make sure she doesn't take off.* I went back out onto the porch and walked down the steps to the sidewalk that led from the driveway to the house. The other officer followed me out. We stood awkwardly while avoiding looking at each other. A few minutes later Officer Jones came back out along with the officer who had gone around the back.

"Where are the Greens?" I asked, trying to look past the officers toward the house.

"No one's in there. The place is empty," Officer Jones said.

Empty? Although empty was better than him saying there was someone dead in there. "I saw them go in there a half hour ago." It hit me that it didn't take a half hour to make coffee. But I'd been busy enough that until now I hadn't realized how much time had passed. I paused. "By empty, do you mean empty of people?"

"Empty of almost everything," the other officer said. He didn't look at me, but at Jones. They both looked at all the furniture on the lawn.

"This didn't come from the house, did it?" I asked. I didn't have to wait for an answer. I could tell by the expression on the officer's face it must have. How could I have been so naive?

I turned to look at the house again. It had one of those historic plaques by the door that said it had been built in the early 1700s. Where were the Greens? If only the plaque could tell me that. The house was a colonial style from the early eighteenth century. It was at the top of a hill. I'd read a bit about its history. The house had been a place where the townspeople went during Indian attacks. It had a tunnel that led from the basement to the nearby woods that was a last-resort escape route if things went south. The woods were long gone, and in their place were rows of small houses with small yards.

"There's a tunnel. From the basement to some-place around the back. Maybe they went out that way," I said. The officers just looked at me. "If this is all stolen, they're the ones that did it. Shouldn't you send someone after them? They *stole* the stuff."

The smaller officer stepped away and talked into his shoulder mike.

Jones turned to me. "Do you know where the entrance to the tunnel is?"

I nodded. "Yes. Do you want me to show you?"

* * *

Minutes later I was down in the basement or cellar or whatever people from New England called them. Basements were few and far between where I grew up in Pacific Grove, California. This one had rough dirt walls and wasn't fit to be a rec room or man cave. It was creepy enough to be a madman's cave, though. Damp air flowed around us with its musty, rotting smell.

Jones and the two other officers studied the primitive-looking wooden door with its rusty lock, hinges, and doorknob. It was set into the back wall of the foundation.

"So if you didn't know anything about this house, how did you know this was here?" Jones asked.

"I noticed the historic plaque by the front door the first time I came over, so I read about the history of the house online."

"When was the first time you came over?"

"Two days ago. To see where I could set everything up."

Jones and one of the other officers looked at each other. All of this exchanging looks and no explanations was making me very nervous. Cops. Jones reached over and turned the knob on the door to the tunnel. It moved easily in his hand, but as he pulled on the door the hinges groaned, resisting. The door snagged on the rough dirt floor. Even only open an inch, the smell of stagnant air pushed me back a couple of steps.

"I don't think I need to be here for this," I said. I was afraid of what was on the other side of that door. Spiders, rats, bats—with my luck a dead body.

But Jones lifted the door just enough to clear the spot where the door had snagged. We all peered in but saw nothing but darkness.

Grab These Cozy Mysteries
from
Kensington Books

Follow P.I. Savannah Reid
with
G.A. McKevett

"That sounds like Becky. She always wants everything to be just so." It took a second for the implication to hit me. Poison. You would want to make sure the right person got the glass with the poison.

"Why are you asking all this? It's strange."

"I know. I'm trying to piece things together. Who all was at the board meeting?"

"Becky, of course, me, Judy Bruce, Delaney, Alicia, Cindy, and Ginger."

Did any of them have a reason to kill Alicia? "Okay. Thanks." So much for letting this all go. Even though Frank didn't want me to be involved any longer, I knew too much to give up now. And Becky knew that too.

I worked for an hour before I realized I was hungry. As I ate my lobster rolls, I thought about Fake Troy. About seeing him at DiNapoli's. Could it mean he was local? Did he have some connection to Jeannette's brother Troy? Someone had set up that camera, and the most logical person was Fake Troy or the other person who had been in the house. I kept feeling like this house had secrets. Maybe it was time to find out what they were.

Zoey sent a text saying she wasn't feeling good and couldn't come in. I sent a text to Harriet on the off chance she had a little time to help. The sale was Saturday and that left four days to finish everything. Harriet responded that she could come over for an hour or two before she had to take her niece to an appointment.

Fifteen minutes later Harriet showed up in a paisley, swirling dress that was reminiscent of hippies or gypsies. Scarves decked out her neck and bangles jangled on both arms. Her only nod to winter was the purple leggings that must be keeping her legs warm. Her hair was braided. I'd never seen a woman who went from one drastic style to another like Harriet did. It seemed like most people settled in to a certain aesthetic. But I didn't know Harriet well enough to comment.

"Thanks for coming over on such short notice," I said.

She tugged at the scarves like they weren't entirely comfortable. "Your other helper doesn't seem too reliable."

"She seemed like she was at first."

"Where do you want me to work?" Harriet asked.

"Let's work on pricing all the items hanging on the walls in the hall."

The hall was narrow so we started at opposite ends. Harriet turned out to be quite knowledgeable about where different masks were from, along with paintings.

"Where are you from, Harriet?"

"Here and there," she answered.

Harriet was a tough person to get to open up. "Military family? Salesman?"

"Military. My dad was in the Navy."

"Did you settle in one place as an adult?" It seemed like military kids went one of two ways—they continued moving from place to place or settled and couldn't be blasted out of their homes.

"No. My job moved me around a lot and I traveled a lot on top of that."

"What was your job?"

Harriet took a mask off the wall and turned it over

Available Wherever Books Are Sold!

All available as e-books, too!

Visit our website at **www.kensingtonbooks.com**

Follow P.I. Savannah Reid
with
G.A. McKevett